VERMILLION DAYS

VERMILLION DAYS

Ann Lilley

Matador
Unit E2 Airfield Business Park,
Harrison Road, Market Harborough,
Leicestershire. LE16 7UL
Tel: 0116 2792299
Email: books@troubador.co.uk
Web: www.troubador.co.uk/matador
Twitter: @matadorbooks

ISBN 978 1805140 054

British Library Cataloguing in Publication Data.
A catalogue record for this book is available from the British Library.

Printed and bound by CPI Group (UK) Ltd, Croydon, CR0 4YY
Typeset in 11pt Minion Pro by Troubador Publishing Ltd, Leicester, UK

Matador is an imprint of Troubador Publishing Ltd

for Maggie

PROLOGUE

I took another sip of water and checked the time. Vermillion was due on stage in fifteen minutes. And not just any stage. They were due on the John Peel stage at Glastonbury, no less. I was sporting all five wristband passes so I could, in theory, go everywhere. But I appeared to be going nowhere. They'd forgotten about me – that was the only explanation. I would be left here, in the hospitality tent of the VIP area, forever.

I looked at my phone again. Maybe I could find the way on my own. I turned towards the tent flap just as Damien, Vermillion's manager, appeared in the gap.

'Jo-D!' he yelled over the crowd.

Everyone's head seemed to turn in my direction.

'Move it, love!' he hollered, clapping his hands at me. Actually clapping his hands.

I lowered my oversized sunglasses onto my nose and hurried outside after him. He'd set off across the quagmire at full stride, splashing through the mud without a care. He had his jeans tucked into his wellies, but there was mud right up past his bum. I followed as quickly as I could, tiptoeing around the slush, trying to pick out the firmer areas. I held my wrist up to security at the other side of the bog and stepped onto firm plywood, stopping to stamp the worst of the mud off my own green Wellington boots. When I looked up, Damien was disappearing between two lorries. I tugged my very short denim shorts down a bit and jogged after him. I dodged roadies and security people, and emerged from between the trucks, right into the line of a TV camera.

'Oh, for fuck's sake,' screamed the journalist I'd interrupted.

I mumbled 'sorry' but didn't stop. Ahead of me, Damien was climbing a set of metal stairs into a vast black tent. I showed my passes again and followed him up into the darkness.

'Ok?' Damien shouted at me over the music.

I nodded, waiting for my eyes to adjust. We were in a long, wide corridor. There were dozens of black crates on wheels and dozens more burly roadies all either loading in or loading out. Damien was still moving quickly, and I hurried on. I needed a pee, but this didn't seem the time to mention it.

At the end of the corridor, we took a left and climbed some more narrow dark stairs into bright light and the source of the noise. We'd arrived at the side of the massive stage. Right then, the PA system announced Vermillion, and the crowd roared. I saw the band, minus Ricky, jog out onto the stage as I followed Damien. They looked like they'd done this hundreds of times.

Damien took hold of my arm and elbowed his way through a group of half a dozen onlookers, one of which looked suspiciously like Russell Brand. He stopped just behind a massive amp at the very edge of the stage and leaned towards my ear.

'See that white line there?' He pointed at a painted line on the floor at my feet. 'Do not cross that line. Got it?'

I nodded.

'Enjoy.' And with that, he was gone.

I peeked round the amp. The crowd was endless and stretched off into darkness at the back of the tent. It would take some nerve to walk out in front of that. But Ricky had the nerve. I pushed my sunglasses up onto the top of my head and peered across the stage. Ricky was staring right back at me, waving. I threw him two big kisses with both hands as his band mates started the intro to 'Give In'.

My heart was beating loudly in my chest. Ricky rubbed his hands on the side of his jeans, gave me a quick thumbs up, and launched himself out onto the stage. He skidded to the microphone stand, grabbed it to slow his progress, and raised both arms straight up above his head.

'Hello Glastonbury! We are Vermillion!'

CHAPTER 1

'Well, this is going to be noisy and shit,' Tanya said as she checked her hair in the mirror that ran along the back of the bar.

'Eh,' I said. 'A little help here?'

She glanced down at me, taking in the empty beer crate and the full shelves, then returned to smoothing her hair. 'Nah, you're ok.'

I clambered to my feet and dusted off my knees. Typical Tanya to be no help whatsoever. Up on the stage, Jim, our manager, was securing the ties that held the Battle of the Bands banner in place. This annual fixture was, indeed, usually shit. But not this year.

'Vermillion are playing,' I said.

'Who?'

'Ricky's band.'

'Oh, Ricky's band,' Tanya said, joining me to fill a pint glass from the tap.

A slow trickle of students were making their way down here to the Dungeon from the upstairs bar, but there was no sign of Ricky yet.

'They're actually very good,' I replied haughtily.

I wasn't sure if this was true. Ricky certainly practised enough. And it was, literally, the only thing he thought about, other than sex. But the rest of the band were just Ricky's mates from his engineering course, and I didn't think they were quite as keen.

'He is hot, don't you think?' Tanya tilted the glass to catch the froth. 'You still sharing a flat with him?'

'Yes.'

'Yes, you're sharing a flat or yes, he's hot?'

'I'm sharing a flat.' I bristled slightly. Sometimes – most of the time – I couldn't stand Tanya. And the thought of her getting together with Ricky was too much. 'And he's not your type.' I took an order and reached behind me for the vodka, flipping two glasses onto the bar at the same time.

'What do you mean, he's not my type?' She laughed, shaking her hair back over her shoulder and exchanging the pint for some cash. 'Or are you after him?'

'Don't be stupid,' I snapped as Jim arrived behind the bar to check the till.

'Tanya, take your break now. Then you're upstairs,' he said, counting money. 'Jo, you're down here with Alan.'

'You're joking,' I moaned. Working with Alan was worse than a back shift with Tanya.

'Well, it's you or Tanya. Alan can't work on his own yet.'

'Fine,' I said. I definitely didn't want to miss Vermillion playing.

Jim slammed the till shut and marched off.

'Don't work too hard,' Tanya smirked as she flounced off after him.

By half seven, the Dungeon was filling up. Alan, who had been working for two weeks and should've got the hang of it by now, was far too slow, so I was busy. The first band was already on stage when I spotted Bob, the bass player in Vermillion, at the bar. It was hard to miss his bald head. I ignored the queue to serve him straightaway.

'Four pints, please, Jo.'

'Is Mhairi not here?'

He nodded his head to the back of the room and, right enough, I could see my best mate and Bob's girlfriend, Mhairi, standing with the boys. Bob and Mhairi had been together forever. Well, since I'd introduced them in first year, not long after I started sharing a flat with Ricky.

'Better give me a vodka Red Bull too, then.'

I picked up two glasses and started pouring. 'When are you on?' I shouted above the music.

'Last.' Bob was watching the band on stage. They didn't sound too bad, although they looked a bit bored.

I glanced back at the boys and caught Ricky's eye. He looked pale. I sent him a confident smile and a thumbs up.

'All set?' I asked Bob as I placed the drinks onto a tray.

'Too late if we're not,' he mumbled.

As the night wore on, I kept glancing at Ricky. He was either studiously observing the band on stage or enthusiastically greeting acquaintances. I could tell he was getting drunk. So when the drummer, Dinger, came up for the next round, I told him not to let Ricky drink too much. He gave me a wink and a slow head nod, which made me laugh. Dinger had a habit of making me laugh. He was short and looked much younger than he actually was. He was always getting ID'd. To compensate, he'd acquired the habits of a much older bloke, like sitting with his legs wide apart and drinking his pint with his elbow sticking out. But I liked him. He was honest and trustworthy and funny – even when he wasn't intending to be funny.

Eventually, Vermillion's turn came, and I watched Bob, Gary and Dinger get set up. There was no sign of Ricky.

Jim marched onto the stage. 'Right, folks,' he bellowed through the microphone. 'That's nearly us. This is the final band of the night and then the judges are going to take a quick break to decide the winner of the 2011 Glasgow Students' Union Battle of the Bands competition. So, without further ado, last, but by no means least, it's…' He checked his sheet. 'Vermillion.'

There was still no sign of Ricky. I'd given up any pretence of serving now. I just watched as Gary, the guitarist, counted them in and they started playing. Then, suddenly, Ricky was running out onto the stage – but he was running too fast. He began to skid. He grabbed the microphone, which slowed his progress, but his feet went out in front of him and he landed on his arse. My hands flew up to my mouth in horror and the crowd jeered with laughter. He bounced right back up again.

'Hello, the Dungeon,' he shouted into the mic, holding his arms straight up above his head.

The crowd cheered in reply, and Ricky launched into the first song. I let out the breath I'd been holding and looked around the crowded room. Did they like it? At least three people were filming on their phones.

'Hello,' a girl hollered at me, waving an empty glass and I started serving again while I listened to them play. I wasn't convinced Bob's bass was in time with Dinger's drumming. I was also pretty sure they were getting faster. Ricky was prancing about like a maniac and visibly sweating. But the audience were waving their arms and cheering. They seemed to be enjoying it.

I looked back at the stage. Ok, they sounded pretty rubbish, but Ricky was going down well. Gary played a guitar solo and Ricky leapt up on an amp to stare menacingly at the crowd before jumping back down to finish the song.

At the end of their final song, Dinger clashed his cymbals repeatedly and Gary drew out the long last chord as Ricky grabbed the mic and brushed his damp hair out of his eyes.

'We have been Vermillion,' he roared. 'You saw us here first. Thank you and good night.'

I laughed with relief as the crowd cheered and clapped. They'd done it. They'd pulled it off. I felt a little bit proud of Ricky.

Mhairi arrived at the bar. 'How good was that?' she screamed.

'I know. Not a complete disaster.'

'Total legend! They're so going to be famous.'

'Well...' I raised my eyebrows, but she was already running off towards the side of the stage to hug Bob, and Ricky was making his way to the bar. Complete strangers were slapping him on the back and shaking his hand. I filled a pint and put it down in front of him.

'You're a star already,' I said.

He grinned and took a big gulp of beer. A trickle of sweat was running down his cheek. 'How was it?'

'Great. You were great.'

5

'I don't have any money.'

'I know.' I flapped my hand at him in dismissal.

He leaned across the bar, grabbed my head with his free hand, and smacked a wet kiss on my forehead. 'You're the best, Jo.'

About ten minutes later, one of the judges, a local radio DJ who no one had heard of, came on stage and called for silence.

'We had a tough decision tonight,' he began and continued on for an age about the high quality of talent, the state of the record industry, and what was coming up in his next radio show. 'But there can be only one winner.' He looked down at his notes. 'Oh, wait. First, we have tonight's runner-up. What they lacked in musical ability, they certainly made up for in enthusiasm. In second place, Vermillion.'

The crowd roared. Ricky was smiling. If he was disappointed, he certainly wasn't showing it. Instead, he looked self-assured, chuffed, and a bit more handsome than he'd been before. I let out a weary sigh.

CHAPTER 2

Even though I'd spent the weekend working back shifts, and even though I had a seminar the next morning, and an unfinished story to finish, I couldn't resist popping into Bob and Mhairi's on my way home from work. Their flat was only a five-minute walk from Uni and I could hear the party from the end of their street. As soon as I opened the door, it was clear that most of the people who'd been in the Dungeon were now in this flat.

I threw my jacket on the pile in the tiny bedroom and squeezed into the living room, stepping over a group of boys who were sitting on the floor skinning up. Mhairi was in the kitchen, which was really just a cupboard off the living room, emptying a family bag of Ready-Salted crisps into a bowl.

'Don't give these away,' I said, putting a crisp in my mouth. 'No one's here for food.'

'Drink?' She pointed at a near-empty slab of beer and another full one underneath.

'Who brought that?'

'I did.' Dinger's head appeared round the door.

'That was dead good tonight, Dinger,' I said enthusiastically.

He went pink from his collar up. 'You think?'

'Definitely. Dead good,' Mhairi agreed.

'Well, cheers,' he said. 'Pass us out the beer, eh?'

'Ah, bless his heart. He was so nervous,' Mhairi said once he'd gone. 'What did you really think?'

'About Vermillion? Better than expected.'

Mhairi took a swig of her beer. 'Ricky got off to a flying start.'

I rolled my eyes. 'I know. What a tit. Bob was really good.'

'Yeah. But Ricky stole the show.'

'He was pretty wild,' I agreed. 'Have you seen him? I should say hi.'

'Not since he arrived.' She raised her eyebrows. 'With Tanya.'

'Shut up! Tanya is here?'

'I know! Since when was *this* her scene?' Mhairi scoffed. She meant a student party. Tanya, being one of the beautiful people, spent most of her time in the trendy footballer-filled pubs in town. This was lowbrow for her.

I sighed. 'Probably since she set her sights on Ricky.'

'No!' Mhairi exclaimed, then thought for a moment. 'Well, with the reputation those two have, it was only a matter of time. Oh, speaking of inevitable, have you sent that story yet?'

I shrugged. 'No. It needs work.'

'Your tutor didn't think so. And the deadline's Friday.'

I pulled a face.

'You've got to be in it to win it.'

'I'd never win it. Kate Clanchy won that prize a few years ago, for fuck's sake.'

'Jo! Jesus!' Mhairi poked a crisp at me. 'You've got the ego of a shrimp. Let me remind you, one more time, that you are a first class honours student, and that you beat thousands...'

'Hundreds.'

'... of applicants to get that scholarship. You are in one of the greatest creative writing courses in the world. You are a great writer.' She pushed the bowl of crisps against my belly. 'Send the bloody story!'

I wobbled my head. I should send the story. I'd have another think.

'Now, take these through, will you?'

Back out in the hall, Tanya found me. 'Your Ricky is very drunk,' she said. She had taken off her Union t-shirt to reveal a strappy vest top that did not cover her lacy bra. 'I'm leaving.'

'He's not my Ricky.' I pushed past her.

'Jo!' Ricky shouted, squeezing sideways through the crowd towards me.

'How you doing?' I asked as he flung an arm round my shoulder.

His head lunged down, then snapped back up. 'Tickety boo,' he slurred.

I laughed, struggling to hold him up. Then I noticed, under his other shoulder, a small blonde first year.

'Jo, this is the delicious and delightful Danielle,' he said, bending his head to kiss her. 'Now that I'm a rock god,' he continued, 'you two can be my first groupies.'

'Ugh! Get off me, you dick.' I struggled away from his

weight, and he stumbled against the girl before regaining his balance.

'Where's that beer, Dinger?' he hollered.

Dinger handed him a can from the slab.

'Here's to fame and fortune!'

'The greatest band in the world!' Bob roared from near the bathroom.

A few beers later, I was sitting on the floor by the kitchen door with Bob's mates, smoking their hash. Dinger was curled up beside me, sound asleep, and the last I'd seen of Mhairi she'd been on the way to the bathroom – with a vomiting Bob. I became aware of someone tapping me continuously on the shoulder and lifted my head slowly to look.

'Are you stoned?' Gary, the guitarist, was standing above me and I had to close one eye to focus on him.

'Maybe.'

I didn't like Gary. He was a lecherous sod and an angry drunk.

'Ricky needs to go home.'

'Not my problem.'

'Not mine either. I'm off.'

I rose to my feet and staggered through the hall to the bedroom. Ricky was alone, fully clothed and face down on the pile of coats. I shook him.

'Ricky, time to go home.'

'I'm a rock god,' he mumbled, rolling over.

'I know. But let's go home, eh?'

I manhandled him to his feet and found our jackets. As I was fastening his zip, he swayed towards me.

'We make a great team, don't we?' he slurred.

'We sure do.' I slung his arm round my shoulder and started towards the door.

'You're the best, Jo.'

'I bet you say that to all the girls.'

The music had stopped, and there were sleeping bodies everywhere. We negotiated them with concentrated care. I could hear someone throwing up in the bathroom.

'I only mean it when I say it to you,' he replied, poking me in the belly with his free hand.

Out on the street, the wind had died, but it was a bitterly cold November night. The chilly air sobered us both up a bit and Ricky could walk without support.

'So,' I said, crossing my arms for warmth. 'You and Danielle?'

Ricky stuck his hands in his jeans' pockets. 'Too young.'

'Tanya?'

'Too much make-up.'

I wanted to sit down with relief.

'What about you?' He swallowed a hiccup. 'Meet anyone tonight?'

'I was working, in case you'd forgotten.'

'What about Gary?'

'Fuck off, Ricky. I'm not going out with Gary.'

'He's got the hots for you.'

I didn't know if he was joking or not. 'I'm not shagging your mate just so you can all sit around in the pub and talk about it.'

'We wouldn't do that!'

I looked sideways at him with my most disparaging look, eyebrows high, until he shrugged.

'Maybe we would. Who do you want to go out with then? Anyone you want. I'll set it up.'

I glanced at him again. I loved looking at him: his dark hair, the way it flopped down over his eyes so his head was permanently cocked to one side; that small mole on his cheek just below his left eye; his hands, strong like workman's hands, although he hadn't done a day's work in his life.

'Anyone?' I asked.

He stopped and turned to look right at me. 'Anyone.'

'Russell Brand.' I didn't even slow down.

Ricky laughed and jogged after me. 'Well, you'd certainly be in there. It would be handy if I knew him. But, fine, Russell fucking Brand. I'll see what I can do.'

We walked on in silence until Ricky accidentally bumped into me. He did it again on purpose, and I pushed him back.

'How come we've never got together?' he asked.

I sighed dramatically. This was a well-rehearsed ritual, usually performed when we were drunk. 'I'm too good for you,' I answered. 'That's why.'

'No, no, no, Miss Duncan, that is not the case. I am too good for you.'

'No, Mister Steele, you're quite mistaken,' I said, smiling. 'I'm too good for you.'

'Nope, that's where you're wrong.' He dunted my arm again. 'I'm too good for you.'

I uncrossed my arms and pushed him hard. He staggered off balance into a lamppost.

'Right!' he laughed wickedly.

I screamed and ran, but he caught me round the waist

within a couple of paces and easily swung me up over his shoulder.

'Put me down!' I wailed in delight.

He lowered me onto the ground head first and ran off whooping. I clambered up and chased after him to the end of the street, where he was waiting with his arms out in front of him to hold me back. I bent over to catch my breath and slapped him on the thigh.

'Come on.' He took my hand. 'Let's go home.'

I let him lead me. 'You were very good tonight, you know,' I said.

'You think so?'

'Sure. You owned that stage. I think you're going to go all the way.'

CHAPTER 3

Of course, it had nothing to do with who was too good for who. I just knew Ricky too well. He chose quantity over quality and had an allergy to monogamy. I did not want to be just one more conquest. But my feelings were making me vulnerable.

I was on my last bit of toast, still pondering this quandary, when I heard Ricky moving around in his bedroom. It was a Friday, and I knew he had lectures all day. I padded through the hall and chapped his door.

'What?'

'Morning to you too,' I said as I entered.

He had the bigger room because it was his flat – or his dad's flat, anyway. Which was another reason not to get involved with him. I was the lodger. When he got bored and dumped me, I'd have to move, and I couldn't afford to move. His dad hadn't put my rent up in four years.

Ricky was frantically shoving paper and folders into his canvas bag while simultaneously trying to get his arm in a t-shirt. 'I'm going to be late. What do you want?'

'My laptop keeps crashing. Can I use your Mac?'

'Sure.' He pushed past me, lifting the toast out of my fingers with his teeth.

'Oi!'

He stopped halfway across the hall. 'Actually,' he mumbled, spraying crumbs. 'It's your birthday tomorrow, isn't it?'

He'd remembered. I felt a swirl of delight in my stomach and shrugged.

'Here's the plan. Get yourself all tarted up and I'll take you out.'

'I'm working tomorrow.'

'No, you're not. I squared it with Jim.'

'What? Ricky, I need to work. I need the money.'

'You can't work on your birthday.'

I crossed my arms. I was pathetically pleased. 'Well, who else is coming?'

'Just us. Seven o'clock.' He hoisted his bag over his head. 'And make an effort.'

'I always make an effort.'

'No, you don't,' he said as he banged out the front door.

By late afternoon, I had written less than a thousand words of the promised three thousand towards my portfolio. And my one-to-one tutorial was Monday. Why just the two of us – for my birthday, I mean. Was it a date? I spun on Ricky's chair, taking in his familiar room: the unmade bed, the Pearl Jam poster, his three guitars under the window, the open wardrobe spilling clothes out across the carpet. And then it dawned on me. A terrible realisation.

I crossed the hall to my room, trying to calm my breathing. I pulled open my wardrobe and stared at the worn-out, scruffy piles of fabric that were my clothes. I pulled a black skirt from under a torn Primark hoodie. It was short and straight and shiny at the seams. I turned it round and spotted the lump of chewing gum imbedded in the material. I sat down on my bed in despair. There was nothing in there that even remotely suggested that I'd 'made an effort'.

I changed into my work clothes, pulled my hair up into a ponytail, and hurried off to the Union.

Tanya, the most glamorous person I knew, was in her usual position leaning on the bar, flicking through Glamour magazine.

'Great,' she said when I arrived in front of her. 'You're early. I'm off.'

'No, wait. I need a favour.'

She folded the magazine. 'I'm not doing your shift. I'm going out.'

'No, it's not that. I need to borrow your purple dress.' I smiled as sweetly as I could. 'The chiffony one. The one you wore to the summer dance last year.'

'It's mauve.'

'Please.'

'Why?'

'I'm going out tomorrow night. I've nothing nice.' I sounded as desperate as I felt.

'Where are you going?'

'Out. And the shoes. I need the shoes too. And a bag, a clutch bag. Whatever you used at the dance.'

She considered this, watching me steadily. I kept my sweet smile fixed on my face as if we were best pals, as if I didn't, in fact, hate that I was having to asking her for anything.

'Why not,' she eventually said, heading round the end of the bar. 'I'll drop it off tomorrow.'

'Are you sure?' I couldn't believe my luck.

'No problem.' As the door swung shut behind her, I thought I heard her laughing, but I was too relieved to care.

*

I considered myself in the mirror the next evening. Tanya's dress hung nearly to my knees, skimmed my thin hips and, having only one batwing sleeve, veered off across my chest asymmetrically. It was gorgeous. And thanks, again, to Tanya, who had just left with her suitcase of products, I was pulling it off. She'd straightened my crazy hair so it was smooth as silk, swishing on my shoulder, and I had make-up on.

'I don't do make-up,' I'd insisted when she emptied her trolley onto my bed.

'I know,' she'd replied. 'But you've never worn a dress like this.'

I turned my head to catch the light. I definitely did not look like a clown, as I had feared.

Bang on seven, I tottered through to the kitchen in Tanya's very high heels. Ricky was lying on the sofa, flicking through the channels.

He glanced at me when I came in, then jumped up to stand. 'Fuck's sake!' he exclaimed. 'You scrub up well.'

'Is that a compliment?'

He squeezed past me, laughing. 'Yes, it's a compliment. You are totally hot.' He smelt gorgeous. 'Let's get going. Where's your jacket?'

'I don't think you're meant to wear a jacket with this dress.'

'No matter. We're getting a taxi anyway,' he said, opening the front door. 'Give me your keys. I can't find mine.'

I opened Tanya's silver clutch bag and handed him my keys. 'Can you afford a taxi?'

'Yeah, yeah,' he said, locking the door.

'Where are we going?'

'Milngavie.' He pocketed my keys and started down the close stairs.

I stayed where I was. 'Milngavie?'

'Yeah. Mum's doing a roast. She's gone all out. I think she's baked a cake. Chop chop.'

'Ricky, why didn't you say that before? I'm dressed up like a fucking fanny and we're only going to Milngavie!'

But he was already out the tenement door.

And so, the evening of my twenty-third birthday found me in Glasgow's dreariest suburb, sunk deep in the Steeles' floral sofa, nursing a stomach full of roast beef and balancing a slab of pink-iced cake on my knee.

'And what about the flat, you two? How's that boiler?' Mr Steele was standing by the mantlepiece in his beige slacks and brown V-neck, whisky in hand.

'Fine now, Mr Steele,' I said. 'But the toaster seems to be broken.' I shrugged as if I hadn't a clue how this had happened when I knew full well that Ricky had made a cheese toasty in it late one drunken night and it had simply never recovered.

'I'll drop one round this week,' Mr Steele replied. 'And what are your Christmas plans, Jo?'

'Just home.' I smiled politely.

'Yes, the island. Which island is it again?'

'Barinner.'

'Ah, the Highlands and Islands.' Mr Steele took a sip of his drink. 'It's all about New Year up there, isn't it? Hogmanay and all that.'

'Your parents will be looking forward to seeing you,' Mrs Steele said from the other sofa, where she was trying to tuck Ricky's heavy fringe behind his ear. 'And it's a sister you've got, didn't you say?'

'Mm-hmm.'

'And no nice young man to take home with you?'

Ricky snorted out some cake.

'Ricky!' Mrs Steele slapped him lightly on the leg. 'A nice-looking girl like Jo should have boys lining up at her door.'

Ricky's eyes danced with delight. 'I completely agree, Mum.'

'I actually always thought you two would be perfect together,' she continued.

Ricky laughed out loud. 'That ain't going to happen!'

I giggled demurely. This was torture. Absolute torture. I was going to make Ricky pay for this. Big time.

'And how's the studying going, young man?' Mr Steele asked. 'I certainly hope you're knuckling down to the books after last year's fiasco.'

Ricky had spectacularly failed the fourth year of his Civil Engineering degree, and was now repeating it.

'I'm not made of money, remember,' his dad went on, when Ricky failed to reply.

I saw my chance for revenge and hauled myself

forward. 'Did Ricky tell you Vermillion got runner-up in the Battle of the Bands competition?'

There was a deafening silence.

'And he's been writing loads of new songs.' I met Ricky's glare with an innocent smile.

Mr Steele carefully placed his glass on the mantlepiece. 'Ricky–'

'Don't start, Dad.'

'We've talked about this. You promised to stop wasting time with that band malarkey. You promised to knuckle down to the books.'

Ricky stood up. 'Time to go.'

'Already?' Mrs Steele asked.

'It's time you put all that behind you,' Mr Steele continued. 'You're not a boy any more. It's time to concentrate. Look to the future.'

'I'm on it, Dad,' Ricky said through clenched teeth. He bent to hug his mum. 'Thanks, Mum.'

I got up too. 'Thank you very much for having me.'

'Oh, Jo. Always a pleasure,' Mrs Steele replied, giving me a squeeze. 'And a very Happy Birthday.'

Ricky marched half a pace ahead of me down the driveway and out onto the pavement before he stopped.

'I can't believe you brought up Vermillion.'

'I can't believe you took me to Milngavie for my birthday.'

'I'm skint! Where else would I have taken you?'

'Literally anywhere else. I got all dressed up, Ricky.'

We stood in a grumpy silence. The hum of the sodium streetlight was the loudest noise.

I shivered. 'There better be money for a taxi. I'm freezing my tits off.'

Ricky peeled off his jacket and swung it round my shoulders. 'We'll get one at the station. Come on.'

'I'm sorry,' I said as we started down the hill. 'The food was nice.'

'My dad is such a tosser.'

'He's better than some.'

'Oh?' Ricky draped his arm around me. 'Did your folks forget your birthday?'

'No. I got money.' I remembered the twenty pounds I'd been sent.

'I'm not wasting my time, you know.'

'With what?'

'With the band. I can make it work. I know I can.'

'I know,' I replied.

We took a taxi home and Ricky rang the doorbell as he was putting the key in.

'What did you do that for?'

'What?'

'Ring the bell?'

He shook his head and gave a laugh. 'Go and put the kettle on. I'm going for a slash.'

I sighed out all the disappointment of the evening and pushed open the kitchen door.

'SURPRISE!'

I stumbled in fright, struggling to comprehend the sight in front of me. The kitchen was full of people.

'Surprise!'

'Happy Birthday!'

Whooping and cheering roared at me in a wave. People, lots of people, were clapping and waving and grinning at me. And here was Mhairi coming towards me through the crowd as everyone started singing *Happy Birthday*.

'Ha! Ha!' She laughed. 'You didn't suspect a thing, did you?'

I glanced over my shoulder and there was Ricky, arms crossed, with a self-satisfied look on his face. 'Did you know about this?' I asked. But I'd already worked out the answer.

I summoned all my strength and fixed a big smile on my face as Mhairi led the three cheers. With my hand on my chest, I did my best to look astonished and delighted. People were hugging me, kissing me, thrusting cards and gifts at me. There were Bob and Dinger, Tanya and her Theatre Studies pals. There were people from my course, from Ricky's course. Gary pushed a bottle of beer into my hand.

'This is amazing,' I stammered. 'I don't know what to say.'

'It was all Mhairi's idea,' Ricky said.

'But you had the important bit, Ricky,' she replied, laughing in delight. 'You really didn't have a clue, did you?'

'I never suspected a thing,' I said. 'I love it.' My eyes were filling up. 'I'll just nip to the loo.'

'Oh, what a sweetie,' I heard Mhairi say. 'She's all emotional.'

I locked the door and sat down on the toilet, leaning forward to let the tears fall onto the tiles. Wondering why I was so upset. And knowing it was because, deep down, I'd hoped Ricky would be interested in me. Finally. How could I have been so stupid? I'd lost all sense of reality. And the surprise party! It was so fucking obvious now. If he'd wanted me, he would have just got drunk and jumped me without preamble. God, I'd been so stupid.

'Jo? You ok in there?' It was Mhairi.

'I'll be out in a minute.'

I unrolled some toilet paper, blew my nose, and wiped away the black streaks of mascara. All I wanted to do was crawl into bed and feel sorry for myself. But that would have to wait. I picked up my beer, stuck a smile on my face, and opened the door.

The hours passed, the party thinned out, and I reckoned I could feasibly withdraw to bed. Quick teeth brush, don't worry about the make-up. I stepped over some bodies on the floor to get to the bathroom, opened the door, and stuck my head in to check it was free. I'd thought Tanya had left ages ago, but there she was now, leaning against the sink, snogging Ricky's face off. Ricky had his back to me, but Tanya opened her eyes and gave me a dismissive wave. I closed the door quietly behind me.

CHAPTER 4

A few weeks later, I was frying some bacon and eggs in the kitchen when Ricky appeared, naked from the waist up, his hair still wet from the shower.

'I can't find my blue t-shirt,' he said.

I pointed up at the pulley where all his best t-shirts were hanging. I'd scooped them up the day before and washed them, anticipating the 'what will I wear' drama.

'You're a bloody lifesaver.'

'The blue one's a good choice,' I said. 'Want some breakfast? I bought bacon.'

'I can't eat food.' He sat down at the table.

I put a plate in front of him and he crammed a piece of bacon into his mouth with his fingers.

I sat down opposite him. 'All set?'

He nodded, spreading egg yolk on his toast. 'God! Winston's.'

'I cannot believe you wangled a gig at Winston's.'

'The old Steele charm,' he said, winking at me. 'Gary thinks we're not ready. But we're ready. And anyway, we can't learn how to play gigs sitting in Dinger's garage.'

He folded the toast and shoved it into his mouth. 'I can't believe you won't be there,' he mumbled.

He'd been irritated when I'd told him I couldn't go. This support slot at one of Glasgow's premier music venues was a massive deal. But Tanya had got to Jim before me.

'I've got to work,' I said.

'But I want you there. I don't want Tanya there.'

'Well, she is your girlfriend.'

'I wouldn't call her that.'

'She's pretty keen on you.'

'So you keep saying.'

'All she talks about.'

Ricky frowned at his plate. It was this easy to freak him out. It wouldn't last with Tanya. It never lasted with any of Ricky's girls. He only liked the excitement at the start. After that, his interest in them became inversely proportional to their interest in him.

'How long's that now?' I continued. 'Must be nearly a month.'

'Anyway,' he said, scraping his chair back and grabbing for the clean blue t-shirt. 'Come see what I've got.'

I followed him through to his room and perched on his bed. 'What?'

From the corner by the wardrobe, he produced a shiny white guitar.

'Ta dah!' he exclaimed proudly.

'Very nice.'

'Nice? She's beautiful.'

'She?'

'Yes, *she*. A Fender Mustang.'

'Where did you get her?'

'The shop behind St Enoch's Centre. I've had my eye on her for weeks.'

'Where did you get the money?'

'I told my dad I needed textbooks.'

I shook my head slowly at him.

'What? He can afford it,' he said, shrugging. 'Want to hold her?'

Ricky clambered onto the bed behind me and reached round my shoulders. I breathed in his smell.

'Like this.' He positioned my fingers on different strings. 'Kurt Cobain had one the same. Well, his was blue, but…'

'Who?'

'I know you know who he is.' Ricky sighed.

'An old musician?'

'A dead musician.'

He reached his right hand round my waist and played the chord. 'Look, that's a D. You're playing guitar.'

I pulled away. 'You play something.'

He slipped the strap over his head. 'Hmm, something Jo'll like,' he mused and then started singing 'Angels'.

'I don't like Take That.' I laughed.

'It's Robbie Williams,' he said, stopping. 'And it's a good song.'

I lay down on my side, cradling my head. 'You surprise me.'

'I didn't say I liked it, but it's a hit song. I need to know why it's a hit so I can write one too. It's the same for you and your writing.'

'What do you mean?'

'You know,' he said. 'All this reading you're doing. You're just immersing yourself in your craft, same as me.'

I sat up again. 'But I've hardly written anything. You've written so many songs.'

'You've written loads, Jo. You're literally always writing.'

'But nothing good. I'm still learning.'

Ricky shook his head. 'I don't think you can be taught stuff like this. You've just got to do it. You learn by doing.'

I picked at my cuticles, and Ricky pulled himself forward to sit beside me.

'Don't worry about good. That's the mistake. Just write. Write everything. Anything.'

'Well, I've got three empty weeks at home to fill, so I might do just that.'

'When you off?'

'Bus is at eight tomorrow.'

'The island.'

'Yip.'

'God, I can't imagine growing up on an island. What was it like? Is there even a school?'

I collapsed backwards onto his bed and let out a loud fake snore.

'What?' He laughed.

'Boring.' I yawned.

He shook his head, still laughing. 'You never talk about your home. Tell me something. Anything. What sort of kid were you?'

Bang on cue, the doorbell rang and I sprang up with relief. 'The past is a foreign country, Ricky.'

'Oh, that's good. Can I steal that?'

I was laughing when I opened the door to let a very nervous-looking Dinger in.

'Is he ready?'

'I'm ready. I'm ready,' Ricky replied from his room. 'Five minutes.'

'It'll be fine, Dinger,' I said. 'You can play these songs in your sleep.'

'You haven't heard us. Gary's shite. He won't do anything we want. Wants to do it all his own way. Fucking instrumentals everywhere. And he's shite.' He looked close to losing it. 'Jesus, Jo. If I ever get through this, I'm never doing another gig again.'

'Oh, you don't mean that.'

'Don't I?' He walked across the hall. 'Ricky, hurry the fuck up.'

'I'm here, I'm here,' Ricky said, dressed and hauling his gig bag and guitar case out behind him. 'You're coming to Bob's after?' he asked me.

'As soon as I finish work.'

I spent the evening reorganising glasses in the bar while everyone else was at Winston's. The torture of missing the gig would've been easier if I'd been busy, but most of the students had already gone home for the Christmas holidays. Jim said I could close up at eleven. I could not wait to get to Mhairi's and hear all about the gig.

I was lifting stools onto tables and cajoling the last dozen drinkers to finish up, when Tanya came marching into the bar, her floor-length red coat flying behind her.

'You're a cow, Jo Duncan,' she started before she'd even reached me.

'Excuse me?'

'I know you did this.' Her cheeks flushed with rage.

'Did what, Tanya?' I noticed more than a few heads turning in our direction.

'Ricky's dumped me and it's your fault.'

I bit my cheeks to try not to smile. 'Oh Tanya,' I said, placing my hand over my heart. 'I'm so sorry.'

'Don't you fucking 'sorry' me, you bitch. You told him I was keen on him. That I kept going on about him.'

I held out my hands, shrugging. 'Reporting the facts.'

'Nobody dumps me.' She tapped herself on the chest. 'Nobody. You're going to get round there and sort this out. Right now!'

I laughed openly in her face. 'Tanya, Ricky's big enough to make up his own mind. He knows trash when he sees it. So, you got dumped. Boo-fucking-hoo. Move on.' I waved my hand dismissively at her.

She stared at me, her mouth twitching.

'However,' I continued, 'if you're not going to the party, you could finish up here for me.'

'There is no party.'

'Why? What happened?'

Some of her anger seemed to melt as her lips curled into a sneer. 'The gig happened.'

'What happened at the gig?'

'Gary happened at the gig.' She let out a single chuckle. 'They got booed off stage in the end.' She crossed her arms. 'It was actually very funny, now I come to think about it.'

'It doesn't sound funny,' I snapped. 'Where's Ricky now?'

Tanya eyed me over her crossed arms and her bulging chest. 'You know what, Jo? You're welcome to him. Fuck the two of you.' And with that, she flounced back out.

I manhandled the stragglers out of the bar and ran all the way home. The flat was in darkness, but Ricky's gig bag was lying in the hall. I kicked my shoes off and dropped my jacket before quietly knocking on his door.

'You ok?' I whispered, pushing it open.

'No.'

'I heard. Want to talk?'

'No.' He rolled onto his back. The glow from the streetlight lit some of his bed, but his face was in darkness. 'Gary's a fucking dickhead.'

I walked over and knelt beside him.

'First, he broke a string and we had to stop until he fixed it.'

'Well, that happens,' I said. 'That's not so bad.'

'Then he blew his amp and he just totally threw his guitar down and stormed off stage.'

'Tell me you're joking?'

He shook his head. 'He just walked right out the door.'

I tried to imagine the scene. 'Oh, Ricky. I'm sorry.'

'We started another song, but it sounded crap with just drums and bass.' He sniffed. 'He walked off in the middle of the set, Jo. Just left us there like three spare pricks. It was humiliating.'

I squeezed his arm.

'And we totally got booed off stage. Seriously, they were booing. This is the worst night of my life.'

'I'm so sorry,' I said, shivering.

'Are you cold?' He pulled back the covers and I climbed in, curling up on my side with my back to him.

'What are you going to do now?' I asked.

He tucked his knees behind mine and wrapped an arm around me. 'Nothing. It's over. I can't work with an arsehole like that. Vermillion is no more.'

'But you love the band. Get a new guitarist.'

He scoffed. 'You can't just magic a guitarist up when it suits you.'

'Course you can. Lots of people play guitar. Advertise. You could hold auditions.'

He didn't reply for a while. I could almost hear him thinking. 'I guess I could put the word out,' he said at last. 'I could put a notice up in that guitar shop in town.'

I smiled into the pillow. Ricky would be fine. He had a plan. He always had to have a plan. I lay still, feeling his body pressing against mine. His arm was resting in the dip of my waist, his heart beating on my back, his breath slowing towards sleep.

CHAPTER 5

Three long weeks later, I was back behind the Union bar having survived the Christmas holidays, and my pain-in-the-arse sister, intact. I'd even got some writing done. Quite a lot of writing, actually. And I wouldn't have to go home again until the summer, and summer felt very far away.

The bar was heaving for a Sunday. It was the night before the start of term, and everyone was getting reacquainted.

'Glasses are getting low,' Tanya hollered from her end of the bar.

'I'll go,' I replied, grabbing a tray.

Mhairi had just come in, and I greeted her with a hug.

'Hello, stranger,' she said.

I'd only got off the bus an hour before, dumping my rucksack in the empty flat and coming straight to work.

'Oh, it's great to be back. Where is everyone?'

'Rehearsals,' she said, rolling her eyes. 'Again. How was home?'

'Never mind about that. Tell me how the new guitarist's going?'

'Malcky?' She pulled a face. 'You'll see. They'll be in in a bit.'

Jim marched past me, clapping his hands. 'More work. Less chat.'

I tugged Mhairi's sleeve. 'Walk with me,' I said, picking up a couple of empties and balancing them on my tray. 'What's wrong with Malcky?'

'Nothing,' she said, following me between tables. 'I don't know. It's just, he's been here, like, five minutes, and suddenly he's all everyone talks about. And it's like Ricky and him are joined at the hip. Like they're best pals, or whatever. Bob's feeling a bit left out.'

'Ricky's always like that with new people. It'll pass.'

I laid the full tray on the bar in front of Alan, who tugged it towards him, toppling the glasses. The sound of smashing glass brought a cheer from the students.

'I'd better get on.' I sighed.

The boys appeared just after ten and I dodged round Tanya and Alan to serve them.

Ricky grinned his wide grin at me. 'Jo!'

'Hey, you.'

'Missed you.'

'Missed you, too.'

He twisted away from the bar. 'Malcky. Malcky! Over here.'

The new guitarist turned at his name and came towards us. He had on black jeans and a too small black t-shirt which stretched over his lumpy torso. He was as tall as Ricky and sported a buzz cut that drew all my attention to his tiny blue eyes and flat nose.

'Malcky,' Ricky said proudly. 'This is Jo.'

Malcky took my extended hand in both of his. 'So, you're Ricky's girl,' he said without letting go.

'Ricky's flatmate,' I replied.

He bent his head and kissed my hand. And then sniffed it. And then, lifting his eyes to meet my startled expression, he slowly licked it.

I snatched my hand away and wiped it on my jeans. 'What the fuck?'

His eyes creased with mischief. 'You can tell a lot about a girl by her scent and her flavour.'

'Ew,' was all I could manage as Ricky burst out laughing.

'We need shots, Ricky,' the weird new bloke said before walking away.

'On it,' Ricky replied. 'Line them up, Jo.'

'What the fuck was that?' I asked. 'He *licked* me.'

Ricky continued to chuckle. 'That was Malcky Chalmers. Isn't he something?'

'He's something all right.' I laid out four shot glasses and reached for the Jägermeister. 'And where did you find him?'

'I advertised. Just like you said. Total fluke, he was just back off tour and was looking for a band.'

'Off tour?'

'He's a roadie. He was away with Rancid Empire on their European tour.'

'Never heard of them.'

Ricky picked up the shots, two in each fist. 'Death metal band. Top of their game.'

I took an order and joined Tanya at the taps.

'Who was that with Ricky?' she asked, dunting me with her hip.

I looked at her, surprised. 'I thought you weren't speaking to me.'

'I'm not.'

I glanced at the boys who were downing the shots at their table. 'That's Malcky. Ricky's new guitarist.'

'I've never seen him before.'

'No, he's not a student.'

'Look at those muscles.'

'I think that's flab.'

Ricky, on the other hand, was not flabby. There wasn't an ounce of fat on him. He was sitting wide-legged on a stool, bouncing his knee repetitively like he always did when he was excited. He kept pushing his hair back, and it kept falling forward again.

'I'll just go say hi.' Tanya grabbed a tray.

I looked at her in alarm. 'You back on with Ricky?'

'God no. Ancient history,' she replied, flouncing off.

Students were waving their Christmas money at me, demanding attention, so I got busy. I loved when it was busy. I got a buzz from being rushed off my feet. It made the time fly.

Jim appeared with some bags of change as I was finishing a sale at the till.

'Where's Tanya?' he shouted above the noise.

I glanced along the bar, but there was only Alan spilling beer and looking confused.

'Collecting glasses,' I replied. But it had been ages since she'd set off with the tray. I scanned the room. There was no sign of her. She'd be in deep shit if she got caught skiving when the bar was this busy.

Jim had turned to look, too. 'I don't see her.'

'Bathroom?'

He dumped the bags of coins in my hands. 'Sort this out,' he said, stomping off towards the doors just as Tanya swanned back in, followed closely by Malcky. I could see Jim shouting at her.

Malcky, meanwhile, walked the length of the bar, winked at me as he passed, checked over his shoulder to make sure Jim was still distracted, then leaped up onto the bar, snatched a bottle of vodka that Alan had left out, and did a crouch jog back to the boys with it.

I couldn't believe it!

'That was close,' Tanya said, arriving beside me and taking an order without a pause.

'Where have you been?'

'Having fun.' She poured two sambucas, slamming the glasses on the bar, and poured two more. 'That Malcky's a damn fine snog.'

'He just nicked a bottle of vodka,' I said.

Tanya shrugged as Jim arrived back in front of us.

'Jo, sort the change already,' he said. 'What is it with you two tonight? Alan's working harder.'

Finally, N Synch's 'Bye Bye Bye' came on, which always cleared the room at the end of the night. The lights went up, and I started sweeping the slow customers out the door. Ricky flung his arms round me as I passed.

'Get off.' I struggled out of his grasp. 'Go home.'

Malcky, who could clearly tolerate alcohol better than Ricky, took his arm. 'We'll see you two back at the flat,' he said.

'What?'

'Tanya and you. Back at the flat.'

'Oh, I think Ricky's had enough. And I'm knackered. I've got a seminar at nine.'

'A seminar at nine, have you?' Malcky sneered, half walking, half dragging Ricky to the door. 'Then you can go straight to bed.'

I watched them leave in disbelief, then turned to glare at Tanya. 'My flat is not a knocking shop.'

'Don't be a snob.' She carried on wiping the bar. 'Ricky said it was fine.'

Back home, I went straight to my room. I was damned if I was going to join them in the kitchen and be all jolly.

I pulled the duvet over my head and must have drifted off because I woke with a start, knowing someone was there.

'Only me,' Ricky whispered, lifting my covers. 'Can I sleep here? My bed's occupied.'

'No, you fucking can't,' I said, shifting over to make room. 'Piss off.'

'You're the best, Jo.' He snuggled in against my back. 'So, what do you think of Malcky?'

I 'humphed' into my pillow.

'He's great, isn't he? He thinks we should do a demo. Like properly. In a studio. And I totally agree. And he's got loads of contacts from his job. He's going to try and line up some gigs.'

'I'll reserve my judgement,' I mumbled.

Ricky kicked my foot. 'What? Cause he licked your hand?'

'And he stole a bottle of vodka.'

'So what? He was just having fun.'

'Showing off.'

'Well, he's different from us. He's never been to Uni. He's been out there, living. He knows more than us.'

'Bollocks. That doesn't make him better than us.'

'I never said that. I just mean he knows stuff. He's been round the block a bit.'

'I just found him a bit…' I hesitated. 'Cocky.'

Ricky let out a slow sigh. 'You can be such a snob sometimes.'

That was the second time someone had called me a snob today. 'I'm not a snob.'

'Are too. Anything new, anyone different, and you're all up on your high horse. He was just being friendly.'

I shifted away from him until I was hugging the edge of the bed.

'Malcky's just direct.' Ricky rolled onto his back. 'He knows what he wants, and he goes and gets it. There's nothing wrong with that. He's not a threat, you know.'

'I know he's not a threat. I don't feel threatened. What are you talking about?'

'Malcky said people often feel threatened by him because he's so confident.'

'Did he?' I took a deep breath. 'Look, I'm tired. I've been on a bus all day.'

'Just don't judge him too soon.'

'I'm not judging him.' I propped myself up on my elbow. 'If you're happy, I'm happy.'

'I hate fighting with you.'

'We're not fighting. We're discussing.'

'Disgusting?'

'Discussing.' I laughed.

Ricky held his arm out and I rested my head on his

shoulder, tucking myself into his body. I knew Malcky wasn't a threat to us – I mean to Ricky and me. Malcky could never come between us. And if he was going to be around for a while, then I was sure I'd cope. I'd coped with much worse.

CHAPTER 6

'Have you no other shoes? Take my arm,' Mhairi said, breathing out a cloud of frosty air. It was the middle of February and Glasgow was deep in a cold snap. 'What you doing this avo? Want to hang at mine?'

I shuffled across the icy pavement towards her. The soles of my trainers were shiny with wear. 'Nah, I've got the flat to myself,' I said, grabbing her sleeve. 'And I'm so behind with the word count for my final assessment. Are you missing Bob?'

'Yes! All they do is rehearse,' Mhairi said. 'This better bloody work, I tell you.'

'What? The gig?'

Mhairi set off down the path, towing me behind her. 'I still can't believe Malcky promised Jim two hundred quid at the door.'

'I know,' I agreed. 'Who's going to pay to see them?'

'And on a Thursday night, for fuck's sake.'

'Everyone's in town on a Thursday. The Union's always dead.'

'And did you hear what Malcky said to Bob?'

'About being in the band?'

'You've got to shape up or ship out. That's actually what he said. To Bob. Who is raging, by the way. I mean, who died and made Malcky God? He basically told Bob it wasn't his decision. And Ricky kept his mouth shut. Didn't say a word. It's like it's Malcky's band now.'

'Slower, Mhairi,' I said. 'I'm going to fall.'

'And him and Tanya swanning around like stupid lovebirds. It's pathetic.' She guided us over to the grass and I gratefully stepped onto firmer ground.

'Is he still bringing her back to yours?'

I shook my head. 'No. That stopped.'

'Well, he's not getting a penny out of me and Bob, that's for sure. Who's got two hundred quid, for fuck's sake?'

'If it doesn't work, it's not from the want of trying.' I pointed at a lamppost which was sporting a pasted-on poster for Vermillion's gig the next night. 'There're flyers literally everywhere.'

As we looked, a couple of first years stopped.

'It doesn't say where to get tickets,' one girl said to the other as she snapped the poster with her phone.

'From the Union bar,' I said automatically.

'We'd better get them now,' the girl said to her friend.

Mhairi snorted. 'You're going to pay money to see Vermillion?'

'It's the gig of the year,' the girl scoffed as they set off back up the hill. 'Everyone's going.'

Mhairi and I raised our eyebrows at each other in surprise.

*

41

B ack at the flat, Ricky was in the kitchen spooning food into his mouth straight from the pot.

'That's my lunch,' I said. 'I made that for me.'

'Look,' he said through a mouthful of cheesy potato. 'It's Valentine's Day.' He nodded at the pile of pink and red envelopes on the table. 'And you got one this year.'

'Aren't you going to open yours?'

'You do it. I'm eating and then I'm out of here.'

I shrugged off my jacket and sat down opposite him, lifting the first of his seven cards.

'All set for tomorrow?' I asked.

'All set. Tickets are selling.'

'So I hear.'

'Jim's had to print more.'

'Shut up.'

Ricky chuckled. 'Over a hundred already.'

'Go you.'

'Go Malcky. He's a bloody miracle worker.'

'And you're ready? Is Dinger ready?'

'He's shitting himself. But gigs get us practise and local support and online reviews.' He stopped eating to stare intensely at me. 'We've got to get our name out there. Start building a following.'

'Did Malcky say all that?' I didn't bother to hide my sarcasm.

Ricky shrugged his shoulders. 'It's true, though. Now that Gary's gone and Malcky's on board, we've got the makings of a great band.'

'Well, I'm going to sell my story to the tabloids when you're famous,' I said, splaying the open cards out on the table. 'Now, which one do you like best?' I pointed to the card I'd sent. 'What about that one?' I'd carefully chosen a slightly cheeky but not crude, bright pink card with no animals on it.

Ricky screwed up his face. 'Boring.' He flicked it open, shaking his head dismissively. 'There's no effort involved. She's obviously just grabbed the first card she saw and flung it in an envelope. I prefer a girl that puts in a bit more work, stands out a bit.' He closed the card. 'And look at that picture. Not exactly kinky, is it?'

I was devastated. 'You don't know that. You can't read all that into it.'

'Course I can.' He picked up another card with a cartoon devil on the front. 'Now, this one, on the other hand, this one screams fornication. *This* girl is most definitely up for it.'

I was cut to the bone.

'Well, let's see yours then,' Ricky said.

'What?'

'Your card. Your only card.' He picked it up and ripped open the envelope.

'Give it here.' I snatched it from him. It was scarily like the one I'd sent Ricky. It was pink and nice and had 'Guess Who?' printed inside in biro.

Ricky was grinning at me mischievously.

'What?' I snapped.

'I know who it's from.'

'Who?'

'My lips are sealed.'

'I don't care anyway,' I said, reaching for the remains of my lunch.

'Ok, it was Dinger.'

I heaped some potato onto the spoon. 'Dinger? Why?'

Ricky scraped his chair back, laughing. 'Because he's got a thing for you.' He stood up. 'I'm off. What are you going to do?'

'Write. Go to work.'

'No, about Dinger. He's my mate. I know you don't fancy him.'

I let out a guffaw.

'Jo. Don't be a bitch about it.'

'Yeah, yeah.' I batted him away with the spoon. 'I'll handle it.'

When I heard the front door shut behind Ricky, I padded through to my room and looked in the mirror at my baggy jeans and stained hoodie. He was right. I was boring.

I tugged my clothes off, pulled out my scrunchy, and took a deep breath before looking in the mirror again. My body wasn't too bad. My legs were good, and I had a flat belly, which made up for my pathetically small boobs. I took a step closer and peered at my face. I'd always had good skin, which is why I'd never bothered with make-up. But I wasn't sixteen anymore. And my wardrobe was holding me back. It was holding my life back.

I got dressed and left the flat. At the cash machine by the bridge, I took out a hundred and fifty pounds of rent money, and jumped the underground into town. I was going shopping.

*

When I turned up for work the next night in my new mini-skirt and 'Flame Red' dyed hair, Jim raised

44

an eyebrow, but managed not to comment. The Union was heaving, and there was a bouncer at the door. We were fully staffed. The Dungeon felt like a Saturday night, but there were no disco lights and people weren't dancing. There was hardly room to move on the floor as the crowd vied for standing room.

'There's two hundred and thirty people in,' Jim shouted in my ear.

I quickly did the maths. That was four hundred and sixty quid at the door. 'Do the boys get the profit?' I shouted back.

'That's the deal,' he shrugged, slamming the till shut and turning back to the bar.

'What is this like?' I shouted at Tanya as we passed.

'My Malcky's a genius.'

'It might have been Malcky's idea, but they're coming to see my Ricky.'

'He's not your Ricky,' she called. 'Love the hair, by the way.' She grabbed the fabric of my t-shirt. 'Wait,' she said as she tied it in a knot behind my back. 'A new look for your new look.'

We were low on bottled beer, so I headed to the storeroom behind the stage, which doubled as a dressing room. Only Malcky looked up when I came in. He wolf-whistled, and I ignored him. Bob was tuning his bass and Ricky was doing star jumps in the corner.

'Bloody hell,' he said when he spotted me. 'What happened to your hair?'

'Fuck off.'

'No, it's great. You look fantastic. Doesn't she look fantastic, Dinger?'

Dinger and Malcky were sitting on crates smoking.

'What are you doing?' I said in alarm. 'It stinks of hash. You can't smoke in here.'

Malcky stood up. 'Well, make sure no one else comes in then, Jo.'

I gave him a look and started moving crates to get to the bottles I wanted.

'Want a hand?' Dinger asked.

I picked up two cases of beer. 'You do not want to go out there.'

'Why?'

'It's busy.'

'Oh, god,' Dinger groaned and took another long drag of the joint. 'Half of Glasgow are going to watch us bomb just like last time.'

'Rubbish,' Bob said. 'That was all down to Gary. You're a great drummer.'

Malcky held the door open for me. 'Don't wish us luck,' he said. 'We don't need it.'

The lights went down bang on nine o'clock, and the crowd surged to the front of the stage. Dinger, Bob and Malcky came on first, just like before, and started playing. Then Ricky ran on, sliding across to grab the mic. He did not fall this time.

'Hello, the Dungeon!' he screamed, then started to sing.

I laughed out loud as the crowd went nuts. I could hardly believe it. It was better than I could have ever imagined. Ricky strutted up and down the stage, and the crowd loved it. The sound was really tight. They sounded like a proper band. Malcky just concentrated on his guitar and on Dinger and let Ricky totally do his own thing. The stage was Ricky's, and the audience was at his beck and call. There were girls dancing and boys cheering. People were holding up their phones and at the end of each song, everyone whistled and clapped.

An hour later, they were offstage, and then back on again when the crowd demanded an encore. I gave up serving and sat on the end of the bar nearest the stage to watch.

'Can I just say…' Ricky raised his hands above his head for attention. 'You guys have been great.' He bent to pick up his pint as the room cheered and whistled. 'Remember where you saw us first, eh? Here's to you all.'

Everyone roared. He had them in the palm of his hand. The music kicked in and the crowd started bouncing up and down in time. 'This is our last song of the night, so let's see you guys rock,' he roared.

I was grinning fit to burst. Was this the same bloke who'd been sitting in a grotty kitchen eating cheesy potato the day before? Now he looked like a proper rock star. Ricky belonged on stage. He totally owned it.

CHAPTER 7

Next Thursday night, and for the second week in a row, Vermillion was playing in the Union.

'Jo, get downstairs and open up the Dungeon,' Jim called from his office at the end of the bar.

Right enough, it was nearly half eight. I finished serving my customer and headed down.

After the success of the previous week, Jim had offered them a four-week residency. They were to play from nine until ten thirty in exchange for a hundred quid and a free round at the bar. There was no door charge and a disco until two after the gig, in an attempt to compete with the big venues in town. I wasn't convinced it would work. Thursdays were when the entire west end of Glasgow relocated to the city centre student nights.

The boys were setting up on stage as I started counting the float.

'Hiya.' Dinger appeared and leaned across the bar.

'Want your free drink now?'

'Sure. Why not?' He slurred his words and swayed a bit when he slapped the bar. This was obviously not his first drink.

I avoided his gaze and picked up a pint glass. 'Beer?'

'No. Something stronger.' He studied the bottles behind me, chewing his lip. 'Give me a jack and coke.'

'Ooh.' I turned to pour his drink. 'How very rock 'n' roll.'

'So, I take it Ricky told you?' he blurted.

I hadn't thought he'd bring it up. 'Told me what?'

He chuckled, dropping his eyes. He knew I knew.

I put his drink in front of him, squirming with awkwardness. 'He mentioned the card, yes.'

'Yeah, anyway, it's no big deal. I know you don't fancy me.' He picked up his glass and took a big gulp.

God, this was awful. 'I liked the card. It cheered me up. I liked it.' I hunted around for a new topic. 'And the studio was a success?'

'Guess so.' He shrugged. 'I'm to pick up the CDs tomorrow.'

Malcky had booked twelve hours in a recording studio with last week's profit. Much to Mhairi's annoyance. She'd had plans for Bob's share of that cash.

'And I'm expected to write a bio for the sleeve.' He took another big slug of his drink. 'Don't know where to start.'

'Vermillion are an up-and-coming, four-piece rock band with huge ambition,' I began, polishing a glass with a dishtowel. 'With their cutting-edge, original sound and infectious melodies, their talent is undeniable.'

Dinger fumbled in his pockets. 'That's it! Wait till I find a pen.'

'I'll help you later,' I said, laughing. 'And then you sell them?'

He shook his head. 'And then we send them to all Malcky's contacts, apparently. And anyone else we can think of. A&R guys, record companies, radio stations. Ricky's in charge of the artwork. He knows a girl at the art school.'

'Of course he does.'

I looked across at the stage. Ricky was on his knees, contemplating Malcky's pedal board with rapt attention. Only the overhead lights were on, casting him in heavy shadow. He'd never looked so sexy. He had on his old Diesel jeans that hung perfectly from his hipbones. He got up and started walking back and forth with one finger in his ear as Malcky plucked at his guitar.

'I'm not sorry I sent it. The Valentine's card,' Dinger said. He'd been watching me watching the stage. 'Even though nothing's going to happen.'

I smiled bravely at him. 'I'm flattered, Dinger. I am, but…'

He chuckled. 'I guess you of all people know what it's like to fancy someone without standing a chance, eh?'

'Dinger!' Malcky shouted over. 'Get your butt over here, you useless prick.'

Dinger downed his drink.

'What do you mean?' I frowned.

He walked backwards, away from the bar. 'You know – Ricky.'

'I don't fancy Ricky,' I said too fast, and Dinger just shrugged.

This was not good. If Dinger had guessed, who else had guessed? I kept my eyes off the stage as I finished counting the float.

*

The gig went well, and it looked as busy as it had been the week before. The disco started up as soon as they finished playing, drowning out the applause and whistles of the crowd. I kept an eye on my gang, scattered round the room. Mhairi and her pals were in and dancing. Bob and Dinger were downing pints with some of their mates at a table. And Ricky and Malcky were holding forth beside the stage with a constantly altering group of unknown faces, usually female, but with the odd back-slapping bloke in there for good measure. Ricky looked quite the star. But there was no sign of Tanya. She had the night off, but I'd expected her to be at the gig. Maybe all was not perfect in paradise.

My shift finished at midnight, and I nipped upstairs to change. I pulled out my ponytail, brushed my hair and smeared on some lip-gloss before joining everyone back downstairs. The place was still jumping.

'I've saved you a seat,' Mhairi screeched in my ear, stumbling into me.

This was a lie, but everyone moved over so I could squeeze onto the end of the bench. Mhairi screamed, flung her arms in the air and took off onto the dance floor to accost someone she knew.

'Sounded good tonight,' I shouted at Bob.

'Aye.' He rubbed a large hand over his hairless scalp.

'I'm getting to know the songs. I was singing along.'

'Aye.'

'What songs did you choose for the CD?'

'Um… 'Rude'; 'My Conscience'; 'Give In'; 'Touch and Go'.'

'*I thought I had you. It was touch and go,*' I sang. '*You never need me, you just touch and go.*'

'Jesus!' Bob stared at me. 'I didn't know you could sing. That was really good.'

I burst out laughing, shaking my head. 'Oh, I can't sing.' I turned away to look at the dance floor. 'Someone's happy.'

Mhairi was flinging herself about to the music.

'Aye, she's had a few. There'll be tears tomorrow.'

With that, Mhairi's legs went out from under her and she tumbled to the ground, snorting with laughter.

Bob finished his pint. 'Think I'll get her home.'

'I'll help you,' I said, getting up. 'Just let me say bye to Ricky.'

Ricky and Malcky were still by the stage, engaged in lively conversation with two girls. Malcky saw me approach and sipped his beer as he watched me.

'No Tanya tonight?' I asked him.

'Not tonight, no,' he said, still staring at me. 'I'm all yours.'

I pulled a face. 'Eh, no thanks.'

'I won't tell if you don't. Or maybe a threesome's more your thing?'

'Jo!' Ricky noticed me and reached between the girls to give me a hug. 'Well? How were we?'

'Very good.' I smiled, turning my back on Malcky. 'Mhairi's drunk. I'm going to help get her home. Coming?'

'Oh, don't go,' one girl said, taking hold of Ricky's arm.

'I'm sure Bob and you can manage,' Malcky said.

'Is this your girlfriend, Ricky?' The other girl folded her arms, looking at me. I'd never seen them before, but they looked very young.

Before I could answer, Ricky flapped his hand towards me. 'Don't worry about her. She's just my flatmate.'

Malcky guffawed and smacked my bum as I stomped away, swallowing my humiliation.

CHAPTER 8

What I needed was a night out. A night out to get my mind off work, off Uni, and, especially, off Ricky. And after badgering Mhairi a bit, that's exactly what I got. It was Saturday and not only was I not working, but I was on a night out. In town. To Glasgow's newest, most talked about nightclub. I was beyond excited.

'I can't believe we have to queue.' Mhairi groaned as we waited outside The Shrine. 'And I can't believe it's so cold.' She handed me the plastic water bottle that we'd filled with vodka before setting off. 'My tits are going to fall off.'

'At least you've got tits to fall off,' I said, taking a swig as my phone rang. I glanced at the screen and turned it off.

'Shut up,' she replied. 'You're gorgeous. Look at you with your foxy red hair and your skinny legs. I haven't got away with a skirt that short since I was twelve.'

'My feet are killing me already,' I moaned. 'I can't do heels.'

'Who are you blanking?' She nodded at my phone.

'Jim. He'll just want me to work. Tanya's probably pulled another sickie. I had to work a double shift yesterday. Lazy cow.'

'Maybe she was sick.'

'She's never sick. She'd have been out with Malcky.' I handed the bottle back, nodding at the boy in front of us in the queue. 'Don't you think that bloke looks like Danny O'Donoghue?'

'No,' she said. 'When was the last time you had a snog?'

'Bloody ages.'

'Right.' She tapped the stranger on the shoulder. 'Excuse me. Has anyone ever told you that you look like Danny O'Donoghue?'

His mate answered for him. 'All the time. And he's got the reputation to match. Why? You interested?'

Mhairi laughed too loudly. 'And who are you? His pimp?'

And then the third member of their group turned round. It was Dinger. He grinned and squeezed between the others to reach me.

'Hey,' he said.

'Friends of yours?'

'Mates from school, aye.'

In my heels, I towered above him. He pulled at his nose several times and kept his chin raised, trying to appear taller. I felt awkward as we watched the Danny lookalike taking a gulp of my vodka.

'Hey Dinger!' Mhairi said. 'How was band practice?' She snorted out a drunken laugh.

'Rehearsal was fine, thank you, Mhairi.'

'Have you grown?'

I turned a full circle to avoid getting caught laughing.

*

All our shuffling was finally rewarded, and I pretended not to see Dinger getting asked for ID as we stepped inside the club. The music got louder and our spirits rose as we climbed the carpeted stairs, giggling with relief at being inside.

'Let's get a drink first, then have a look about,' Mhairi shouted.

The place was jumping already, and we joined the crush at the bar with Dinger and his mates.

'Can I get you a drink?' Dinger yelled.

'No. Mhairi's on it.'

He leaned closer to my ear. 'Jo, actually, can we talk? I've been meaning to speak to you.'

I was cringing inside. He was going to bring up the Valentine's card again. I just knew it. Or even worse – he was going to ask me out. Luckily, the Danny lookalike pulled us apart.

'And who's this lovely lady?' he asked.

Dinger sighed, looked at his feet, then answered. 'Steve, meet Jo.'

Steve's eyebrows shot up. 'This is Jo?'

'Don't.' Dinger shook his head at his pal.

'This is the Jo we never stop hearing about?'

I pretended I hadn't heard. 'So, you went to school with Dinger here?'

'Dinger?' Steve's eyebrows shot up again and Dinger screwed up his face in agony.

'It's just a nickname,' Dinger answered.

'Hey Neil. Neil!' Steve shouted over his shoulder in glee. 'Wait till you hear this.'

Mhairi was still nowhere near the front of the bar, and

I tugged her arm.

'Forget the drinks. Let's dance.'

We squeezed our way into the middle of the dance floor and began to sway. I could feel the bass thumping through my bones and I closed my eyes, raising my hands above my head. This was more like it. This was fun. I opened them again when the tune changed and locked eyes with a boy standing at the edge of the floor.

'Fuck,' I exclaimed.

'What?' Mhairi spun round to look.

'No, don't look!'

'Who is it?'

'Gary.'

'Gary? Rubbish guitarist Gary?'

I nodded frantically. 'Shit, he's coming over.'

'Keep dancing,' Mhairi urged, trying to manoeuvre us across the floor, but it didn't work. Gary arrived and started swaying in front of me. He'd brought a friend, and the friend was thrusting his hips at Mhairi, separating us further.

Gary looked me up and down. 'Hey Jo. Looking good.'

'Not in the mood, Gary.'

'Dance with me,' he shouted. 'Old times' sake.'

I didn't want to go back to the bar to talk to Dinger, and I was enjoying dancing and what was the harm? I danced to the music, trying my best to ignore my partner, but he danced me right across the floor until my back was nearly on the wall at the far side. He caught my arm as I tried to step past him.

'Not so fast. Come here.' He jerked me back, and I staggered in my heels, my bare back touching the damp wall. 'Let's catch up a bit,' he said, leaning towards me. 'I think we'd have been good together, Jo.' He ground his hips against mine and sucked my ear.

I got my arms between us and pushed hard. 'Fuck off, Gary,' I shouted as he staggered into the crowd.

'Stupid bitch,' I heard him say.

I burst through the door of the toilets and stood with my hands on each side of a sink, taking deep breaths.

'Not having a good night?' the girl beside me asked, her lipstick poised in front of her mouth.

'Not the best, no.'

A cubicle door opened and Mhairi came out, still buttoning up her trousers.

'There you are!' She lunged at me in drunken delight.

'Hands!'

'Sorry.' She detached herself and turned on a tap. 'Where did you go?'

'Gary tried to snog me,' I huffed.

Mhairi finished her quick hand wash and shook her wrists violently up and down. 'Aye? His mate had his hand on my arse the minute your back was turned. But guess what? My new pals are in. Let's go dance with them.'

I'd met Mhairi's new pals from her teacher training course before. I hadn't liked them much.

'I need a drink,' I said. 'I'll find you.'

Back at the bar, Dinger immediately handed me a drink. I wasn't even bothered about having to talk to him now. Anything other than Gary.

'Cheers,' I said. I sipped my vodka, realising I would never get a snog when I was surrounded by blokes I didn't want.

'Pretty good in here, eh?' he said, resting an arm on the bar. 'Oh, hi, Gary.'

I took a deep breath and turned to glare at Gary, who had his bloodshot eyes fixed on me. He was obviously far from sober. I stared him out.

'I wouldn't bother with this one, Dinger,' he slurred. 'She's a frigid little cow.'

'Gary, come on,' Dinger said. 'That's not on.'

He didn't answer, just turned and walked off.

Dinger frowned at me. 'That was a bit harsh.'

'A bit?' I said and downed my drink. 'I'm going home. Can you tell Mhairi?'

I didn't wait for a reply. I wanted out of there. This had been far from the night I'd hoped for.

*

Back in the flat, I closed the door behind me as quietly as possible. The place was in darkness. I flipped the light in the kitchen and staggered towards the table, resting my hands on the warm pine to kick off my shoes. It was good to be home.

I heard a yawn behind me and turned. Ricky was stretching his arms round and above his head, resplendent in only his boxer shorts. I let my inebriated eyes linger over his taut stomach and smooth chest and chuckled quietly. Yet another man sent to complicate my ruined night.

'You're home early,' he said, padding past me to fill a glass with water from the tap. 'Malcky's not long gone.' He scratched his hair roughly with his free hand. 'We were working on a song.'

I hobbled over on my sore feet, took the glass, and drained it in one big gulp.

'So,' he said, refilling the glass and handing it back to me. 'How was it? Where did you go?'

'The Shrine.'

'That new club on Bath Street?' Ricky bounced up to sit on the worktop. 'Dinger was going. Did you see him?'

I gulped the water down and placed the glass on the counter. 'Yes, I saw him. And Gary.'

'How's Gary?' Ricky asked, stifling a yawn.

I was suddenly very, very tired. I put my hands on my face and dropped my head.

Ricky jumped off the worktop and took me by the shoulders. 'Hey? What's the matter? What happened?'

'Nothing,' I said, letting my hands drop. 'Just Gary being an arsehole. And then having to deal with Dinger.'

Ricky sniggered quietly and drew me towards him. I slid my hands round his waist.

'It was rubbish,' I mumbled into his shoulder. 'And I just wanted a nice night out.'

'Poor you.'

He swayed me gently to and fro, and I closed my eyes. I could feel his breath on the back of my neck. He was tucking loose strands of hair behind my ear and I relaxed against him, aware of every bit of his body. The alcohol in my blood was telling me not to think further – to just enjoy the moment. I ran a hand slowly up his back, feeling the skin and muscle under my fingers.

And then I felt a movement further down our bodies and I froze, realising what it was. Ricky tensed up too, trying to shift his hips back against the kitchen units.

He was getting a hard-on. I slowly lifted my head from his shoulder, trying not to laugh. He was looking ahead, blinking, obviously searching for control. He swallowed once and then dropped his eyes to mine. Absolutely refusing to think any further about what I was doing, I covered the short distance to his lips and kissed him. And he kissed me back. Properly. Not the usual quick peck on the lips, but a soft, lingering caress. I felt like I was flying. Then, at exactly the same moment, our lips opened and just the very tips of our tongues met. It was like an electric shock and our heads sprang apart. It was over.

We stared at each other. I was suddenly very sober.

'What's going on?' Ricky asked, quietly.

'I'm drunk.'

He let go of me and turned his body towards the kitchen units, clearing his throat. 'I don't know if we should...'

'Neither do I.'

He stood a moment longer, then practically ran out of the room, leaving me to die a slow death of embarrassment.

CHAPTER 9

I'd woken the next day consumed by a thumping headache and waves of self-loathing. What the fuck had I been thinking? I'd ruined everything. The years of easy friendship, gone. All that awaited us was awkwardness and embarrassment.

But the hangover waned, and I came to the conclusion that I had two options – apologise or pretend it didn't happen. I was choosing to pretend it didn't happen. I was going to ignore the whole bloody thing. Which included ignoring Ricky.

My plan got off to a flying start, aided by Ricky, who was ignoring me better than I was ignoring him. In fact, he was nowhere to be found for the whole of Sunday. But Monday evening loomed ahead of me. There'd be no avoiding him then.

I caught up with Mhairi as she headed off campus on Monday afternoon.

'You coming round tonight?'

'For the listening event of the century?' she replied, steering us through the throng of students. 'Wouldn't miss it. I wonder what song they'll play.'

The CDs, complete with the bio I'd written and a tasteful, not too swirly, Vermillion graphic on embossed purple card, had been posted the week before. And Malcky had got word that one of the songs was to be played on Radio Glasgow that very night.

'Want to grab lunch?'

'No can do,' I replied, pulling my hood up against the chilly drizzle. 'Library. I'm so behind. That Tanya pulled another sickie. Can you believe her? I had to do another double shift. Honestly, wait till I see her.'

Mhairi nodded down the path. 'You won't have long. Here comes Tanya now.'

And, right enough, there she was, sauntering towards us with her long red coat swinging out like lady muck.

'Would you look at the sunglasses,' I growled. 'It's raining, for fuck's sake.'

'I'm looking forward to this.' Mhairi giggled.

Tanya was almost upon us. I stepped in front of her and she ground to a halt.

'Feeling better?' I stood up straight, but in her heeled boots, she was way taller.

She flicked her hair over one shoulder and adjusted her sunglasses.

'Only, your pals said you weren't sick at all. Your pals said you were out with Malcky.'

She turned her head away, looking somewhere past us.

'I had to work a double shift. That's two weeks in a row. Did you think I would just not mind?'

I paused, but still she had nothing to say. I was losing my temper. 'And what's with the shades? It's winter, for fuck's sake.' I reached up and pulled them off her face, and gasped.

Mhairi gasped, too, stepping forward to have a better look. Tanya tried to turn away, but Mhairi took hold of her shoulder. 'What happened to you?' she asked in horror.

Tanya was sporting a corker of a black eye. It was swollen almost shut, with dark purple bruises round the socket and down over her cheekbone.

She snatched her sunglasses back and slid them carefully into place. 'Nothing happened. It was an accident.'

I couldn't speak. I was just standing there, completely speechless.

'Who did this to you?' Mhairi's face had turned pale, her mouth set tight. 'Tanya, did Malcky do this to you?'

Tanya sniffed loudly. I had never seen her cry before.

'Right!' Mhairi let go of Tanya and set off back the way we'd come.

'No! Mhairi, stop,' Tanya cried, but I held her arms to stop her following.

'Tanya, what the hell happened?' I asked, finding my voice. 'You've got to tell me.'

'Where's she going?' Tanya wailed, watching Mhairi jog across the grass. She was heading in the direction of the engineering building where Bob and Ricky were most likely to be.

I spoke calmly. 'Did Malcky do this to you?'

She shook her head. 'It's not like that. It was my fault.' Her lips had gone all rubbery. 'I hit him first. I provoked him.'

'That doesn't excuse this,' I replied. We'd attracted a few onlookers by now, so I linked her arm and dragged her up the path. 'Come on, let's get a cup of tea.'

Some of Tanya's pals were at a table by the window in

the canteen. She ground to a halt when she spotted them, disentangled herself from me, blew her nose, flicked her hair up and patted her face with powder from her shoulder bag all in lightening-quick time.

'I'm fine,' she said, squeezing my hand. 'Really, I'll be fine. But if you could be a doll and go stop Mhairi doing whatever it is she's going to do, that would be great.' She gave me a final hand pat and swanned off through the tables towards her pals.

I watched as they started flapping around her, their collective high-pitched chatter fluttering across the room. Total drama queens, the lot of them, with Tanya in the centre, loving all the attention. And I had no intention, whatsoever, of stopping Mhairi doing whatever it was she was going to do. I headed to the library instead.

Everyone was due to meet at our flat at six, so I started for home just after that to be sure of not being alone with Ricky. When I got in, Ricky, Bob, and Mhairi were sitting at the kitchen table in silence. Bob had a bag of frozen mixed veg resting on the back of his outstretched hand.

'What's going on?' I asked, dropping my bag.

'We're waiting for Malcky,' Mhairi said.

'What happened to your hand?'

'Bob punched him, but Ricky stopped them fighting.'

'And I said we'd finish it later,' Bob mumbled.

'He's on his way now,' Mhairi concluded.

Ricky had his arms folded and his eyes down. He was still ignoring me better than I was ignoring him.

I shrugged off my jacket and started collecting the empty mugs. 'Shouldn't we turn on the radio?' I asked. 'Wouldn't want to miss it.'

'Shit.' Ricky got up to find the station on his laptop. 'What time is it?'

'Plenty of time.' Mhairi turned to me. 'Sorry, we finished the tea bags.'

I boiled the kettle anyway and retrieved a jar of instant coffee from the back of a cupboard.

'What happens when Malcky gets here?' I couldn't help myself asking. 'What are you going to do?'

'We're going to wait and hear Malcky's side of it,' Ricky answered.

'Malcky's side is spread out across Tanya's face,' Mhairi snapped. 'I can't believe you're taking his side.'

'Just give him a chance to explain,' Ricky mumbled. 'That's all I'm saying.'

'I don't need to hear his excuses.' Bob's voice was lower than usual.

'But you don't know Tanya,' Ricky continued. 'She can be a complete nightmare.'

Mhairi started shouting. 'What? Because she's a strong woman? Because she had the audacity to speak her own mind? There's no fucking excuse, Ricky. None. If he couldn't handle Tanya, he should've just walked away.'

The doorbell rang before she'd finished, and I sprang into the hall to get it. Tanya pushed me out of the way as she came in. Her sunglasses were still in place, but I knew she was raging. Malcky followed her at a slower pace.

Tanya slapped both fists onto the kitchen table and leaned across at Bob. 'How dare you,' she shouted. 'Who the hell do you think you are?'

'Someone had to do it,' Mhairi roared back.

I slid round to the worktop to get a better view, pressing the volume up button on Ricky's Mac.

Tanya turned her body to face Mhairi. 'No, they bloody didn't. He had no right. This is between me and Malcky. And it was sorted long before you stuck your nose in.'

'Oh, it looks sorted.' Mhairi stood up. 'Have you seen yourself, Tanya? Look what he did to you, for fuck's sake.'

'Tanya,' Malcky said from the doorway. 'Sit the fuck down. Let me handle it.'

Bob rose to his feet and pushed Mhairi down. He stepped round the table to square up to Malcky. I braced myself against the work surface and held my breath, but Tanya sprang between them. Malcky physically lifted her out of the way and she stumbled against me. The boys took a step towards each other, puffing out their chests like baboons.

Then Ricky sprang to his feet, knocking over his chair. 'Right! That's enough.' He bolted round the table and positioned himself between the two blokes with his arms stretched. 'That's enough! Come on. Let's talk. Let's hear what Malcky has to say.'

Bob hesitated, then shrugged and sat down. Foster the People's 'Pumped Up Kicks' was playing on the radio, I noticed, keeping half an ear out. Malcky stood where he was. He had a faint yellow swelling on his right cheekbone, but no other evidence of the morning's events.

'First of all,' he began, holding out his palms. 'I am, in no way, trying to excuse my behaviour.'

Mhairi got up, tutting in disgust, and joined Tanya and me at the worktop.

'What I did was wrong. I have wronged Tanya. I have no excuse, although I had had a few drinks.'

'That doesn't make it alright,' Mhairi said.

'Shut up,' Tanya told her. 'You weren't there. I was winding him up.'

'I know I have a problem with my temper,' Malcky continued. 'And I need to deal with that. But I've never hit a woman before and I don't plan to again.'

'That's what they all say,' Mhairi said.

'Tanya has forgiven me.' He held out his hand, and she took it, slipping off her sunglasses to gaze pathetically at him.

'Jesus Christ, Malcky,' Ricky said. It was his first sight of Tanya's face.

Malcky reached up and cupped her cheek. 'I have to look at what I did to this beautiful face every single day. That's my punishment.' Malcky let Tanya go and turned back to the boys. 'Bob, you were right to do what you did this afternoon. Any man would've done the same. If you feel there's more to do, we can finish it now.'

All eyes turned to Bob. The song had finished, and the DJ's voice was droning on in the background.

'No, I've done what needed done and I've said my piece.'

'Are you joking?' I scoffed. 'Look at her face, Bob.'

Bob pulled his shoulders back but didn't reply.

'Ricky?' I said.

'It's not your fight, Jo.'

'Not my fight?!' I was raising my voice. 'It shouldn't be anyone's fight. Especially not Tanya's fight.' I looked around the room. 'I can't believe you're swallowing this bullshit! The lot of you.'

'Jo–'

'No, Ricky.' I held a hand up at him. 'Tanya, there are non-negotiables,' I continued, turning to her. 'Violence and infidelity.'

Tanya lifted her shoulders. 'Oh, you naïve little sausage,' she sneered. 'You have no idea.'

I threw my arms out. 'Enlighten me.'

'Just shut up, Jo,' Ricky shouted.

'What did you say to me?' I yelled.

Ricky ran at me and covered my mouth with his hand. 'Just shush! It's on!'

And, right enough, the familiar chords of Vermillion's 'Give In' could be heard over Ricky's speakers. Everyone froze where they were, and listened in silence, breathing in the tension.

'... *And I try to quit baby*
But you're hard to resist
My mind is saying give up
But my body just insists I give in...'

I kept my eyes fixed on the far side of the room, listening to my heartbeat until the song finished and the DJ started speaking again.

'...*That was Vermillion, our unsigned band of the week, with 'Give In'. You can catch these guys playing the Dungeon at the GSU on Thursday night. Next up, we've a classic from...*'

Ricky dropped his hand from my mouth just as Dinger burst in through the door.

'Have I missed it?' He was panting, his eyes scanning the room until they alighted on Tanya. 'Oh my god! What happened to your face?'

CHAPTER 10

Thursday rolled around, and a packed Dungeon kept us busy behind the bar. It was Vermillion's last Union gig, but instead of giving them more Thursdays, Jim was planning a 'Live at the Dungeon' night instead, where he intended to promote different bands with the same free disco after. Vermillion's run was over.

'Jo!'

'Not now, Ricky. I'm busy.' I walked down the bar to the beer taps, even though there were perfectly good ones right in front of me.

Ricky dodged the waiting punters to catch me up. 'Stop avoiding me.'

'Not avoiding. Busy.' I willed the glass to fill up quicker.

'I know you're angry with me.' He leaned over the bar, trying to catch my eye. 'Jo.'

I walked back up the bar with the full pint and exchanged it for cash. Ricky kept pace with me on the other side.

'Aren't you meant to be on-stage?' I asked.

'We need to talk, Jo.' He reached across to hold my forearm. 'Please.'

I sighed dramatically. It looked like my pretend-it-hadn't-happened time had run out. I was going to have to apologise.

I stomped out from behind the bar and through the door into the toilet corridor.

'What?' I said firmly when he arrived.

'Last Saturday night. We need to talk about it.' His face was grim.

'What about it?' I asked, crossing my arms. I hated apologising and wasn't about to rush into it.

He sighed and put a hand on his hip. 'The thing. The kissing thing.'

'Ah,' I said, slowly. 'The thing.'

'Don't laugh at me,' he snapped. 'This is really hard. I mean, difficult for me.'

Was he flustered? Was Ricky Steele flustered?

He took another deep breath. 'The thing is, we need to talk. We need to clear the air. There's air to be cleared.' He ran a hand through his hair as he waited for a girl to pass, still buttoning up her jeans. 'So, now, Saturday night, the kissing thing, in the kitchen. The thing is, about the thing...'

It was pathetic to watch. 'Ricky, I know about the thing. I was there.'

'Jesus! Jo, shut up. You know how difficult this is for me. I never apologise and you're making it impossible.'

He was trying to apologise? 'Apologise?'

'I'm trying to! Just let me say my piece. I've got it all planned and everything.'

I stood up straighter and unfolded my arms. 'Carry on.'

'Thank you. Right, the thing is, I never meant to kiss you. I mean, I wasn't trying to kiss you, but I did. Not that I didn't want to kiss you. Well, I didn't not want to kiss you. I mean, I don't fancy you. No, that's not it. I do fancy you. But not in an active way. You're a good-looking girl. Any boy would be happy to… you know. But you're, like, my pal. And I shouldn't have kissed you. And there's no excuse for it. I was out of order.'

I was silent for a moment after he'd finished. 'Right,' I said, eventually, for want of anything better to say.

'So,' he continued, 'my point is, I'm sorry. For the kissing thing and…' He waved his hand briefly over his nether regions. 'The other thing.'

I was now as flustered as he was. 'Don't worry about it,' I said.

'But I have been worrying about it. It was out of order. You're my friend.'

'Ricky, it's fine. Really.'

He put a hand on my shoulder and leaned down to look me in the eye. 'Is it?'

'Yes. It wasn't all you. I'd had too much to drink and was being inappropriate.'

'So, we're ok then?' He cocked his head to one side. He had the longest eyelashes in the world.

'Of course we are.'

'Cause I hate it when we're not speaking.'

'Me too.'

'There's no one else to talk to. You're the only one that understands me.' He pulled me forward into a hug. 'You're my best friend in the whole world, Jo. I won't do anything like that ever again. Promise.'

I felt a lump in the back of my throat. Was I ever going to get over him?

The door banged open. 'Aye, aye,' Malcky jeered. 'What's all this then?'

'Nothing,' Ricky replied, letting me go.

'Well, get your skinny arse onstage, you prick. We're waiting.'

Ricky jogged off, ducking under Malcky's arm as Malcky held two fingers up to his mouth and waggled his tongue between them at me.

I stuck one finger up at him in reply.

I returned to the bar, where Tanya was waiting, her face like fizz.

'Oh, you are here?' she said. 'Planning on doing any work tonight?'

Her eye had lost the puffiness in the preceding week, and her years of make-up practice were paying off. All remaining bruising was well hidden. We hadn't revisited our spat in the kitchen. As far as I was concerned, she was welcome to Malcky.

I ignored her and turned to serve. 'What can I get you?'

'Pint of lager,' my customer replied without making eye contact. He was leaning one elbow on the bar, looking around the room. I knew, instantly, that he wasn't a student. Students lean halfway across the bar, never taking their eyes off their chosen barperson and wave fivers like little flags to attract attention. I started pouring and had another look at him – and then I nearly dropped the glass in shock. It was Mick Dumfries, the DJ from Radio Glasgow.

He wandered off across the room with his drink as

Vermillion took to the stage. I continued working, my eyes flitting between Ricky and Mick Dumfries. People were dancing. A lot of the crowd was actually singing along. Mick Dumfries was sipping his pint, watching all of it. On stage, Ricky was on top form, swinging himself across the floor, being a total rock star.

As soon as they finished their set, the crowd bore down on the bar, but I ignored them all and waited while Mick Dumfries approached.

'Another lager?' I asked him.

'Well remembered. Yes, please.'

I picked up a glass and began pouring. The tap was right in front of him. 'Did you enjoy the gig?'

'Pardon?'

I cocked my head at the now empty stage. 'Vermillion. What did you think?'

He nodded his head.

'I'm Jo. I live with the singer, Ricky.' I was feeling very brave. 'They'll be chuffed you came.' I placed his drink in front of him.

'Actually, I was hoping to have a word with them,' he said, taking a first sip.

'I'll take you straight through.'

I was round the front of the bar before Tanya could notice, pushing my way to the side of the stage and down the corridor towards the storeroom. I opened the door without knocking.

'Mick Dumfries is here.'

'What?' Ricky was standing with a beer bottle in hand, naked from the waist up.

But I didn't have time for a naked Ricky. 'Mick

Dumfries. Here,' I repeated, glaring at Malcky who was stubbing out a joint. 'Now!'

Ricky grabbed his t-shirt from the top of a crate of beer as I slowly swung the door wider for Mick Dumfries, who walked straight past me into the room and kicked the door shut behind him. I pressed my ear to the door but could hear nothing.

Back at the bar, I avoided Tanya's venomous glares and worked fast to clear the queue. 'What are you so fidgety about tonight?' she asked as we both pulled pints.

'I was just wondering what Mick Dumfries was speaking to the boys about,' I replied innocently.

'What? Mick Dumfries is here?'

'Didn't you see him? He's been here all night.'

We both looked over at the corridor just as Mick Dumfries appeared. He walked the length of the bar with our eyes on him, dropped off his empty glass and swung out the door. Our eyes swung back to the corridor. Only Dinger had appeared.

'What did he want?' Tanya hollered as he sped past.

'He wants us to play on his show on Easter Monday,' he said, making a beeline for the toilets. 'I'm going to be sick.'

CHAPTER 11

I zipped my bomber jacket right up to the neck. It was pissing from the heavens, and I was wearing tights. But I only had an hour's break, so I started down the Union steps; I needed to eat and I needed to get my notebook. It was Saturday, but it was the Easter weekend and the Union was dead, so plenty of time for some writing.

I could hear music thumping from the flat as I dripped up the close stairs. Ricky's bedroom door was lying open and his speakers were blaring from within, but I could hear laughter from the kitchen. Probably Malcky. It was always bloody Malcky. But food could not wait. My stomach was rumbling as I walked in. But the scene I saw stopped me in my tracks.

Ricky was sitting with his back to me, head bent over the table. Malcky was facing me, and he looked up when I entered.

'Evening, Jo,' he said, leaning back in his chair.

I didn't answer.

Ricky spun round, wiping his nose. 'I thought you were working.'

I looked at Ricky, then at Malcky, and then at the table, which Ricky was not managing to conceal.

'What's going on?' I asked, stepping forward to see better. Beside Ricky's cash-line card and some square scraps of magazine paper was an empty CD box with two neat white lines of powder still in place.

'We're celebrating,' Malcky replied.

'We've got a gig!' Ricky explained. 'In Winston's. A week on Friday.'

'Winston's?' I said, eyes still on the table. Was this cocaine? 'After last time? After Gary?'

'That was ages ago.' Ricky swept his hand through his hair. 'That was before Malcky. We'll be fine this time.'

'Oh, before Malcky,' I said sarcastically.

'Here she goes,' Malcky scoffed, getting up. 'I'm going for a slash.' He placed a hand on my shoulder as he passed, leaning into my ear. 'Chillax, little lady.'

I jerked free of him and sat down in his seat. 'Is this cocaine?'

'It's no big deal.'

'Where did you get it?'

'Malcky got it. It's fine. It's good. You should try some.'

'Not my thing,' I said, scanning Ricky's face. He shrugged at me, grinning. 'Ricky, this is not cool.'

He stopped smiling. 'And what the fuck do you know about cool?'

His words stung, and I scraped my chair back, shoving past Malcky in my haste to leave.

'Going so soon?' Malcky laughed.

As I pulled the front door open, I could hear Ricky say, 'Just leave her, Malcky. Forget it.'

*

I woke up at noon the next day with another stinking hangover. I'd gone round to Mhairi's after work and let her vodka take the sting out of Ricky's words.

I listened carefully. I had no idea if Ricky was home or not, but all I could hear was my own head pounding. There was paracetamol in the kitchen and I swung my legs out of bed, bracing myself against the wave of pain.

I was staggering across the hall when the doorbell rang loudly right beside me and I'd opened it before I remembered I was only wearing a t-shirt.

Mr Steele stood filling the entrance. 'Hello, Jo. Happy Easter.' He walked past me into the flat. 'Did I wake you?'

'Bit of a lie in,' I replied, stretching the fabric of my t-shirt down. 'I was working last night.'

'Thought you'd have gone home for the holidays,' he said. 'But you can come for Sunday lunch instead. Plenty of room for one more. I've been sent down to collect himself personally.' He turned to Ricky's room. 'He'll still be in bed too, I expect, eh? Off you go and get dressed and I'll get him up.'

Mr Steele swung open Ricky's door and flicked on the light switch. From where I was standing, I could clearly see a large hump under the duvet, so at least Ricky was home.

'Come on, son,' Mr Steele said firmly. 'Time to get up. Your mother's waiting.' He grabbed the duvet and whipped it off in one pull.

I heard the scream, high-pitched and female, before the duvet had hit the floor. Mr Steele staggered backwards, and I tiptoed forward, snorting out a giggle. Ricky rolled off the far side of the bed in alarm, grabbing for his shorts, while the bed's other naked occupant curled herself into a bashful ball, muffling her continued screams.

'Dad! What the fuck are you doing here?' Ricky spluttered. His legs were in the air as he tried to hastily manoeuvre them into his boxer shorts.

'Language, Richard,' Mr Steele replied automatically.

I coughed out an audible laugh. Bad language seemed to be the least of Ricky's problems right then.

'Easter Sunday. Your mother's expecting you,' Mr Steele snapped. 'I'll be in the kitchen.'

I moved to let him pass. The naked blonde had retrieved the duvet by this time and Ricky was standing in his shorts, glaring at me. I laughed again, right from the belly. Ricky marched round the bed and slammed the door in my face.

I stood in the hall, giggling. I had an inbuilt immunity to Ricky's one-night stands, so this latest one didn't bother me too much. And his humiliation this morning was more than making up for his mean words to me last night. Then I remembered last night. The kitchen. Ricky's dad was in the kitchen.

Shit, shit, shit. I crossed the hall, panicking at what I would find.

Mr Steele was inspecting the table. 'Taking up origami, Jo?' he asked.

'Sure am,' I replied, with a big, fake smile as I swept the folded squares of paper into my hands and left the room.

*

I had a quick shower and was still drying my feet when a fully dressed Ricky barged in, shutting my bedroom door behind him.

'How could you just let my dad in like that?' he stage-whispered.

I retrieved my towel and covered myself. 'I'm naked, Ricky!'

'I know you're pissed off with me, but letting my dad into my room like that. I mean, that's low, even for you.'

'He rang the doorbell. I opened the door,' I stage-whispered back. 'I didn't know you were entertaining, did I?'

Ricky snorted. 'Entertaining! And you can forget about Easter dinner. You're uninvited.'

'Do you really think I'd have let your dad in if I'd had the faintest clue?'

He folded his arms.

'Who was she anyway?'

Ricky shrugged. 'No idea.'

'Seriously?'

He shrugged again.

'You're unbelievable.' I fastened my towel more securely. 'And I just saved your ass, by the way. You left your drugs all over the kitchen.'

Ricky rolled his eyes. 'Right. Let's have it out. This isn't about the coke. This is about Malcky. What is your problem with Malcky?'

'I'm not doing this now.'

'You've never liked him since the moment you met him.'

I clamped my lips together in an attempt to not speak, but it was no good. 'I don't trust him.'

Ricky crossed his arms and leaned back on one hip.

'He's bad news. Look what he did to Tanya. And the way he speaks to Dinger. He's a bully. And he's a thief. And now he's got you doing cocaine.'

'It's no big deal. Everyone does it.'

'Everyone does not do it.' I put a hand on my hip. 'And anyway, it's not just about that. It's Malcky. He's not like us. He's not like anyone we know. He's changing you, Ricky. Suddenly you're doing coke, and what's next?'

He rolled his eyes, again. 'Nothing's next. Fuck's sake, it's like talking to my mother.'

I clamped my mouth shut properly this time.

'Look,' Ricky said. 'I don't want to fall out again. You're, like, my best friend. You're practically family. I hate it when we argue.' He looked serious and open and genuine. 'Malcky is different from us. I know that. But different is good. He knows things I don't. He knows how to make the band work. I really think we're going to make it this time. I know you don't trust him and I can see his faults. But with the band, I do trust him. And I'm not walking away from this just because you don't like him.'

'I never asked you to walk away from anything, Ricky. And I don't want to fall out about this either.'

'Hurry up, Richard!' Mr Steele called from the kitchen.

'And I'm happy for you about Winston's. And everything.' I smiled at him. 'Just, please, be careful.'

'I am careful.'

'And please let me come to Easter dinner.'

'No,' he said, opening the door. 'You blew that.'

'Please,' I wailed as he left.

He stuck his head back in. 'Ok. But only because I got a look at your bum.'

CHAPTER 12

'What is the point of Easter?' Mhairi was stretched out on her sofa, nursing a can of diet coke. It was Easter Monday, and the radio was on in the background in anticipation of Vermillion's live radio appearance.

'I didn't even get a chocolate egg,' I said, popping a greasy chip into my mouth. 'Have you heard about your placement yet?'

'Clydebank Academy.'

'Oh, that's handy.'

'Yeah. I can jump the train.'

'You nervous about it?'

'Shitting myself. No idea how I'm going to handle a room full of smelly teenagers. They don't teach you how to actually teach. Teacher training, my arse.'

'I might apply for next year,' I said.

'To what?'

'Teacher training.'

'What? No!' Mhairi swung her legs off the sofa. 'Why?'

I shrugged. 'I need a proper job. I can't work a bar forever.'

'But you're going to be a writer!'

I rolled my eyes and tutted.

'What's happened?'

'I don't know. I don't think I've got anything to say. Or certainly nothing interesting.'

There was a loud knock on the front door.

'Who'll that be?' I asked.

'Tanya,' Mhairi got to her feet.

'Tanya? Why?'

'Because I invited her,' she said. 'She's part of our group now.'

'No, she's bloody not.'

'Be nice,' she hissed, opening the door.

'Am I late?' Tanya asked, sweeping in with a breeze of perfume.

'No,' I said. 'Anytime from half seven, they said. Want a chip?'

She was unbuttoning her coat. 'No, thank you.'

'Tea?' Mhairi asked.

'Tea would be lovely. Should we turn it up a bit?' She turned the radio up a bit.

'I wonder if they're nervous,' Mhairi said, pouring Tanya some tea from my pot.

'Malcky doesn't get nervous.' Tanya laughed. 'He's so confident. I often wonder how he does it? And Bob always seems so calm,' she continued. 'But I suppose he's always stoned, so that helps.'

'He's not always stoned,' Mhairi replied.

'Malcky doesn't smoke at all. He's just naturally laid-back.'

I was chewing my cheeks to refrain from uttering the

cutting remark I was forming, trying, instead, to keep one ear on the radio. But Mhairi was riled. No one talks down Bob and gets away with it.

'Maybe Malcky gets his confidence from other sources,' she said, glaring at Tanya.

'What's that supposed to mean?'

I sunk into my seat. Here we go.

Mhairi took a deep breath. 'Maybe it's the cocaine he's snorting that makes him so confident.'

'Malcky does not do cocaine.'

I was momentarily pleased to note that I knew something Tanya didn't. Then Mhairi said, 'He does, too. Ask Jo.'

Tanya glared at me. 'What have you been stirring up this time, Jo?'

'I'm not getting into this,' I said, holding up my palms.

'Jo caught Malcky and Ricky snorting coke in her flat.'

'Bullshit. I don't believe you.'

'Well, it's true.'

Tanya looked at me.

'It's true,' I said, shrugging.

She hesitated, then flicked her hair and sat back.

But Mhairi hadn't finished. 'So don't be making any more comments about Bob being a stoner. At least he's not a druggy.'

'Malcky is not a druggy!'

'And neither is Ricky,' I said, pulling myself forward. 'Now, can we please just listen?'

The song on the radio was finishing, and Mick Dumfries was talking again. '*I'd like to welcome to the studio Glasgow's newest talent in the form of Vermillion. Good to see you boys.*'

'Thank you, Mick. Good to be here.'

'Oh my God! That's Ricky!' Mhairi laughed.

'Now, I've met you all a few times before, but for the benefit of our listeners, why don't you introduce yourselves?'

'Sure. Well, we've got Donald Bell, aka Dinger, back there on drums. This is Bob McFarlane here beside me on bass guitar. And Malcky Chalmers on my other side, doing a fine job playing lead. And I'm Ricky Steele, remember the name listeners. And I hold the whole thing together.'

'Aye right!'

Malcky's voice sounded far away, and I was delighted to realise he didn't have a microphone.

'Hahaha. Well, let's see what you've got. What are you going to play for us first?'

'This is a song off our EP called 'Touch and Go'.'

'Oh, I love this one,' Mhairi said.

'Shhhh!' I nearly spilled my tea with annoyance.

'Everyone be quiet so she can hear her Ricky,' Tanya said.

'He's not my Ricky,' I shouted.

'Shut up,' Mhairi wailed. 'We're missing the song!'

The boys were on the second verse by this time. But we all managed to keep our respective mouths shut for the rest of the session. And once I'd calmed down and could listen properly, I could hear that Ricky was coping remarkably well. He sounded completely at ease. You'd never have guessed it was his first interview. They played two more songs, mentioned the Winston's gig several times, and got an invitation back to the show in the future. And then they were done.

'Well, that went well,' I said. 'When are we meeting them in the pub?'

'Not until ten.' There was tension in Mhairi's voice. She was still angry.

'Maybe we could drink this first, then.' Tanya pulled a bottle of Smirnoff out of her bag. 'I know you girls like your vodka.'

Mhairi hesitated for only a moment, then stood up and reached for the bottle. She snapped the lid off, took a long swig, and held it out to Tanya. Tanya stood and lifted the bottle to her lips, pulling a face as she swallowed a mouthful.

I laughed. 'That's not something you see every day. Tanya Rossini drinking straight from a bottle.'

'And you won't be seeing it again,' Tanya replied, coughing and handing me the vodka. 'There better be something to mix this with.'

*

We met the boys in town later. The mood was ecstatic and celebratory, but Malcky was working at the Barrowlands the next day and left early, Tanya in tow. Dinger disappeared to catch the last train and the four of us left decided to walk home. There wasn't a breath of wind and it was almost mild. I linked arms with Ricky as we walked along behind Bob and Mhairi.

'Do you think they'll always be together?'

'Who?' Ricky asked.

'Bob and Mhairi.'

'Don't see why not. Look at my parents – they've been married for twenty-five years.'

'Blimey.'

'How long have your parents been married?'

'Not long enough,' I replied absently.

'Are they divorced?'

'No,' I said, blinking to attention. 'Yes.'

Ricky laughed. 'Which?'

I laughed too, louder than necessary. 'They're not together.'

'Ah,' he smiled, nodding. 'Separated.'

'Something like that. Twenty-five years, huh? I can't imagine being with someone that long.'

'Me neither,' he said. 'Mind you, I've been shacked up with you for nearly five.'

'I don't think that's the same.'

'How come we've never got together?' he asked, laughter in his voice.

'Oh no!' I pulled away from him. 'You're not going to try and snog me again, are you?'

'Jesus! Will you never forget about that?'

He reached for my arm and I jumped away.

'Don't you be trying anything, Ricky Steele.'

He grabbed me easily around the waist, and I screamed in delight. His other arm slipped round my front, and he lifted me into the air. I kicked frantically, but he still managed to turn me upside down.

Bob and Mhairi had stopped to watch. 'What are you two up to?'

'He's trying to snog me! Help!'

'It doesn't look like he's trying to snog you, Jo.' Bob chuckled.

Ricky dropped me to the pavement, then manhandled me back onto my feet, keeping hold of me to stop me from staggering. Mhairi and Bob set off ahead of us again.

'Bastard.' I grinned at him.

'If I was trying to snog you, I wouldn't have missed,' he said, grinning back.

'Is that right?'

'That's right.'

CHAPTER 13

By Thursday, I still hadn't started the poems that were due after the Easter holidays. But I had a completely empty day and grand plans to crack on. My tutor had suggested a pivot to poetry because of my persistent inability to get a longer piece of writing finished.

Ricky was out with Bob, playing pool, thank god. He'd been at a loose end and driving me crazy since Malcky had got a temporary guitar tech job in town. I'd suggested he study, and he'd replied with a roll of the eyes.

'I doubt I'll be at Uni much longer, Jo. So I'm not entirely sure of the point of studying.'

The bloody band. Since they'd been on the radio – and a very local radio at that – Ricky imagined they were one step away from making it.

I shifted all my books and notes through to the kitchen table and settled down to work. He'd likely go to Bob's after to get stoned, so I had all afternoon.

When the doorbell rang, I looked up at the clock and was surprised to see it was after five; I'd been sitting there for four hours. I stood up and stretched, and my stomach rumbled. The doorbell rang again.

'Coming,' I shouted, even though the storm door was shut, and I was two rooms away.

It was Malcky.

'Ricky's not here,' I said. His bulk filled the doorway, blocking out the light from the close. 'He's playing pool with Bob, or he was. He's probably round at Bob's now.'

Malcky pushed past me into the hall. 'Not Ricky I came to see, actually.'

He continued walking into the kitchen, so I closed the door and followed him.

'Can you not touch that, please?' I snapped.

Malcky turned round, holding my pages of poetry in his hand. The corner of his lip curled up. He dropped the paper, and it fell on the floor, one page sliding across towards the sofa. I looked at him, and he stared back at me. I walked to the sink and filled a glass of water. My mouth was very dry.

'So, Jo, how are you?'

'Malcky, what do you want?'

He laughed. 'To be rich and famous, mainly. But I can see that's not what you meant.'

I kept my back to him and sipped my water.

'Thought I'd come round and have a bit of a chat. Spend some time getting to know you. Find out what makes you tick, Jo. Because it occurred to me, we may have got off on the wrong foot.'

I turned round and leaned back against the sink.

'Truth be told,' he went on, 'I get the distinct impression that you don't like me.' His voice was oozing sarcasm. 'So, what's the problem?'

'I don't know what you're talking about.'

'What exactly is it between Ricky and you?'

'Ricky's my friend. *That's* what it is.'

'Ah, I see. 'Friends'.' He actually made air quotes with his fingers. 'No ulterior motives?'

'Don't be ridiculous.' I took a deep breath; my voice was shaking. 'Now, if there wasn't anything else, I'd be grateful if you would leave. I've got work to do.'

Malcky took a step towards me, and I realised he was now directly between me and the door.

'What you've got to understand, Jo, is that Ricky and me… well, we're different from you. We have bigger lives than you. We're a team.' He wasn't laughing anymore. 'I've been looking for someone like Ricky longer than I care to remember. And now I've found him, I'm not going to let him go.' He took another step towards me. 'The coke thing? Just part of his education. Part of the plan. It won't be the last time he comes across it, and I want him to be prepared. I'm taking this band to the top, Jo, and Ricky is the key. Doors are opening for us. I can do the knocking, but Ricky is going to get us inside.' He took another step, and I had to look up to keep eye contact. 'We're going all the way. And I know it's pissing you off, Jo. You're going to be left behind and there's nothing you can do about it. You're losing him. Maybe you've already lost him. And your little games are not going to work on me.' He poked me firmly in the shoulder.

'Get your hands off me,' I warned.

'So, from now on, I don't want to hear Ricky giving it 'Jo said this' or 'Jo said that'. Do you hear? I'm sick of it. I don't give a flying fuck what you think.'

A bit of spit landed on my face, and I flinched.

He leaned towards me. 'Ricky knows what he's doing. I know what I'm doing. What we need you to do is to keep your pretty little red head down and keep your nose out of things you will never understand. Capiche?'

'Fuck off, Malcky,' I said as firmly as I could.

'Strong words.'

He placed a hand on the work surface beside me. I slid the other way, but he quickly blocked me with his other hand.

A picture of Tanya's bruised face came into my head. 'Get away from me.'

As if reading my mind, Malcky continued. 'And another thing – Tanya. Honestly, I have to admire your shit-stirring skills. But what is your point? You'll never split us up. We're rock solid. But maybe you're jealous.' He leaned against me, pressing his crotch into my belly. 'Perhaps you want rid of Tanya so you can have me all to yourself.'

'I don't *think* so,' I managed to say. I struggled to move, but he just leaned against me harder. I was trapped.

'Now, Jo, I'm not objecting to that, per se.'

I could feel his breath and turned my head away. He took hold of my chin and steered me back to face him.

'I'm guessing you're pretty tight. Maybe we *should* hook up. Maybe I should give you a go.'

I jerked my head backwards away from his grasp, lifted my hands to his chest, and pushed for all I was worth. But Malcky simply adjusted his footing and crushed my body harder against the sink. He took hold of my hands and lifted them easily above my head, holding them in one hand, the other coming back to grab my chin again. I kicked at his ankles and he chuckled.

'Like a bit of rough, do you?'

His fingers dug into my jaw as he raised my head and placed his mouth over mine. I was breathing hard through my nose as he forced his tongue into my mouth. I tried to scream. He pulled his face away, laughing, and I summoned all my strength. My adrenalin was pumping, and I managed to twist my hands out of his. I went straight for his face, digging my nails in where they landed and clawed downwards. He pulled back enough for me to thrust my body out from under his. But I was only two steps towards the door when he grabbed me round the waist and kicked my legs from under me, sending us both crashing to the floor. I landed heavily on my hip and then smashed my forehead off the lino as Malcky landed on me. He wrestled me over onto my back, keeping his full weight on top of me, and pinned my hands above my head again. I had my face turned to the side, fighting for air. His breath was hot in my ear.

'Now, where were we?'

He bit my earlobe, and I realised, right then, that there was nothing I could do. He was twice my size. I started to cry.

'Malcky, please. No.'

My anger had gone. I was just very, very scared.

He stopped what he was doing and lay still. I could feel my heart hammering against his chest. From my position, I could see right under the fridge and I noticed it was filthy. He still hadn't moved, and I gathered my thoughts. I realised he wouldn't dare carry this through. He'd never get away with it. And I realised he was just trying to scare me. Well, he'd succeeded. A flicker of anger sparked in my belly.

Slowly, I turned my head, and he lifted his face away from my neck.

'You've made your point,' I said as firmly and calmly as I could. 'Let me go.'

His eyes were an inch from mine. 'So we understand each other?'

'Perfectly.' I was still in no position to argue.

'If you want a fight, you'll get one.' He pushed himself up onto his knees. 'But I will win, Jo.' He slowly let go of my hands. 'Now, I expect you to start as you mean to go on by not mentioning this to Ricky.' He bounced up onto his haunches, still squatting over me. 'You're quite a girl, Jo.' He laughed. 'Fiery. That was fun.' He stood up. 'I'll let myself out.'

I lay where I was until I heard the door close with a single click, then I rolled over onto my side, curling my legs up to my chest and stared at the crumbs under the fridge. I waited until my heart beat came back to normal, then I got up. I started preparing my dinner, cracking eggs into a bowl and slicing some onion. My hip ached, and I knew I'd bruised my forehead, but I didn't go to look in a mirror. I removed some skin from my knuckles while grating the cheese.

I was trying to think about what to do next, not about what had just happened. I had to use both hands to pour the egg mixture into the frying pan because they were shaking.

Malcky wanted Ricky to himself, and all my sniping was undermining him. At least I was getting to him. But I couldn't win a physical fight with Malcky. And all my moaning to Ricky was doing no good. I continued moving the omelette around the pan until it was black and smoking. Then I tipped it straight into the bin and sat down at the kitchen table. Malcky was here to stay. This wasn't like Ricky's girlfriends, who had come and gone over the years. I was losing him. He was going to end up needing Malcky more than he needed me.

I picked up the remote control and turned the TV on. As soon as the sound kicked in, I turned it back off. I was losing Ricky. I swallowed down some vomit. My hip throbbed. I lay both palms on the table and pressed as hard as I could to stop them shaking. I couldn't lose Ricky. I needed a plan. If he needed me, he wouldn't leave me. I needed a way to keep Ricky needing me.

I fetched a bag of frozen veg from the freezer and held it to my forehead. There was only one thing left I could do – one more roll of the dice. I was going to have to go all in.

CHAPTER 14

'...*And tonight, live at Winston's, let's welcome on stage... VERMILLION.*'

I peered over the crowd, and could just make out Ricky taking centre stage. Or at least I thought it was Ricky. I was too far away to know for sure. Winston's was full to capacity. How the hell had they managed that? I pushed my way through the crowd as the music started. I had no idea where Mhairi was, but I could only look.

This was the night. This was my chance. I'd bought a tiny leopard print dress from Quiz and re-dyed my hair, hence the fact I was running late.

The first song finished and Ricky was rousing the crowd with his usual Glasgow banter. I was still miles from the stage and I craned my neck to see over the heads, standing up on my tip-toes. He was looking more gorgeous than ever. They launched into the next song and the crowd went wild. I was whipped off my feet and carried forward with the press of people. Adrenalin rushed through my veins. I'd been to concerts before and, small as I was, had been lost in the crush on many occasions, but never while wearing backless sandals and a boob tube. I curled up my toes to save my shoes, took hold of my top with one hand and with the other grabbed the shoulder of the bloke nearest me. We surged forwards in a diagonal direction towards the far side of the stage and, as soon as I felt my feet touch the ground again, I was off, pushing and shoving with all my might.

And then a hand grabbed my arm and hauled me upwards.

'What are you doing here?'

Mhairi had secured a small ledge against the wall, just down from the toilets. I steadied myself beside her.

'You look amazing,' she shouted. 'Why aren't you at work?'

Mhairi was dressed in her battered Levi's and a slouchy white t-shirt.

'Pulled a sickie,' I shouted back, taking the proffered plastic tumbler.

'Jim'll kill you.'

I took a sip. Vodka and Coke, watered down by the melted ice. Ricky was running from one side of the stage to the other, leaping on and off the amps as he went. I could see the sweat on his face and his hair was separating into damp strands. He looked fantastic. He looked like a rock star.

'Didn't want to miss it,' I shouted in Mhairi's ear.

'It's sold out. Dinger actually vomited when he heard.'

'No!'

'He's got a bucket behind the drum kit.'

I scanned the crowd, picking out familiar faces mixed in with so many that I'd never seen before. People who had never spoken to Ricky, or to any of them, but who had parted with their hard-earned cash to come and see them play. I didn't think I would ever get used to that.

Back on stage, Dinger had his head down, thrashing wildly at the drums. I couldn't see his bucket. Bob was pacing calmly to the right of Dinger, his bald head shiny with sweat, and bent over his bass in concentration. Malcky was nearest to us, his full focus on Ricky. As I watched, he stepped forward to his pedal board and started a guitar solo while Ricky dropped his mic, leapt onto the monitor, and clapped his hands in time above his head. The crowd instantly raised their hands to mimic him. It was amazing. He looked supremely confident as he clapped and nodded at the crowd in time with Malcky's guitar. Then, with no warning, he flung himself off the stage, straight onto the clapping hands in front of him.

'Holy fuck!' Mhairi shrieked beside me.

I nearly fell off the ledge as I tried to see. Ricky had dropped down, but then reappeared, floating sideways on a bumpy sea of hands towards us. I held my breath, paralysed with disbelief. Bouncers appeared from nowhere, forcing a path through the throng towards him. Suddenly, he went down head first and I had a glimpse of his feet before he disappeared completely. I grabbed Mhairi to steady myself. But there he was! The bouncers had him. They hoisted him back onto the stage and he picked up his microphone, nodded to Malcky, and started into the chorus.

Mhairi turned to me, and we screamed into each other's faces.

Fifty minutes and one encore later, they were done.

'You've been amazing! Glasgow rocks!' Ricky roared before disappearing off stage to deafening amounts of howling, clapping and whistling.

'We're to meet them over at The Shrine,' Mhairi said as we stepped down off the ledge. 'And if we're in before eleven, it's half price. Move!'

There was hardly any queue at The Shrine and once inside I took up position at the bar with a good view of the door, and refused to budge.

Tanya and her gaggle of pals arrived, and set up at the other end of the bar, after telling me I was 'so fired'. Dinger's pals, Neil and Steve, turned up too, and Mhairi went off to dance with them.

People were pouring into the club by this stage, pushing and shoving to get to the bar, but I didn't give an inch.

What actually was hours later, Dinger and Bob arrived. I waved until they saw me.

'Where's Ricky?' I asked without preamble.

'Still talking,' Bob replied. 'He'll be over in a minute.'

I patted Dinger on the arm. 'You were great. Fantastic.'

Dinger nodded, his face still pale, and turned to talk to Neil.

'Mhairi's dancing,' I said to Bob.

'Well, I'm not. Want a drink?'

'Vodka Red Bull. Who's Ricky talking to?'

'Mick Dumfries.' Bob was trying to attract the attention of the barman. 'He was introducing us to Damien Dwyer.'

'Who?'

'The guy who manages Antalis.'

'Who?'

'Antalis. They're huge. Or they're about to be. They've just released their first album. We supported them last year. Gary's last gig? Winston's, part one?'

'Ah.'

'Anyway, this bloke, Damien Dwyer, wants us to support them next week at King Tut's.'

Suddenly, he had my full attention. 'You're joking. King Tut's?'

'Straight up.'

'But that's mental! Oasis have played there. Coldplay played there, for fuck's sake.'

The barman appeared, and I glanced at the door again. And there was Ricky, at last, with Malcky in tow.

Like the parting of the Red Sea, the crowd suddenly separated. Ricky spotted me, turned away, then turned back to stare. I leaned against the bar, stretching my arms out against the crowd, and smiled seductively. Ricky grinned and stomped over. I cupped his face in my hands and kissed him firmly on the lips. His eyes popped in surprise, but his hands came to rest on my hips.

'You were amazing.'

'You look amazing,' he replied.

He held me out at arm's length and looked me up and down.

'Dance with me,' I said, tugging him towards the floor.

Ricky could dance, and so could I, especially with half a dozen vodkas inside me. The floor was packed, and I pressed my body against his, face to face, eye to eye, as we moved with the crowd. He was grinning, but I didn't grin back – just gazed up at him through my (actually quite heavy) mascara.

His eyes narrowed. 'You're not going to snog me again, are you?'

'What if I am?' My heart was hammering in my chest.

He stopped smiling, and I raised my chin just a fraction. It was enough. He lowered his head and before I could take a breath, his lips were on mine. I closed my eyes and slid my arms up and around his neck while his arms encircled my waist. And we were kissing. It was better than before. We totally fitted. There was no awkward nose banging or teeth knocking, just perfectly synchronised snogging.

Ricky pulled away and frowned at me. 'I don't know what you're up to, Jo Duncan,' he said, then kissed me again, quickly and thoroughly. 'Let's get a drink. I need a drink.'

He led me through the dancers, holding my hand, straight past Tanya, who could have caught a passing train in her open mouth as she gaped at me.

'Bar's shut,' Bob informed us on our return. 'Party's back at ours.'

Ricky leaned into my ear. 'There's beer at the flat. Let's get a taxi.'

I nodded, and he headed immediately towards the exit. Tanya had returned from the dance floor to animatedly relay her news to a startled Mhairi. I'd deal with that lot later, I thought as I hurried after Ricky.

In the taxi, I had a moment to consider the consequences of what I was doing. A small wave of panic rose in my belly. This was what I'd always wanted. It was finally happening. But there was so much at stake. I was shaking with nerves.

Back at the flat, I left Ricky to pay and dashed upstairs to the loo. I scrubbed my teeth and brushed my hair, then looked at myself in the mirror. This was it then. No backing out. My mind was made up.

'Do not fuck this up,' I said to my reflection.

I felt very sober. I could hear Ricky banging about in the kitchen, so I took a deep breath and opened the door, kicking my shoes off in the hall as I went through. Ricky had laid out the beer on the kitchen table, but he didn't lift it when I came in. We watched each other across the room.

'So,' he said. 'Will we walk round to Bob's?'

I crossed the floor in a couple of steps and put my mouth back on his. He grabbed me by the waist and kissed me hard, walking me backwards into the hall. Halfway across, he stopped. The light wasn't on and his face was deep in shadow.

'Are you sure about this?' he asked.

'Yes.'

He reached down, tucked his arm under my legs, and swept me off my feet. I shrieked with laughter.

'Let's get to it, then!' And he carried me into his room, slamming the door shut behind us with his foot.

*

I woke up, startled and disorientated, and pushed myself upright. Ricky's room. I looked to my right. No Ricky. Fuck. It was daylight outside and I could hear the morning traffic. I let my head fall back against the pillow. Ricky had obviously woken up, seen me, and been too embarrassed to hang around.

I'd given it my best shot, and it hadn't worked. I was no closer to my goal of being indispensable to Ricky than

I had been the day before. And now, I'd made everything worse. I needed to get back to my room and hide. Forever.

The door banged open. 'Wakey, wakey! Rise and shine!' Ricky, in his boxer shorts, was balancing a tray in his hands. 'Breakfast in bed,' he announced.

I pulled myself up again. 'Wow.'

He lowered the tray onto my lap and bounced over me and under the covers. Tea and toast. The tea was almost white with milk and the toast was covered in half a jar of jam, just the way Ricky liked it.

'I made it for you,' he said, grinning. 'I've had mine. I've been up for ages.'

'You should've woken me.' I took a sip of tea. It had at least two sugars in it. I took mine very weak and black.

'Nah. You looked like an angel.'

'I doubt that.'

'Are you going to eat the toast?'

'Not right now.'

Ricky picked up the plate and devoured it in a few easy bites. 'I've never made anyone breakfast in bed before,' he mumbled with his mouth full.

I put the tray down on the floor, then rolled over to face him, sliding my hand under the cover and onto his belly. The corner of his mouth twitched, and he cupped my bum, pulling me on top of him.

'How come it's taken us so long to get together?' He traced a line down the side of my body with his fingers.

I nuzzled into his neck. 'Circumstances. Consequences,' I mumbled. 'I don't know.'

'If I'd known you were such a great shag,' he breathed. 'We'd have got together years ago.'

CHAPTER 15

Much as I'd have liked to stay in bed with Ricky for the rest of my life, I had work that evening. Or I had to show up to work in the vain hope I still had a job.

I was clomping down the close stairs just as Malcky was on his way up. He blocked my path, slow clapping.

'Get out my way, Malcky.'

'Nicely played,' he said, still clapping. 'I didn't think you had the bottle for it. You seemed like a bit of a tease to me. But there you go.' He shrugged. 'Shows what I know.'

'This has nothing to do with you.'

He laughed. 'Of course it does. You could have been shagging him years ago if you'd wanted. You planned all this, Jo. You're a manipulative little bitch.' He smiled his nasty smile and put his hands into his jeans' pockets, getting himself comfortable. 'But your little plan will never work. You'll never manage to keep him and you know it. Deep down, you know it.'

'Fuck you, Malcky.'

He laughed again, stepping to the side and signalling

for me to pass. I steadied my nerves and made a dash for the door, but he caught my arm.

'You're not good enough for him,' he said, leaning into my ear. 'He'll get bored. He'll get sick of you.'

I twisted away and banged out of the close onto the street as my phone began to ring in my pocket. I took a deep breath of fresh air as I answered.

'Hi, Mhairi.'

'Oh, so you are alive! I'm not disturbing anything, am I?' Mhairi sounded thoroughly amused.

'Everything's normal here,' I replied. 'On my way to work. Good party?'

'Wicked party,' she said. 'But that will not be the subject of this call. I want to hear all about it.'

'I will not be discussing it,' I replied haughtily.

'Don't be boring.'

'I wouldn't ask you about Bob.'

'Do you want to know about Bob?'

I screwed my face up. 'No!'

Mhairi laughed down the phone. 'So, what? Are you two, like, an item now?'

'I don't know yet.'

'Seriously, when did all this happen? I mean, was it just last night? Or has this been on the go a while?'

'No,' I said. 'Just last night. I'd have told you. You'd have known.'

Neither of us spoke for a while.

'Do you like him?' she asked at last.

'Yes.'

'Do you love him?'

I slowed my pace and let out a long sigh.

'Fuck, Jo. Ricky?' She chuckled softly. 'I did not see that coming.'

'I'm a master of disguise.'

'I feel like I should say something,' she continued. 'I want to give you advice or something.'

'It's fine, Mhairi. It'll be fine. I know what he's like. I know him.' I paused at the bottom of the Union steps. 'But I want to give it a shot.'

'Fair enough.'

'I'm at the Union. I've got to go see if I still have a job.'

'Ooh.' She inhaled. 'Big and brave, then, with Jim.'

Tanya had arrived at the same time as me. She waited as I climbed the steps. 'You are so getting fired.'

I blew my cheeks out.

'So, what's the score with you and Ricky?'

'None of your business.'

'Like that, is it? Well, just don't get your hopes up, that's all I'm saying. Ricky's not one for commitment. Not like my Malcky.'

'I think I know him better than you do,' I snapped. 'I've been living with him for years.'

She smiled, holding the door open for me. 'But you've never shagged him before. I have.'

I didn't have time to reply as Jim was waiting in the foyer.

'Tanya, get to work. You, in my office, now.'

I got a warning and a bollocking, but I kept my job. I'd never taken the piss before. In three years, I hadn't missed a shift. And I didn't mind when Jim let everyone away early, leaving me to clear up after closing.

It was nearly half two when I finally left, zipping up

my jacket as I stepped outside. This late at night, there was no one about.

A shadow moved on the steps below me, and I gave a small shriek.

'It's only me.'

'Ricky! What are you doing hiding out here?'

'Waiting for you, of course. Can't have my woman walking home alone at this time of night.'

I jogged down the steps, straight into his arms. He kissed me and I leaned in towards him. I was his woman. Oh, hallelujah! Maybe I didn't know the future, but right at that moment, we were most definitely an item.

'Here.' He pulled away and handed me one of his earphones. 'Listen to this.'

The music sounded loud, trashy. There was a lot of guitar. 'Who is it?'

'Antalis.' He linked my arm as we set off for home. 'They've just made the Radio One playlist. They're big news. King Tut's is going to be huge. And if we get this gig right, maybe we get to support them again?' He widened his eyes at me.

'Wow! That is exciting.'

We strolled along quietly for a bit. Even with the rubbish music in my ear, I didn't think I'd ever been happier.

'I've been thinking,' he said, after a bit.

'What about?'

'Us.'

I glanced at him in alarm, but his long eyelashes were hiding his eyes. 'What about us?'

'I know why we never got together sooner.'

'Why?'

He looked down at me. 'Because you thought I'd just shag you and dump you. And you're better than that. You're not that type of girl.'

'Aren't I?'

'No. And I'm not going to. Well, I'll shag you, but I'm not going to dump you. I'm going to prove you wrong.'

'You are?'

'Yes. I'm going to treat you really well. I'm not going to be a bastard in any way. I've turned a corner.' He flicked his hair back, looking very pleased with himself.

There was a long pause. Obviously, I was expected to say something here.

'I can't make the gig on Saturday.'

Ricky's hair flopped back into place. 'No!'

'Jim won't hear of it. And he'll fire me this time if I don't show.'

This was the truth. But Ricky could take it either way. He might not like being crowded, but the gig at King Tut's was the most important one yet.

'I'm sorry.'

Ricky shrugged. 'It is what it is.'

'But I'll be there when you get home.' I stopped walking and slid my hand between his thighs. The corner of his mouth twitched. 'And I'll make it up to you then.'

'I'm going to need a down payment now,' he said. 'Come on. Let's get home.'

*

A week later, I did the same walk again. Alone this time. The night was still and almost warm. I hadn't heard from Ricky, or anyone, and it wasn't a surprise to find the flat empty. I dithered in the hall, deciding which bed to sleep in before plumping for mine.

Ricky woke me an unknown time later as he crawled in. I shifted to make room, and he wrapped an arm over me and snuggled his legs into the back of mine.

'You smell of perfume,' I mumbled. He smelt of other things too: smoke and beer and sweat.

'Do I?'

I knew he was drunk, even from those two words. 'How did it go?'

'Fan-fucking-tastic,' he slurred. 'Best one yet.'

'Wish I'd been there.'

'Yeah, it was the real thing. And an after party at the Hilton. With a free bar.' His hand cupped my breast, his thumb sliding idly over my nipple. 'There were record company guys from London. They loved us. Obviously.' He lifted one leg over my hips and reached for a condom from my bedside table.

I tried to turn to face him, but he pushed me back onto my stomach, tearing the wrapper with his teeth.

'And the best bit,' he said, working my pants down with a practised hand. 'That Damien Dwyer bloke wants us to support Antalis in Edinburgh next month.'

I let out a low moan of pleasure as he slid into me. 'You've got exams next month.'

'Shh.' He sighed, scraping my hair off my neck, his beery breath hot against my cheek as he pressed into me.

*

Glasgow's annual heatwave arrived in the second week of May, to coincide, as usual, with the end-of-year exams and assignments. Classes were suspended, leaving empty hot days for me to fill with rewrite after rewrite of my poetry portfolio. I swivelled on Ricky's chair to look at him. He was sound asleep, face down and spreadeagled diagonally across his bed, having given up all pretence of taking his studies seriously. I was wondering whether to wake him when the doorbell rang.

Malcky still had his finger on the bell when I unlocked the door. He pushed past me into the flat. Ricky was standing in his doorway, rubbing his eyes. Malcky grabbed him by the shoulders and roared in his face.

'What the fuck?'

'Guess who just phoned me on my fucking phone?' Malcky bellowed. I'd never seen him like this. He was completely overexcited.

'Who?' I asked, because Ricky was still yawning.

'Only Damien fucking Dwyer, that's who.'

Ricky snapped to attention. 'What did he want?'

'Only to fly us to London.'

'What?'

'This weekend.'

'What?'

'To meet those record company guys.'

Ricky took hold of Malcky's arms. 'Fuck right off.'

'I'm serious. They want to meet us. Like, at a meeting.'

'Lava Records?'

'And they're going to fly us down. In a plane. Put us up in a hotel. And, fuck, I nearly forgot, Damien Dwyer? He wants to be our manager.' Malcky finished his speech and let go of Ricky with a small shove.

'Oh, my god! We're going to London. We've got a manager!' Ricky grabbed Malcky again, and they both started roaring and jumping around the hall.

I closed the front door and squeezed past them to the kitchen to fill the kettle. I wasn't sure what I felt. Even with this amazing turn of events, I couldn't help but feel that Malcky had trumped me somehow. Like, it was all still a competition for Ricky's attention.

'Get Bob and Dinger over right now,' Malcky said as they tumbled their way into the kitchen.

Ricky grabbed his phone off the table. 'Look,' he said. 'Missed call from Damien Dwyer.'

Malcky raised his eyebrows and shook his head. 'Luckily someone was paying attention.'

'So tell me exactly what he said.' Ricky quickly fired off a text.

'I'll just have to repeat it when the others get here.'

'So?' Ricky said, pulling open the fridge and handing me the milk. 'I want to hear it twice.'

'He just wanted to hear 'yes', then he's phoning back with arrangements.'

'And you said 'yes'?'

Malcky gave him a withering look. 'Some big shot manager offered to be *our* manager. And a bloody international record label wants to fly us to London to sweet talk us. I said 'yes.''

Ricky paused for a moment, then burst out laughing. 'It's happening!'

I left them to it, taking my tea back to Ricky's room, but I couldn't get my concentration back. I was packing up my notes to head to the library when Dinger and Bob arrived.

'This better be important,' Dinger began when Ricky opened the door. 'I've got a shit ton of work to do.'

'Oh, it's important.' Ricky grinned, bowing low and holding an arm out. 'To the kitchen, if you may.'

I steadied myself on Ricky's shoulder to pull on my trainers.

'Where you off to?' he asked.

'Library. I need to work.' I smiled up at him. 'I'm totally chuffed for you. But exams start Monday.'

'I'm about to get handed a record contract, Jo. I don't think I'm going to be a bloody engineer anymore.'

'You don't know anything yet. You don't know what's going to happen in London.'

'Have a little faith.'

'I have faith,' I said. 'But it's about keeping your options open until you know for sure. You've got to at least try to pass these exams.'

He swept a hand through his hair and rolled his eyes. 'I'll try, for fuck's sake. I'll sit them. It'll be fine. I'm a genius, you know that. I don't need to study.' He leaned down and planted a kiss on my lips, then patted me on the bum out the door. 'Off you go. Don't worry about me. You're the one who needs to work.'

As the door shut behind me, I could hear Bob's deep voice from the kitchen, saying, 'There's no fucking way I'm going to London this weekend.'

CHAPTER 16

Ricky and Malcky left for London on Friday afternoon, alone. Bob and Dinger had refused to go, what with their final presentations looming. And Damien Dwyer seemed to think it wouldn't matter.

As their taxi turned the corner, I let the close door bang shut against the blue sky and the smell of cut grass from the park. I dragged my mind off the glorious weather, off London, and off Ricky, as I walked back up the stairs to the flat. I absolutely had to get my head down and work. I'd cobbled together a hybrid narrative poem, combining classical bardic school rules from thirteenth century Gaelic poetry, with experimental open form, all set in a Glasgow tenement. It was hopeless, but it was all I had.

I doggedly fiddled about with it through Friday night and into Saturday, stopping only for food and a few hours of sleep. I worked a quiet shift on Saturday night, mainly sitting on a bar stool tinkering with word placements, then got back up about six on Sunday morning to tinker some more. I'd set myself up at the kitchen table, wearing one of Ricky's dirty t-shirts and not much else. I'd pull a handful of fabric to my nose every now and again, inhaling his smell.

By late afternoon, I had a strong final draft. I jumped in the shower and was at Mhairi's just as their plane was due to land.

'All good?' she asked. 'Any word?'

'Not a peep.'

Tanya was already there, sitting cross-legged on the armchair behind the door. 'They're in a taxi. Landed early,' she said, not taking her eyes off her split ends, which she was deeply involved in separating one at a time.

'Have you got exams tomorrow?' I asked.

'She doesn't know the meaning of exams,' Mhairi replied, kneeling down in a pile of notes. 'She's studying drama.'

'It's not drama,' Tanya snapped back. 'It's Theatre Studies, Arts and Media Information, actually.'

'Where're Bob and Dinger?' I asked.

'Bedroom. Practising for their orals.'

I sat on the sofa as a flash of lightning lit up the room, making us all jump.

'That'll be the summer done then,' I said as the thunder rumbled.

After the next crack of lightning, the rain began in earnest. As it gathered force, I could hear it drumming against the windowsill. I couldn't concentrate on the conversation. Ricky walking through the door was the only thing on my mind. I was looking at the window when the next flash lit up the sky. The room seemed to fill with electricity. The thunder followed immediately and was deafeningly loud. The storm was right on us.

As the noise fell away, it left a faint ringing in the room. We were all looking at each other, holding our breath. And then the next ring began.

'Door!' Tanya shouted, springing to her feet.

I followed as she swung the front door open and launched herself at Malcky. I squeezed past them and out into the close to get at Ricky.

And there he was. He raised his chin sharply in a backward nod and I obediently moved towards him and into his arms. He held my head against his chest, his other hand low on my back. I could hear him inhale deeply. He smelt of airplanes and smoke and I lifted my face to kiss him.

'Hey,' he whispered.

His eyes were bloodshot and rimmed with dark circles. His mouth was a hard, straight line and there was a crease on his forehead.

I frowned. 'Are you ok?'

'Tired. I'm just tired.' He took my hand, leading me back into the flat. 'Let's get this over with.'

'Get this over with' were not the words of a man happily in receipt of a record contract, I thought as I followed him into the living room.

Ricky slumped onto the sofa beside Dinger, who'd appeared from the bedroom with Bob. Dinger was still clutching a pile of handwritten index cards. There were dark stains of dried blood round his fingertips where he'd bitten his nails down to the quick. Malcky was standing in front of the TV, hands in pockets, waiting for us all to settle.

'Spit it out, Malcky,' Bob said.

'Right.' Malcky nodded slowly. 'Good news and bad news.'

He looked at Ricky, and Ricky dropped his gaze to his knees. I put a protective arm round his shoulder, unsure what was going on.

'Good news first,' Malcky continued. 'We met with Damien Dwyer Friday night and agreed, officially, for him to be our manager.'

'We know that bit,' Dinger said.

'Then on Saturday we went to Lava Records. And the bottom line is, they're impressed.'

Ricky changed position, but his eyes were still fixed on his knees.

'They've offered us a contract.'

'A record contract?' Bob spluttered.

'Yes.' Malcky nodded. He didn't exactly look overjoyed.

'Oh, my god!' Dinger came to life and slapped Ricky on the shoulder.

'I knew it!' Bob laughed. 'I fucking knew it.'

But I was watching Malcky. 'What's the catch?' I asked.

Malcky waited for quiet before continuing. 'The catch is, they want us in London.'

'When?' Bob asked.

'End of the month.' Malcky shifted his weight, straightening his back.

'That's fine,' Dinger said. 'We're all done by the end of this week.'

Bob ran a hand over his bald head. 'As long as they're paying again.'

'How long for?' Dinger asked. 'I've got two weeks before my placement starts.'

Malcky shifted his weight again. 'They want us in London at the end of the month, permanently.'

'What?' Dinger choked out. 'Move down there? Are you joking?'

Mhairi reached up to take hold of Bob's hand. 'We can't move to London. That's crazy.'

'The main condition of the contract is that we move to London by the end of the month on a permanent basis.' Malcky's eyes flicked over to Ricky, who was still studying his knees.

'And if we don't go?' Bob asked.

'Then no contract.'

The room was silent as everyone took this in.

'Well, that's it then,' Bob said. 'We can't just fucking move country.'

'Why though?' Dinger asked. 'What's wrong with Glasgow? What difference does it make where we live?'

Malcky sighed. 'Obviously we asked why we have to move and they said it was impossible, logistically, to make it work from up here. They're wanting to fast-track us and all the media outlets are down there. And the people they want us to work with for the album are down there.'

'The album?' Dinger spluttered.

'Record contract equals album,' Ricky said quietly. They were the first words he'd spoken.

'What does 'fast-track' mean?' Bob asked.

'Just, you know, push us, promote us,' Malcky said with a shrug. 'Get us there quicker.'

'Get us where?' Dinger asked.

'So they can make their fast buck,' Bob said. 'That's what is sounds like to me. Typical record company talk.'

'Some one-hit-wonder nobodies,' Dinger agreed. 'Is that what they want? Did you see the contract? I hope you didn't sign anything, Malcky.'

'No, we didn't fucking sign anything,' Malcky snapped back and took another glance at Ricky.

This time, Ricky was looking right back at him.

'It's a good contract.' This time, Malcky looked away. 'Damien Dwyer doesn't back one-hit wonders. It's a serious offer and Ricky and I know it's a bit of a shock.'

Dinger abruptly stood up. 'I can't deal with this right now. I've got the most important presentation of my life in two days, in case everyone's forgotten.'

Ricky took hold of his arm. 'Dinger. Come on.'

'Come on what, Ricky?' He shook off Ricky's hand. 'I'm up to here with this fucking band right now! And I've got work to do. You might not have, Mr I'm-going-to-be-a-rock-star. But some of us have our heads somewhere beneath the clouds.'

Ricky leapt to his feet. 'What the fuck are you talking about?' he shouted in Dinger's face. 'Are you deaf? This is real. Jesus, Dinger! You're worried about some fucking wee Uni shit? We've got a record contract. In London. With Lava Records. We've made it. We're going to be famous.'

Dinger and Ricky stared at each other.

'Ok,' Malcky said, taking his hands out of his pockets. 'We'll talk about it another time.'

'I'm not moving to London,' Bob said. 'End of.'

'Well,' Malcky said, rubbing his palms together. 'I'll make some calls. See if there's any room for manoeuvre. Let's call it a night.'

'Fine,' Bob said, standing. 'I'll show you all out.'

Out in the close, Dinger was already long gone. Ricky swung his rucksack onto his shoulder, took hold of my hand, and began pulling me down the stairs.

'Told you it would be fine,' Malcky said from above us.

Ricky ground to a halt. 'That was not fine, Malcky. That was not how it was meant to go.'

'It was exactly how it was meant to go. It was never going to be all sweetness and light, Ricky.'

Ricky squeezed my hand hard as his anger boiled. 'They are my friends!'

'And that's why we're doing it like this!'

I caught Tanya's eye, and she raised her eyebrows at me before Ricky started back down the stairs with me in tow.

I didn't ask him what was going on as we walked home through the rain. Nor did I ask him what was going on when we got inside the flat. He kept hold of my hand as he kicked the door shut behind us, dropping his rucksack and pulling me into his bedroom. The street lights were filling the room with their amber glow. He tugged my wet jacket off and then pushed my dripping hair away from my face with both hands. He held my head tight in his grip and stared into my eyes. I stared right back without blinking.

'I need you.'

'I'm yours,' I replied without hesitation.

He pulled me forward and smacked his mouth onto mine so hard that I could taste the metallic tang of blood. Then he was ripping at my clothes, stripping me bare enough to get inside. And I didn't struggle, didn't resist. I gave myself over to him.

The sex was fast and raw and brutal, and it left me

wide awake and stunned. My body was still throbbing as I ran the events of the night through my head while Ricky slept beside me. Something was wrong. Something was seriously wrong. Ricky and Malcky were not telling the truth. But why not?

CHAPTER 17

I woke up to the sun pouring through the open curtains and checked the time.

'Ricky!' I shouted. 'It's after ten.'

His head sprang up, but his body remained motionless.

'Come on! Move it!' I flung myself out of bed, picked up his jeans and threw them on the bed, then looked about for a t-shirt.

'I was sound there,' he said, stifling a yawn.

I found a t-shirt and began turning it the right way out. 'We've slept in. You've got an exam ten minutes ago. I can't believe this.'

He dropped back down onto the bed and turned his head away from me. 'Well, I've missed it now, haven't I,' he mumbled into the duvet.

I looked at the time again in disbelief, feeling slightly sick. 'Well, yes, you've missed the start. But if you go now and explain, you might be able to sit it in another room or something. We'll think up an excuse. You got locked in the flat. You got mugged. Ricky, please, come on.'

I tugged at his limp arm, but he pulled it out of my reach.

'Jo, calm the fuck down,' he said, pulling himself upright. 'I'm not going. All right? I don't know the first thing about Geotechnics. I'd have trouble even defining the word.'

I stared at him in exasperation. 'I know you haven't revised. But you're bright, Ricky. You can blag it. You said so yourself.' I reached my hand out to pull at him. 'Come on.'

'No!' He tugged his body out of my reach and rolled off the bed to stand facing me from the other side. We were both still naked. 'I don't give a shit about the exam,' he yelled. 'I am going to London! What bit of that do you not understand?'

I took a deep breath. 'But Bob and Dinger won't go to London. Lava Records will pull out.'

'We'll go alone. Malcky and I.'

I was stunned. 'What? You can't go without them.'

Ricky just shrugged. 'We'll get new people in.'

'You'll get new people in? They're your friends. What are you saying?' I was incredulous.

Ricky stared at me across the bed. His mouth was that same hard line I'd seen the night before.

'What happened in London?' I asked. 'Tell me the truth.'

He picked up a t-shirt and pulled it on.

'Ricky, tell me.'

'We signed the record contract in London,' he said, without looking at me.

'Ok. But Bob and Dinger didn't. Don't they have to sign it?'

He sat down with his back to me to pull on his jeans. 'They were never going to sign it.'

'I don't know what you mean.'

'They wouldn't even go to London for the meeting, Jo. Their hearts weren't in it. And Damien said just to do it without them. That it was Malcky and me that stood out. And Lava Records had a drummer and a bassist lined up, so–'

'I can't believe I'm hearing this.' I marched out of his room and into mine.

'We knew Bob and Dinger would never agree to move south.' Ricky followed me. 'And Malcky said it would be easier to let them think they'd made their own decision not to go.'

'And what did you think?' I snapped, pulling on a pair of leggings.

Ricky shrugged. 'I thought it was wrong.'

'You thought it was wrong?' I said with scorn. 'That Malcky is one twisted son of a bitch.'

'Oh, don't start that again, Jo! He was doing what he thought was right. He was trying to protect them. Look how far he's brought us.'

'Brought himself, more like,' I said, shaking my head as it popped through my hoodie. 'Ricky, you've lied to your pals. You've betrayed them. This is betrayal.'

'Their hearts were never in it. Not like mine. If they'd been serious about the band, they'd have come to London this weekend.'

'That's ridiculous! You never gave them a chance. You've lied to everyone.'

'I know.' He hung his head. 'But Malcky said–'

'I don't want to hear what Malcky said,' I shouted. 'You are so wrong about him, Ricky.'

'Oh, here we go!' Ricky stomped back out of my room, heading to the kitchen. 'You're like a broken fucking record. Why are you so jealous of Malcky?'

'What?' I marched after him.

'You think he's some kind of threat to you. He says you're always having a go at him.'

'He said what?' I put my hands on my hips.

'I can see it in your eyes when he's around. You can't stand him.'

I took a deep breath. 'I don't like him. I don't. And I'm right not to like him.' I lifted my hand to count off my fingers. 'He lies. He steals. He beats up women. He takes drugs.'

'Can you even hear yourself?' Ricky shouted back from across the table. 'I never thought you were like this. You never used to be like this.'

'Like what?'

He lifted his own fingers to count them off. 'Whiny and annoying and clingy and boring and just the same as all the other girls I've ever shagged.'

Silence fell.

I tried to hold his words outside myself, to stop them getting to my brain, but they slipped through anyway. I held my breath to stop my body reacting as I knew it would, but almost straightaway I felt my throat getting blocked by tears.

'I'm sorry,' Ricky said, walking round the table.

I moved out of his reach. 'Don't be. Say what you think.'

'I didn't mean it. I'm just stressed out my brain.'

I wrapped my arms around myself and sat down. I wasn't sure my legs could have held me much longer. Ricky walked to the sink and ran the tap. I could hear him drinking, then he refilled it and sat down beside me.

He held the glass out. 'You know I don't feel like that. I've never cared for anyone the way I care for you. I've never had a relationship like this, have I? Nothing's ever lasted this long.'

I took the glass. 'It's only been a month, Ricky.'

'It's been years. We've lived together for years.'

I laughed despite myself. 'That doesn't count.'

We were silent for a long time while my tears fell.

'I can't believe you're leaving,' I said at last.

Ricky took the glass from my hands and held them both in his.

'So, I've been thinking,' he said. 'About us.'

'What about us?'

'Well, I'll be travelling up and down a lot, I expect.'

'No, you won't,' I replied.

'You can come down at weekends, then.'

'You'll be too busy.'

'I can make time for my girl,' he said in a forced, jolly voice.

A wave of sadness swept over me. 'I don't think you need a girl right now.'

Ricky squeezed my hands, but couldn't bring himself to look at me. And then I knew what had to be done. It seemed inevitable.

'I think if you're going to make it work down south, you need to be as free as you can be.'

I watched the top of his head until he finally lifted it to look me in the eye.

'Long-distance relationships never work,' I said. 'And I think a clean break. Rather than just letting it peter out.'

Ricky reached across to wipe a tear from my cheek. 'Are we splitting up here?'

'Yes,' I said, while I still had the strength. 'I think that's fairer on us both. Fresh start, and all that.'

Ricky smiled weakly. 'I've never had a break up like this before. There's usually a lot more shouting and quite often slapping.'

I giggled through my tears.

'So have we split up now, or can we wait till I go next week?'

I wasn't sure if he was serious. 'I think we've split up now.' I started laughing.

'Does that mean I have to sleep on my own?'

'Yes, that's what it means.'

'Only...' Ricky screwed up his face.

'Only what?'

'Only, I don't want to sleep on my own and wouldn't it be nice to just have these last few days?'

I smiled, sadly. Ricky was just being Ricky. Same as always. And I loved him. And I wanted to feel it all. All the pain. Night after sleepless night. Hour after sleepless hour.

'Ok,' I began, only to be interrupted by a loud and continuous rapping on the front door.

The hammering didn't stop, getting louder if anything, and Ricky's face fell back into the hard line as he pushed himself up from the table. 'Phone Malcky,' he said.

Bob barged in, trailing Mhairi behind him.

'You signed the contract?' he bellowed, looking twice the height and girth he usually did.

I fired off a text to Malcky on Ricky's phone.

Ricky put his hands in his pockets and hung his head.

'You signed the fucking contract?!' Bob repeated, shoving Ricky's shoulder.

Ricky took a step to keep his balance.

'I thought to myself, something's not right. Something's not adding up.' Bob tapped his finger against his temple. 'So I phoned Damien Dwyer myself. You've played us for a pair of fucking fools.'

He shoved Ricky again. And, again, Ricky just held his ground, head down, hands in pockets.

'He was just trying to make it easier on you,' I said reluctantly.

Mhairi swung towards me. 'Don't you dare defend him.'

'I'm not.'

'And I bet you knew all about it, didn't you?'

'No,' I shook my head. 'No. I'm the same as you.'

'Aye, right,' she scoffed.

'Let's just settle down,' I said as reasonably as I could, looking from Mhairi to Bob, who was white with rage. 'Let's talk about it. Ricky?'

But Ricky just kept staring at the floor.

'Nothing?' Bob asked him. 'You've got nothing to say? Dinger and me are just out with the trash?'

'I think if we just wait for Malcky,' I said, holding out my hands. 'He's on his way. And he'll maybe explain things.'

Mhairi let out a dangerous laugh. 'You phoned Malcky? You called for reinforcements?'

'I'm waiting for nothing,' Bob growled. 'I'm done. We're done. I called you my friend, Ricky Steele. But now? You're nothing to me. You're nothing. I will never forgive you for this.'

Ricky lifted his head and looked right at Bob. They stared at each other in silence. And then Bob shook his head, turned, and stormed back out the door.

Mhairi pointed a finger at Ricky. 'You.' She swivelled to point it at me, too. 'And you, are dead to us.'

'Mhairi, please.' I tried to catch her arm as she headed out the door.

Malcky was holding it open as she passed. 'Word's out then?' He chuckled.

'This is fucked up,' Ricky said.

'All for the best. New day. New start.' Malcky shrugged.

Ricky slammed into his room, kicking his door shut behind him.

'I'll come back when he settles down,' Malcky said.

I followed him into the close. 'This is all your doing,' I hissed.

He turned round. 'It is all my doing, Jo. You are completely correct. I found the manager. I found the record company. And I got rid of those two tossers so we can finally be a proper band.' He stepped towards me and I stepped back. 'You should be congratulating me.'

I glared at him, and he laughed. 'Ah, look at you. What a shame,' he said. 'I was right all along. Wasn't I, Jo? Ricky's way out of your league. And now you've lost him, haven't you? He's leaving you. Leaving you behind, just like I said he would.' He grabbed the front of my hoodie and pulled me towards him. 'You were never anything more than an easy shag.'

'Fuck off, Malcky,' I said through gritted teeth.

'No,' he replied, letting me go. 'You fuck off, Jo.'

CHAPTER 18

'Jo.'

Tanya poked me in the shoulder and I realised I'd been staring at the sink, rinsing the same glass over and over.

'A little help here?'

I brought my mind back to the present and took an order from a bloke waving a twenty-pound note, joining Tanya at the taps with two pint glasses.

'I don't want to be here any more than you do,' she hissed. 'I would much rather be in Edinburgh right now. But we're not. We're here. And it's the end of term and it's fucking mobbed. And you'd better pull your weight tonight, Jo, because I swear to god I'm not in the mood.'

'I've got a lot on my mind,' I replied. 'Give me a break.'

'Oh, poor you,' she sneered sarcastically. 'What unimaginable trauma have you got on your mind?'

'Don't pretend Malcky hasn't told you.'

'Told me what?'

I turned to glare at her. 'That Ricky and me are splitting up?'

'Hello!' My customer was leaning over the bar towards me. 'Are you deaf? I said two pints of heavy. Not that watery pish.'

I picked up fresh glasses and moved down the bar to the other taps. I was tired. That was the problem. I hadn't slept at all the night before. I'd just lain there staring at Ricky, storing him up, cramming in all the images I could get of him before he was gone. He was in Edinburgh tonight, with the others, playing their contracted support gig with Antalis – the last time they would all play together. It seemed like everything was ending.

Suddenly, Tanya came into my line of sight, grabbed my arm and whizzed me off down the bar.

'We're taking a break,' she yelled above the bar noise, not letting go until we were outside, down the steps and onto the grass in the fresh evening air.

'What are you doing?' I was still holding a pint glass. 'Jim'll have a fit.'

'Jim can stuff it,' she replied. 'I didn't know you'd split up.'

I raised my eyebrows at her.

'What happened? I thought you guys were tight.'

'London happened,' I said. 'Ricky's moving to London. So...'

'So what?'

'So he's leaving, Tanya. Jesus!' I could feel my throat closing over again. Do not cry in front of Tanya. Do not cry!

'So go with him.'

I tutted. 'For a hundred reasons, I can't do that. I can't just move to London.'

'Why not?' she asked, folding her arms. 'I am.'

Of course she was moving to London.

'I'm going wherever Malcky is,' she said, smugly. 'Is that why you split up?'

'Kind of.' I looked out over the grass. 'And he lied about signing with Lava Records.'

'Bollocks!' Tanya scoffed. 'That's got nothing to do with you. And anyway, they were only trying to do the right thing. Save bad feelings.'

'Well, that's debatable,' I replied. 'Anyway, Ricky doesn't need me down there. I'd be in the way.'

'Self-pity does not suit you, Jo Duncan,' she said, uncrossing her arms. 'Now, listen to me, because I won't say it twice and I'm only saying it because I feel sorry for you. That boy needs you. And deep down, he knows it. You can't see it because you're too close to him and all mixed up with emotions.' She patted herself on her chest. 'But I know him too, remember. And I can see how he feels about you. It's nothing like when we were together.'

I was too surprised to reply.

'He's going to need all the stability he can get in London. Same as my Malcky. That's why I'm going.'

Was this true? Did he need me?

'Malcky would have a fit,' I said.

'What are you talking about?'

'Malcky hates me, Tanya. He'd hate it if I went to London.'

'Again, what are you talking about? Malcky doesn't care about you. He just… he just thinks you're bonkers. He doesn't hate you. And what do you care what he thinks? That's your whole problem, Jo. You've always got to have someone to fight. It's always got to be a fight. Someone's got to win, someone's got to lose. How about if everyone wins for a change, eh?'

I frowned at her, but I knew it was possible. What she was saying made sense. Made perfect sense. 'I guess I could move to London,' I said, my mind still whirling. 'Do I want to move to London?'

She shook her head. 'That's not the question. The question is, do you love Ricky?'

'Yes,' I said. 'I love Ricky. He's the love of my life.'

'Same with me and Malcky.' She smiled. 'And I wouldn't dream of giving up on us because of a few miles. Jo, you've got to do it. It might not work out, but you've got to try.'

Her words hung in the silent evening air.

'I need to phone Ricky,' I said at last.

'He'll be on stage.'

'God, yes!' I laughed, hopeful excitement stirring my belly. 'I'll see him when he gets home. Thanks, Tanya. God!' I shook my spinning head. 'I'm going to London.'

'That's more like it.' She laughed back. 'We'll be like best friends.'

I laughed a bit more loudly. 'But we'd better get back in or Jim will fire us, for sure.'

I turned towards the Union, but Tanya grabbed my arm again.

'You know that eighties film, 'When Harry met Sally'?'

'I've seen it.'

'Right at the end, when they finally get together?'

I frowned. 'Remind me.'

She flicked her hair off her shoulder and leaned in close. 'So, Harry turns up at some posh party Sally's at in his trainers and old sweatshirt, all out of breath, and she asks him what he's doing there. And he says–'

'Tanya! What's your point?'

She let go of my arm. 'Go tell him right now. Go to Edinburgh. Be spontaneous for once in your life.'

'What? Now?'

Just at that moment, we heard Jim shouting at us from the top of the stairs. Tanya pulled a twenty-pound note out of her trouser pocket and swapped it for my pint glass.

'Go.'

'I'll lose my job.'

'You don't need it. You're moving to London. Go!' she said, laughing.

And I did. I just took off down the grass. I could hear Tanya whooping as I bounced along, arms flailing. And I whooped too. I bloody would go to Edinburgh to tell him. And then I'd bloody well go to London, too.

*

I sped down the road past our flat and round the corner to the Underground. A train was pulling in and I jumped on board, standing the entire way into town even though there were plenty of seats. I dodged past the Saturday revellers in the underpass to Queen Street station and bought my ticket with Tanya's money. The train was in and I leapt aboard, taking the seat closest to the door. It seemed like fate was on my side. I took a deep breath and grinned out the window at the pigeons on the platform. I was going to London with Ricky; I couldn't believe it was that simple. I was going to London and Ricky was going to

London and we were going to live happily ever after. And I kind of knew things didn't work out like that, but I didn't care. Right then, I was refusing to think about anything negative. I would not think about money, or where we'd stay, or where I'd work. I was going to London. I was rushing to Edinburgh to tell Ricky that it wasn't over, that I wouldn't make him go alone, that I was coming to London with him. I repeated this all the way to Waverley station.

It wasn't until I emerged out onto a windy Princes Street that I realised I didn't have a clue where the venue was. I needed a location and directions. I crossed the road, rubbing my bare arms, and jogged up a block to Rose Street, dashing inside the first pub to ask the bar staff. Bar staff know everything.

I was back on the street moments later and heading over to the Old Town. I broke into a run, dodging in and out of the pedestrians over the North Bridge towards the castle. After one wrong turn, I found the alley where the barman had told me the Caverna Club was located.

There was an angry kerfuffle going on at the door as two bouncers manhandled a very drunk bloke out onto the street. I had no money for a ticket, so I seized the chance and dived inside through the heavy curtains.

Antalis were playing, and the noise was thunderous. I had to get backstage. I pushed forward through the crowd towards the bar.

'I need to see the singer from the last band,' I shouted at the barmaid. 'I'm his girlfriend.'

She glanced at me and at my Students' Union staff t-shirt, then continued filling a glass. 'Girlfriend, eh? Lucky you.'

'I've just come through from Glasgow. I need to speak to him,' I hollered. 'It's an emergency.'

She finished her order and turned to the till, then nodded her head towards the end of the bar as she handed her customer his change. I pushed through the crowd to meet her, following her down to the side of the stage and past a bouncer. She held back another heavy curtain.

'Take a right at the end of the corridor. Second door on the left.'

'Cheers.'

It was all going perfectly. The lighting was very subdued in the corridor and I shrieked with surprise when I turned the corner and walked into Bob.

'God! You gave me a fright. How did it go?'

'It went.' He stepped round me, knocking my leg with his guitar case.

'Not hanging around?'

He didn't turn or stop. 'Nope.'

I shrugged my shoulders. An angry Bob would not deflate my mood. Ricky was right through that door and nothing was going to stop me now.

I threw open the door without knocking and looked about. It was a large room, crammed with mismatched chairs and tables. It smelt really dodgy and was as dark as the corridor. There seemed to be about half a dozen people and I squinted to see who they were, and then I heard my name.

Dinger was scrambling up off the floor and stepping over his drum kit towards me.

'Oh, this should be fun.' I couldn't mistake Malcky's voice. He was sitting in the corner with another couple of blokes I didn't recognise.

Dinger reached me and took my arm, steering me back out the door.

'Where's Ricky?' I asked, trying to shake him off.

'He's busy,' Dinger said. 'What are you doing here?'

I laughed as I got my arm free. 'I need to see Ricky.'

Dinger kept on trying to spin me round. I batted his hands away, still laughing, and he actually pushed me into the corridor.

'Let her go, Dinger,' Malcky said. 'Ricky's through there.' He nodded at the back of the room towards another door. 'Off you go, Jo. It'll be a lovely surprise for him.'

'Jo.' Dinger sounded odd. 'Don't.'

I walked past Dinger and glared at Malcky as I crossed the room.

'You're a fucking arsehole, Malcky Chalmers,' Dinger said behind me.

'I completely agree,' I murmured, trying to focus my mind back on what I was about to do. I was about to alter the course of my life forever.

I knocked once and flung open the door.

'Ricky!' I called out.

His name was still forming on my lips when the scene before me registered in my brain. Ricky was sitting facing me on an old computer chair. His head was thrown back, but it sprung forward at the sound of my voice, his hair falling into place over his eyes. But the sight that stopped me in my tracks was the girl kneeling in front of him with her back to me, her blonde head bobbing rhythmically up and down.

CHAPTER 19

I ran. I ran back across the room, past Dinger's outstretched arm. I ran out through the door, skidding to make the turn, hearing laughter behind me – Malcky's laughter. I ran down the corridor, grabbing the wall to make the left turn, glancing behind me to see Dinger at my heels and Ricky already at the door of the room. I ran faster, hauling myself mentally towards the black curtain. Behind me, I could hear my name being called, and then I was through into the club.

But this wasn't right either; the scene in front of me was all wrong. The lights were on. It was brighter than daytime. The club was in chaos, the noise deafening. But it wasn't music. The noise was from people shouting and screaming. I tried to push through the crowd, but it was hopeless. Everyone was moving in different directions, pushing me back, then hauling me over towards the stage. I craned my neck to see above the crowd. A wall of black uniforms were streaming in the door.

The uniforms swiftly created a barrier down the centre of the club, separating me from Ricky and Dinger, and the crowd became calmer, more alert. I stopped pushing and watched as the central line of police began to kettle us into groups of male and female. A police officer took hold of my arm firmly and placed me against the side wall.

'Keep your mouth shut,' a voice hissed in my ear. 'Have you got anything on you?'

I turned to see the barmaid that had helped me get backstage. 'What's going on?'

'Raid. It's happened before. They're looking for drugs. Are you carrying?'

'No.'

'Good. Say nothing. Act normal.'

Before I could answer, another police officer arrived in front of us.

'Are you in possession of any illegal substances?'

'No,' my new best friend replied.

'Are you carrying a weapon?'

'No.'

'ID please.'

'Our bags are in the cloakroom. We're staff.'

The police officer looked at me, and I smiled innocently.

'Proceed to the cloakroom and present to my colleague there,' she said and turned to the next girl along.

The barmaid took my arm. 'Let's get out of here.'

'Wait,' I said. 'My friends. The band.'

'They've had it. Backstage is swimming with coke. Come on.'

We joined the queue at the exit. A male police officer was pushing punters out into the night, one by one.

'We've had our ID checked over there. She said we were free to go.'

He pushed my new pal out the door.

'Me too,' I said as confidently as I could. 'ID checked. Free to go.'

He didn't even look at me, just shoved my shoulder out through the door and into the hazy May night.

'Bloody hell,' I said.

'Honestly, your pals have had it.' She pulled a fag from her back pocket and lit it. 'They'll be here all night. Longer if they're caught carrying.'

She offered me a drag, and I shook my head.

'Just go home,' she said. 'That's what I'm going to do.' And with that, she walked away up the alley.

I stood still amid the sea of police vans and officers, unsure what to do. And then it all came back to me – what I'd seen backstage. Ricky and that girl. Ricky with his head thrown back. That look in his eyes. And straightaway, I didn't give a shit. I didn't care if they caught him with coke. They could lock him up and throw away the key.

I turned on my heel and headed to the station.

*

As soon as I heard the key in the front door, I threw myself off my bed, across the floor and slammed my back against my already closed bedroom door.

'Jo?'

The front door clicked shut.

'Jo?'

I could hear him pacing the hall, checking rooms. And then he was outside mine.

'Jo? You in there?'

I stared straight ahead at my dark window, my reflection stared steadily back.

'Look, I need to talk to you. I'm coming in.'

The door pushed against my back, but I held firm, bracing myself with my hands on the floor.

'Jo, come on, let me in.' He tried the handle again. 'Come on. Don't be like that. I can hear you breathing.'

I held my breath, keeping eye contact with my reflection.

'Fine. We can talk through the door. That's absolutely fine. But I'm going for a slash first.'

I waited until I could hear him peeing, then darted up to grab my pillow and duvet. He was not getting in my room no matter what he said, and if that meant sleeping on the floor, so be it.

He tried the handle again when he came back, and then I could tell he was settling down on the floor. When he next spoke, his voice was right beside my head. 'Didn't get arrested, by the way. Dinger's ok too, in case you were wondering. What a night, eh?' A pause. 'Fuck knows about Malcky.' He sniffed. 'Dinger's dad came through to get us. Now that's a journey I don't want to repeat.'

I wished I'd gone somewhere else, instead of coming home.

'Look.' He lost the chatty tone. 'I'm sorry, Jo. I'm so sorry. It meant nothing. Absolutely nothing. You shouldn't have seen that. I just… I wasn't expecting you.'

I rolled my eyes silently to the ceiling.

'I didn't know you were coming. I thought you were working.' He sighed from the other side of the door. 'And I know Dinger tried to stop you coming in. And that Malcky didn't. Which was really shit of him.'

'What's her name?'

I could almost hear Ricky shaking his head. 'It doesn't matter.'

'What. Is. Her. Name?'

'It's not like I'm going to see her again.' His phone rang, and he turned it to silent.

'What's her fucking name?'

'I don't know,' he mumbled, his phone continuing to rumble in vibrate mode against the floorboards.

'Were you doing coke?'

'No.'

'I don't believe you.'

'Well, I wasn't.'

'I don't believe anything you say anymore.'

'Well, I don't know what I'm meant to say, then. What do you want me to say? I'm sorry. I've said I'm sorry.' He was silent for a while as his phone buzzed on and off. 'And we've more or less already split up, so what did you expect me to do? You, of all people, know what I'm like.'

'Well, why the fuck are you here?' I yelled, my voice cracking. 'Just fuck off.' I drew the duvet tighter round my shoulders and tucked my chin into the folds for comfort.

'Cause you're upset!' he yelled back. 'Cause I've upset you. And *I'm* upset, too. It's like it physically hurts. Dinger, fucking hell, Dinger was raging. Pure nipping my ear all the way in the car. He really likes you, by the way. But he was raging mad. I mean, proper mad. Having a right go.'

He's feeling guilty, I thought. That's all he's feeling.

'I shouldn't be here,' he mumbled. 'Cause we're done, aren't we? I wouldn't usually give a shit. But I do give a shit. It's so weird. I really do give a shit, Jo. The thought of what you saw. Your face. You looked so fucking wiped out.'

I swallowed quietly and wiped a tear off my cheek.

'This is the biggest pile of shit. I hate that I even did that – you know, what you saw. I don't know what I was thinking. I was just being an arsehole.' He sighed. I could almost feel the back of his head through the door. 'But all the way home – that pain in my chest. I'm scared, Jo. I'm scared of losing you. Cause I still care about you. I still feel like we're together, like we shouldn't split up. I don't want to split up with you, Jo. I don't want to lose you.'

I bit the duvet to prevent myself from sobbing.

'That's why I'm apologising. That's why I'm sitting here on the floor like an eejit. I'm sorry. I'm just sorry.'

He was quiet for a long time before he spoke again.

'I love you, Jo.'

Fresh tears spilled over my lids and down onto the duvet. He'd finally said the words I hadn't even allowed myself to hope for. I felt like my heart was being ripped apart.

'It's like, I just thought it was for the best, us splitting up, you know. I'm going to London. New start and all that. But, now, I just don't know. I *feel* so weird. I have all these *feelings*.'

I laid my head back against the door, letting the tears flow freely down my face.

'I mean, it's only cause I'm going to London that we're splitting up, isn't it? But I don't want to lose you, Jo. I need you. You're the best thing that's ever happened to me. Ever. And I've never said anything like this to anyone before.' He chuckled. 'And you know that's the truth.'

I smiled through my tears. He was telling the truth. And I desperately wanted to believe him.

'And then I had an idea. Why don't you just come to London too? I mean, what's keeping you here? You can write anywhere, Jo. I just want us to be together. Then everything will be ok. That's what I want. That's all I want.'

'Me too,' I whispered.

'Jo? Did you say, 'me too'?'

I slid forward a bit and reached up to turn the handle on the door. It swung open and Ricky twisted round onto his knees.

'That's why I was in Edinburgh,' I said, my tears dripping on the floor. 'To tell you I was going to come to London with you.'

'Well, do it. Let's do it!'

He started crawling towards me, but I placed my hand on his chest to stop him. I looked into his eyes. I tried to see everything that he held inside him: all his dreams, all his ambition. And I tried to see myself in there. I tried to see the future, because I knew that if I chose him right then, if I decided right at that moment to be with him, then I was going to lose myself in some way I didn't fully understand.

'Say it again,' I said.

'I love you.'

I let my hand fall, and he kissed me. He kissed me as if he'd lost me and found me again. And part of me melted into him with that kiss. Like I was tethering myself to him in some invisible, indestructible way.

He pulled back and brushed a hair off my forehead. 'I don't want to lose you, Jo. I'm sorry I ever thought I did.'

'You won't lose me.'

'I love you, Jo.'

'I love you too.'

He pulled me into his arms and we clung together for a long moment as his buzzing, vibrating phone jiggled itself about on the floorboards behind us.

I sighed. 'That fucking phone! You'd better see to it.'

'Maybe it's Malcky,' Ricky said, picking it up as the doorbell rang, followed by repetitive knocking.

'Tanya,' I said, as I opened the door. 'What's the matter?'

She was white as a sheet, her mascara smudged and her hair unbrushed. And she was visibly shaking.

'What's the matter?' she wailed. 'Malcky's been arrested, that's what's the matter. Him and half of Antalis. For possession of cocaine.'

'Shit,' Ricky said.

'Get her some water,' I told him. 'Tanya, come and sit.'

'Don't you touch me, Jo Duncan.' She jerked her arm out of my reach. 'This is all your fault.'

'How is this my fault?'

She waggled a finger at me. 'I've been nothing but nice to you, Jo. And you've been nothing but nasty in return.'

'When was I nasty?'

'And when Malcky said you arrived just in time to get Ricky out.' She let out a cackle of a laugh, taking the proffered glass. 'That's when I knew.'

'Knew what, Tanya?' I said calmly. 'This has nothing to do with me. Or Ricky.'

'You've had it in for Malcky since the moment you saw him. This is all some grand plan you've dreamt up.'

'Tanya–'

'And to think it was my fucking twenty quid that got you there! To think I called you my friend. But hear this, Jo Duncan. Your time is up. I am going to drop you in it from a great height.'

I was getting fed up with this. 'And how are you going to do that?'

'Wait until the police hear about your scheming, plotting, evil little games. Then we'll see.'

I crossed my arms. 'Tanya, you're talking rubbish. You're just upset. Malcky was doing cocaine. Again. And he got caught. Open your eyes. It's as clear as day.'

'My Malcky does not do drugs!' she shouted, and threw the contents of her glass into my face.

I stumbled back and wiped my eyes clear. 'What the fuck?'

'I'm going to take you down, Jo Duncan. You're not so fucking special.'

'At least I don't sound like a horse in labour when I'm getting shagged,' I shouted back.

Ricky spluttered out a high-pitched laugh as Tanya stormed out the door.

'That was epic.' Ricky chortled.

'You, call Damien,' I instructed.

'What, now? It's the middle of the night.'

'Call Damien.'

CHAPTER 20

'Right,' I said, holding out my fingers one at a time. 'Tickets, passport, money.'

Ricky was just coming out of the bathroom, still buttoning up his jeans. He shook his head. 'There are no tickets. We're in the digital age. We don't need passports. We're only going to London. And there's no money, we never have any money. Why would you think there was money?'

'It's just a saying.' I huffed. 'And we do need passports. We need photo ID.'

I knew I was driving him nuts, but I was so bloody nervous, I couldn't help myself. I surveyed the pile of luggage on the hall floor.

'It'll all be fine.' Ricky clambered over rucksacks and guitar cases to open the front door. 'You've got to chill. You're acting like you've never been on a plane before.'

'I haven't.'

'What?' He laughed.

I folded my arms. 'When would I have been on a plane? I've never been anywhere.'

'God, no wonder you're like this,' he said as he started hauling his rucksack onto his shoulders.

My bag was leaning against a guitar case. I sat down to slip my arms through the straps. 'I'm fine. I just want to get going. I'll be fine once we're going.' I fastened the buckle around my waist and got onto my knees, holding the door frame as I tried to stand.

'Here, let me help you,' Ricky said, lifting the weight off my back. 'Jesus! What have you got in here?'

'Stuff.'

'What kind of stuff? It's twice the weight of mine. We'll have to swap.'

He pulled the bag right off my shoulders and set it on the floor again while he struggled out of his.

'Do we not even have a tenner for a taxi?' I asked as he settled his rucksack on my back.

'You know we don't. I've looked in every pocket.' He moved away through the hall, in and out of the rooms, checking and turning lights off. 'Anyway, it's more like twenty quid to the airport. We'll get the bus. It'll be fine.'

'What about the emergency credit card?'

'Malcky had it,' he replied, pulling the holdall out into the close. 'Last I saw, he was cutting lines with it. I've cancelled it.'

'God, your dad'll have a fit.' I tested the weight of the guitar cases, picking the lightest. 'When do you think he'll get out?'

'Who? Malcky? No idea. He's probably out already.'

'Seriously?' I looked out the open front door.

Ricky stepped towards me to fasten my waist strap. 'He wouldn't dare come here,' he said, clicking the buckle in place and resting his hands on my shoulders. 'Jo, it's over. He's gone. You don't need to worry about him again.'

Over the weekend, I'd told Ricky exactly what had gone on between me and Malcky without it sounding like I was exaggerating or telling tales. Ricky finally saw him for what he was.

He kissed me on the lips. 'Let's go.'

I stepped out the door and watched Ricky lock up the flat and post the keys through the letterbox.

'Bye flat,' I said. That was it then. We'd left. For good. I took a deep breath. I still couldn't believe this was actually happening.

We'd stayed awake the rest of Saturday night after Tanya's visit, and several heated calls with Damien Dwyer, Ricky insisting he knew nothing about the raid. Then we talked about our future and tried not to think about Malcky. Damien Dwyer phoned back at nine o'clock on Sunday morning to say Malcky no longer had a contract with Lava Records, and that Antalis had been dropped too. But Ricky was still in and I could join him; they had a couple of blokes lined up already to audition for lead guitar. They'd booked the studio for Tuesday morning, and Ricky was to see how he got on with them, although the final decision would be Lava's. They'd already signed up the drummer and bass player, and their first gig was in London a week on Thursday. So that was that. Vermillion was dead. Long live Vermillion. And Malcky was gone, finished, out of my life forever.

The rest of Sunday we spent packing up the flat. We were taking everything we thought we would need. The rest of our stuff we packed into boxes, hoping Ricky's dad would store them for us. His parents had no clue about what was happening. They didn't know about the record contract or about the move to London or about Ricky abandoning university. His dad was going to explode.

We didn't see anyone before we left. No farewell parties or long goodbyes. Bob and Dinger would never forgive Ricky for signing the contract in London without consulting them. And it looked like I'd lost Mhairi, too. She returned none of my calls.

Everyone had laid their cards on the table. There was just going to be Ricky and me. No going back. I turned my attention completely onto the future.

*

Three hours later, we were in London, where Damien Dwyer was waiting for us at the barrier. This was the first time I'd seen him. He was in his early fifties, I'd guess. He wore his thin hair long and tied in a ponytail, which looked ridiculous. He was wearing pale blue jeans, leopard print brothel creepers and a long, wool camel coat with a purple silk lining. He was on his phone, but he waved at us and then set off without waiting.

'Jesus!' Ricky hissed as he manoeuvred the trolley through the arrivals crowd. 'What's the rush?'

'Guess we're in London now,' I replied, jogging along beside him and out into the London air. It was grey, busy, loud, and noticeably warmer than Glasgow.

'Ricky,' I whispered.

'What?'

'I don't think I like it here.'

He laughed and threw an arm around me. 'This is just the airport, silly. You'll love it.'

Just then, Damien finished his call and turned to us, grabbing Ricky's hand. 'Great to see you. Excellent. Flight ok?'

'Great. Good. Yeah,' Ricky replied.

Damien dropped Ricky's hand and grabbed mine. 'And this is Jo Duncan, I presume.'

His grip was like a vice. I tried not to wince.

'Excellent.' He dropped my hand, tapped his phone and stuck it to his ear. 'We're outside.' That was all he said before hanging up and strolling off down the curb, tapping out a message.

'Blimey,' I said, and Ricky squeezed my shoulder.

A black SUV pulled up in front of us and blasted its horn. Damien turned and indicated for us to get in, still distracted with messages.

'Nice wheels,' Ricky said as the driver climbed out and opened the boot. He didn't reply. We packed our luggage in and climbed into the back seat. It was enormous. I'd never been in a car like it. I could put my legs straight out and barely reach the front seat. Everything was cream leather, and the dash was polished wood. With the doors shut, silence enveloped us. We pulled out into the throng and seemed to glide along above the other cars.

'Right.' Damien swivelled round to look at us. 'Welcome to London!'

Ricky and I grinned at him. He didn't grin back.

'Now, listen. I lost one and a half bands this weekend, so I'm presuming you brought your A game.'

'I brought my A game,' Ricky agreed.

'Good. You'll be pleased to hear you've got nothing to do for the rest of the day. We're going straight to the hotel. Pass me that briefcase.' He pointed to the brown leather case at my feet.

'The hotel?' Ricky asked.

'Your apartment won't be ready for a couple of weeks. It's being redecorated. So you're in a hotel.'

I passed the case forward, and Ricky took hold of my hand.

'There are two restaurants. Just charge everything to your room.' He glanced at me as he snapped open the case. 'I've put you on Ricky's tab, love.' He rooted about then handed Ricky an iPhone 5. 'Obviously it comes back out your sales.'

'I already have a phone,' Ricky told him.

'Now you have another one. This one you keep on you at all times. It stays turned on. Got it?'

'Sure.'

'Everyone that needs to get you has the number. Do not give out the number. This is for work. Got it?'

'Yes.'

'Now pull up the diary.'

Ricky swiped the phone on and found the app. I leaned in to look.

'This is your schedule for the next couple of days. Ali, here, will pick you up tomorrow morning. Eight thirty. Sharp. The studio is booked nine to twelve. We want a decision on the guitarist asap. And obviously you need to get the guys up to speed with your songs. First gig a week on Thursday.' He peered at Ricky, waiting.

'Oh, no bother,' Ricky said. 'Plenty of time.'

'Excellent. Then lunch meet at Lava. It's me they want to see, really. Legal stuff. But it's a good idea for you to be there too.'

'What's a stylist?' I asked.

'Ah, yes, two pm. Stylist. She'll come to the hotel. Bring a whole selection.'

'But what's she for?' Ricky asked.

'Style.'

'I have style.'

Damien took a slow breath. 'How do I put this? She'll give you a look, so to speak. Everything you're doing now. Just better. Not so High Street.'

'High Street?'

'Exactly.'

'But I like the way I look.'

Damien coughed away a laugh. 'And so do I. So does everyone. She'll base it on what you have now. But you're not a student anymore. You need to be a bit more...' He waved a hand up and down at Ricky. 'Inspiring. Not so messy. Ok?'

Ricky shrugged.

'Excellent. So, late afternoon free, then meet and greet with Lava etcetera at a club in the West End. I'll brief you on that later. Pick up at eight. And Jo Duncan, I think you could come to that too, if you want.'

'Hey.' Ricky sat forward. 'Jo comes to everything.'

'Not necessary. She can entertain herself through the day. Have a look at the shops. Whatever.'

'No,' Ricky repeated. 'Jo comes with me. I need her with me. She won't get in the way or anything.'

Damien looked steadily at Ricky and then looked steadily at me. 'You really want to do this? Be out there? With him?'

'Yes,' Ricky said. 'She does.'

''Cause it could work,' Damien nodded. 'The whole couple's angle. A take on Kate and Pete. A John and Yoko kind of thing.'

'Everyone hates Yoko,' I said under my breath.

'We'll need a name and a point,' Damien continued.

'Sorry?'

'Name. We need a name. Jo Duncan won't cut it. No offence.'

'You want her to change her name?' Ricky asked, glancing at me with raised eyebrows.

Damien turned to the driver. 'Ali, how about it? Jo Duncan? What have you got?'

'Jo-D,' Ali mumbled.

'Jodie?'

'Nah. Jo hyphen big D.'

'Not being used already?'

'Nah.'

'Not some American rapper?'

'Nah.'

'Excellent.' Damien looked back at us. 'Jo-D it is. Ricky Steele and Jo-D.'

I was speechless.

'And now a point. What is your point?'

'Excuse me?'

'We can't just say you're Ricky's girlfriend. You'd be tabloid fodder. It's weak. We don't need weak. We need definition. We need strength. We need a story. We need a point.' He held out a palm towards me. 'Define yourself. Who are you? Start talking. Go.'

Define myself? I was stupefied. I'd never met anyone like this. But before I could think of anything to say, Ricky piped up.

'She's a writer.'

'Excellent. Well, there we are. We can definitely work with that. But you'll need styled too, Jo-D.' Damien turned back round to attend to his phone.

Ricky and I looked at each other, wide eyed, as Damien made a call.

'Pamela?' he was saying. 'Damien. How are you? Excellent. Now, tomorrow, slight change of plan. I need you to work a female spec too, if you can. Excellent. Yes, about five foot...' He looked over his shoulder at me.

'Five,' I said.

'Five foot five. Clothes size?'

'Eight.'

'Eight. Yes, red hair. Kind of punky, grungy, just now. Yes, definitely change that up. We want an artist. A creative. Excellent. I'll leave it with you.' He hung up. 'I'm really excited about this.' He didn't look excited at all. 'This could really work. A celebrity relationship. A creative team. Excellent. Let's see what Pamela throws in the mix.'

'Damien?' Ricky said.

'Speak.' Damien was still typing into his phone.

'You know Antalis?'

'Dropped. I told you. Lava wanted shot. Drug arrests make international travel a nightmare.'

'You know how they were to play Glastonbury?'

'I do.'

'Well, who's filling the slot?' Ricky asked. 'Vermillion are free.'

Damien looked at Ricky and snorted out a brief laugh.

'In fact, we're free for all their festival slots,' Ricky added.

'I like your style, young man. I'd have to pull some very big strings. Think you could handle it?'

'Definitely.'

'Glastonbury's on the John Peel stage. That's make or break stuff.'

'No bother.'

'Ok. Leave it with me. No promises.'

The car was pulling up under a covered entrance.

'Here we are,' Damien said. 'Right. Eight thirty tomorrow. Got it?'

A uniformed doorman opened my door.

'Got it,' Ricky confirmed as we clambered out onto the outdoor carpet.

Another doorman was piling our luggage onto a cart. He slammed the boot, and the SUV drove away. Ricky and I watched it go, then looked at each other, grinning. And then we both burst out laughing.

'Well, here we are,' I said.

'Here we are.' He grabbed my waist and lifted my legs off the carpet into his arms.

'Put me down, you nutter,' I squealed. 'People are looking.'

'Let them look,' Ricky said. 'Shall we proceed into our new home?'

I laughed and clung on. 'Why not!'

CHAPTER 21

Four months later

I climbed onto the bed beside Ricky, getting my knee caught on the piles of red fabric that made up my skirt. I tried again and managed to lie down on my side, propping my head on my hand.

'Well, this is awkward,' I said.

Ricky grinned at me, his arms behind his head. 'No, it's not. It's fun. Relax.'

He sat up and leaned in for a kiss.

'Ricky!' I said, pulling back. 'He's watching.'

'No, he's not. He's busy. Kiss me.'

I let him pull my face down to his. But as soon as I touched his warm lips, I heard a camera shutter sound in rapid succession and pulled away in alarm.

'Keep going, guys. That's good,' shouted the photographer from across the room.

Ricky smacked his lips back against mine, pulling me over so I lost my balance and collapsed on top of him.

'No kissing shots,' I said, untangling myself. 'We discussed this.'

The photographer approached the bed and began spreading my massive skirt out over the white sheets. I checked my bikini top wasn't gaping, and then looked back at Ricky.

He was smiling at me. 'You're beautiful. I love you.'

'Love you too.'

We listened to our instructions. I was to gaze wistfully out the open French doors while Ricky sniffed my neck and held up my ribcage. Or that's what it looked like to me. But I knew enough not to interfere and to let this very well respected and difficult to book photographer do his business. (I'd literally had to accost him in the toilets at a VIP charity event the month before, when my half a dozen emails produced no response.) He'd nearly finished anyway. This was the last shot of the session and my fourth outfit of the day. It wasn't even half past ten. But soon it would be over and I'd be beside the pool soaking up some Italian rays.

Pamela, our stylist and my new best pal, was behind the photographer, covertly taking some snaps with my phone like she'd promised. I mouthed 'thank you' as Damien came in to call time. He looked sweaty and uncomfortable in his usual London clothes.

'Ricky,' he said, wiping his brow with a Kleenex. 'They're ready for you downstairs. Pamela, I don't know about Zhou's bandana. He looks like the Karate Kid.'

Everyone left the room, and I collapsed back on the bed beside Ricky.

'Thank fuck that's done.' I sighed.

Ricky rolled over on top of me and pinned my arms above my head. 'You are completely gorgeous, you know that?'

I let him kiss me, melting slightly under his body's heat. The breeze from the open doors tickled the back of my arms. But I could hear voices and a great deal of banging from downstairs and I gently pulled back from his lips.

'And so are you, but your day is far from over.'

Ricky groaned and rolled off me onto the floor, landing on his feet. 'I know. I'm on it.'

'Last day,' I said, watching him pull on his t-shirt.

'So they say.' He was already striding towards the door. 'I'm so sick of this song.'

'*And I try to quit, baby, but you're hard to resist,*' I sang deliberately out of tune.

'Shut up!'

'*My mind is saying give up…*' I raised my voice as he hurtled down the stairs, howling in fake distress. '*But my body just insists I give in.*'

Alone at last, I wrestled my way out of the impractical and extremely expensive red skirt, leaving it draped over the clothes rail for Pamela to sort out later. She was going to be busy all day with the video shoot before flying home early evening. I'd thought Italy would be all lying about having fun, but I'd hardly seen her. She was in full work mode. And so was I.

I put on my white bikini and sent her a thank you text, resisting the urge to scroll over the photos she'd taken. I could do that from the sun lounger. I grabbed my laptop, charger, sunglasses and a bottle of water and headed out of the white bedroom, down the white curving stairs, over the white tiles of the hall and out into the white, white Italian September light.

I slipped the sunglasses on and watched the scene

on the terrace to my right. The boys were all in position. Behind Ricky were Zhou, Matteo and Lee, who had replaced Dinger, Malcky and Bob in the band. And the summer months of festival after festival, driving up and down the country, and hopping about Europe had cemented their friendship too.

Ricky was closest to Lee, the bass player. They'd bonded over their love of Stone Temple Pilots. And I got on better with Matteo, the guitarist, who found the business side of things fascinating. He was my sounding board when I needed to run ideas past someone, and Ricky was turning a deaf ear. But I liked the drummer, Zhou, the best. He was quiet and professional and teetotal. If I ever felt overwhelmed, I could hunt Zhou out and imbue a portion of the peace he seemed to ooze at all times.

Some of the crew were rearranging huge reflector panels. Others were scanning clipboards and staring into monitors as a massive camera on wheels was pushed along in front of the band. Ricky was holding the mic stand, head down, all his weight on one leg. Zhou had lost the bandana and was sitting calmly behind his drum kit, sticks crossed on his legs. Matteo had his back to me, his guitar slung across his hip and his arms crossed as he watched Lee fiddle with his bass.

'Stop fuckin' tuning it, man,' he was saying. 'No one'll hear it.'

'Fuck off, Matteo,' Lee replied pleasantly.

'Places,' yelled a woman with her hand in the air from behind the cameraman.

The boys sprung to attention.

'In five… four…' She counted down the rest with her raised fingers.

The track boomed out of the speakers, and the boys began playing. I turned away. I'd heard enough of 'Give In' to last a lifetime. Over and over and over again these last three days while they filmed the video. But it was a big deal. This was Vermillion's first single.

I walked round the corner of the villa and down some stone steps towards the pool, where the sound became muffled by the building and by the crashing waves of the sea far below. I looked over the purple bougainvillea that covered the wall separating the villa from the sheer cliffs. White waves smashed against the rocks far below me and I let my eyes travel out across the waves and the sea, bright and dazzling in the sunlight. I breathed in the fresh, warm, salty air. This was the life. This was *my* life!

Since the moment we'd left Glasgow, this new life had kept hurtling me forward. And forward was the only way to go. I had moments at most to reflect on things before the next thing took over – the next gig, the next interview, the next photo shoot.

But I was on it. And I was loving it. I'd carved out a role as Damien's unpaid deputy, making myself indispensable within weeks, and meaning I got to go everywhere Ricky did. And I had a job – a paying job – as a writer, no less. I was being paid as a columnist for The Sunday Chronicle.

I chose a white lounger angled away from the sun and propped my laptop on a folded towel on my knees. I had a lot of work to do; a dip in the pool would have to wait. I had the blog to write up for the vlog I'd filmed yesterday; to line up at least three Instagram stories, as the last one would've been posted that morning; and a quick glance at my email showed me I also had to re-edit my column.

What they didn't like this time was anyone's guess. I sighed as I snapped the top off my water bottle. I'd start with the column. Get it over with.

I clicked the email open and read what my editor had to say. The trick was to not get offended, to not take it personally. This week's column would be the third I'd written about life with a rock star for this shitty but well-read Sunday rag. It was anonymous, but it was already all over the Internet that I was the author, as I, and everyone involved in it, had assumed it would be. And as Damien had predicted, our profile was growing by the day. Our Instagram, by which I mean my Instagram, or Jo-D's Instagram, was increasing by at least a thousand followers a week, taking it close to twenty thousand already.

The editor's comments about my column were mainly about sentence length and complexity. All too long and too complex. So I put my water down, screwed on my stupid-person head and simplified the life out of it. This I could do; I was getting the hang of what they wanted. I had reattached the file to the email and clicked send when Damien appeared round the side of the villa.

'Excellent.' He bounced down the stairs, phone in hand. 'My main girl, Jo-D.'

I pursed my lips. The Jo-D thing had stuck, but that didn't mean I liked it.

He scraped a free sun-lounger over the stone slabs towards me and sat down, fingers already moving on his phone.

'Right, where we at?' he began, not looking up.

'Me or Ricky?' I pulled up the calendar on my MacBook Air that I'd bought with the money from my first column.

'You.'

'Column's finished and sent. Instagram sitting at… let me see.' I opened the app. 'Nineteen seven.'

Damien raised his eyebrows and nodded. 'Excellent. What about Vermillion's?'

'That isn't working. Just let Matteo do his thing. I'm covering Ricky.'

Damien pulled a face.

'Instagram isn't Facebook,' I said with authority. 'And it certainly isn't MySpace. It's more individual. Matteo's posting about his tattoos and his American take on London and Vermillion's fans love it. It's enough. It's not cool having a Vermillion profile up. Leave it on Facebook.'

'We'll circle back on that. Single is going on pre-release November twentieth. Can you plan something?' He waved his hand about without looking up from his phone.

'Sure.' I typed *talk to R re single* into next Monday's slot.

'Did you get the email about the Lava party Tuesday?'

'Yip. Midweek party. Love it.' I did not smile.

'Plane tickets for tomorrow?'

'Yip. Got them here.' I opened my email to check I had all five, the band and me.

'And when you get to London, do not go through without Zhou, for fuck's sake. That was a pain in the arse after Bilbao.'

On the way back from a festival in Spain in July, Zhou had been detained for seventeen hours. Someone had omitted to update his visa from student to work, or that was the story. Lava's lawyers had had to sort it out.

'He has his visa,' I said. 'And you are the amazing

163

manager who spun the publicity so it was a big win, remember?'

'Oh, and one more thing.' This time, he lifted his reading glasses onto his head to look at me. Not a good sign.

'What?'

'That pap I was talking to you about – Dan?'

'What about him?'

'He's here.'

'Where?'

'I don't know. Down in the village somewhere. Anyway, he's in Italy.'

I tutted. 'I don't get it. I hate them.'

'I know,' Damien said, pulling a face. 'But we've got to play along. And this one's ok. Like I said, he's decent. He always gives me a heads-up before he sells.'

'Well, what a gent.'

'I know, I know. But most don't bother. And he did us, you, a massive favour after Reading.'

I tightened my lips again and looked at him for a moment. 'So? What does he want?'

'Marvellous.' He slapped his thigh and lowered his glasses back onto his nose. 'Photo. You and Ricky, something cosy. He knows you're going to Africana tonight, so if you don't want him there, then give him the shot before. Pick some bar in Praiano. I'm sending you his number now.'

'Why do I have to contact him?'

Damien stood up and tapped my knee with his phone. 'He's good to know. He's a good one. Keep your friends close.'

'And your enemies closer,' I finished as Damien strode off towards the stairs.

'Marvellous,' he called again. 'See you in London.'

I laid my laptop down between my legs and walked over to the balcony. The stone was hot under my feet. I stared out at the endless blue sea. Bloody paparazzi. I hated this lack of control. But Damien was right. I had to keep them close, play along. It was all about impressions. That old saying, first impressions count? Total bullshit. I'd learned, in the preceding months, that *impressions* count. That's it. So, first impressions count, second too, and third, and actually you never get further than impressions. The impression of whatever it is you're trying to sell. And right now, that was Ricky and me.

I tapped open Damien's message, saved Dan's contact details under Pap-Dan, and sent him a brief text with time and place and *Jo-D*. Almost instantly, a thumbs up came back.

CHAPTER 22

The sun had set that evening by the time Ricky and I headed off down the mountain roads to Praiano. I'd suggested a drink first before we met up with the band and crew at Africana, so we'd taken the villa's mint green Vespa and it was thrilling to be hurtling along, arms locked round Ricky, thighs tight against his and the warm wind blowing my hair. I had failed to mention the paparazzi rendezvous. In fact, I was hoping to not have to mention it at all, that the scheme would go unnoticed until the pictures appeared in the papers. As much as I disliked the paps, Ricky hated them. His delight in being photographed everywhere we went had faded as soon as he realised he didn't get to choose what photos got printed, or what was written about him. And now he refused to entertain the idea that the paparazzi could be useful.

The lights of the town appeared ahead, sparkling on the still sea, and we motored on into civilization, drawing to a stop beside a small cafe on the shore. We'd been here the day before for a late lunch with the crew, and the waiter greeted us with a smile.

'I want to sit out by the sea,' I said as Ricky parked the Vespa.

I followed him in as he chatted to the waiter in Italian, securing us a table for two overlooking the small beach. I shuffled my chair round closer to Ricky's and scanned up and down the beach, but it looked deserted. I checked the time on my phone. We were only ten minutes late.

'They've still got polpo. Want some?' Ricky asked, sitting down beside me.

'Polpo?'

'Octopus,' Ricky said. 'Caught this morning.'

I screwed up my face, and Ricky laughed. He babbled to the waiter, who nodded and left us.

'You'll love it and I'll eat it if you don't. And I've ordered a bottle of wine.'

'I don't like wine,' I said, pulling another face.

'We're in Italy. You can't drink vodka Red Bull.'

'Why not?'

'You just can't.'

I put my arms on the table to lean towards him. He covered my hands with his and leaned in to kiss me softly on the lips. I hoped the pap had caught that.

The wine arrived quickly, and Ricky sat back in his chair, gazing out at the sea.

'God, I love Italy. Let's move here.'

'I still can't believe you speak Italian.'

The waiter had uncorked the bottle and filled both our glasses half full before leaving.

'I had a school exchange here when I was fifteen,'

Ricky said, picking up his glass. 'I spent a month in Rome.' He took a sip of wine. 'Carmella.'

'Who?'

He smiled. 'Carmella from Rome. She was my first.'

'Your first what?'

Ricky laughed and clinked his glass against mine. 'Not a patch on Jo from Glasgow.' He tucked my hair behind my ear and ran the back of his fingers gently down my cheek.

I smiled and tipped my face to rest on his fingers. 'I'm not from Glasgow.'

'I know this area too, you know,' Ricky continued, sitting back and taking another sip of the disgusting, saliva-stripping red wine. 'I learned to sail just round the coast from here. In Naples.'

'No way.'

'Way.' He nodded. 'You don't know everything, Jo Duncan.'

'Jo-D, if you don't mind,' I replied as the plate of what was very obviously octopus arrived. 'Oh, good lord.'

Ricky picked up a knife and fork and cut a piece of tentacle off, holding it up to my face. He had to be joking, but he wasn't, and I had half my mind on the whereabouts of the pap, so I gamefully opened my mouth and leaned towards the fork in a seductive manner. I was about to secure the shiny piece of white rubber between my teeth when Ricky's head whipped up towards the beach.

'Did you see that?'

'What?' I asked, momentarily relieved.

'A flash,' Ricky said, looking about. 'A camera flash. There's someone out there. That's the second flash I've seen.'

'Surely not.' I put my hand on his arm. 'Not out here.'

'No, definitely.' He rose from his seat, shaking his head. 'Come on, let's move back a bit.'

'Ricky, sit down,' I said. 'It's fine. It doesn't matter.'

'Jo, someone's out there taking pictures of us.'

'They could be taking pictures of anything.' I tugged at him to sit down. 'Just let's enjoy this.'

He sat, looking at me oddly. 'Why are you not bothered by this?'

'Because.' I picked up my wine, and swept my arm out towards the sea. 'We're in Italy.' I took a sip and swallowed, trying not to gag. 'Let's just enjoy. Relax.'

I took another sip and smiled through a grimace. How anyone enjoyed wine was beyond me.

Ricky narrowed his eyes. 'There is someone out there,' he said. 'And you know it.'

'Maybe.' I set the glass back down.

'What the fuck, Jo?'

'Because he knows we're in town and going to Africana later and it's better to get it over with now.' I resisted the urge to cross my arms.

'Who set this up? Was it Damien?'

'Yes,' I said slowly.

'I'm going to kill him.'

My phone, which was sitting on the table between us, pinged a message and Ricky grabbed it.

'Cheers? Why are you getting a message saying 'Cheers' from…' He paused dramatically and then pointed at the phone with his other hand. 'Pap-Dan?'

'Because,' I grinned a cheesy grin and tilted my head. 'It's nice to be nice?'

Ricky crossed his arms and glared at me, but I knew he wasn't really cross.

'Because now he's finished and we can let our hair down in the club?'

He continued to glare without blinking.

'Because,' I ran a finger along his folded arm; his skin was warm and taut, 'you can punish me later?'

His mouth twitched. 'Maybe I'll punish you now.'

I raised my eyebrows playfully. The crisis appeared to have been averted.

He lifted the fork, and a blob of garlicky oil dripped off the tip of the tentacle. 'Open wide.'

CHAPTER 23

'Well, we're not in Italy anymore,' I said in my best
Southern American accent, pulling my leggings up
above my knees and settling back in the bathtub.

'Maybe not.' Pamela knelt down beside the tub, resting
her arms on the rim and mimicking my American accent.
'But we sure ain't in Kansas either.'

We'd only been back for four days, but Italy seemed
like a distant dream.

I wiggled my toes and turned my phone's camera on.
'Quite,' I replied. 'We're in delightful Hornsey and I don't
know what I'm meant to be doing.'

'We're in Crouch End.' Pamela snatched my phone
from me. 'Give it here.'

'This is definitely not Crouch End.'

'Close enough.' Pamela scrolled through the filters
before handing it back to me. 'And it sounds better. Stop
saying Hornsey.'

I pointed the camera at my toes. 'Just take a picture of
my feet? That's your great idea?'

'No, wait.' Pamela laughed. 'I haven't finished yet.'

She reached through the door behind her and pulled in the large box that had been delivered earlier, ripping the tape off.

'Look, candles!' She lifted out two beautiful glass jars, their scent filling the tiny room.

'I do love it when I get sent things.' I giggled, lifting them from her and placing them at the end of the bath.

Products had started to pour in from all fields in the last few weeks as my Instagram began to take off.

'You'll get tired of it,' Pamela said, lighting the wicks.

'Doubt it.' I took a couple of snaps and tilted the camera towards Pamela to let her see.

'No, lower,' she replied. 'You've got the mould in that one.'

I scooted down a bit in the bath.

'And cross your feet,' Pamela said.

'Like this?'

'No, not like a bloody great ape.' She grabbed my crossed foot and shook it out. 'Relax, don't curl your toes.'

I took some more snaps and handed the phone to Pamela. She flicked through the photos and stood up, so I guessed I'd done ok.

'Let's open the other box,' I said, climbing out the tub.

'Make-up,' she said, kicking it towards me with her heel as she stepped through into the other room.

There were only two rooms: the tiny bathroom – which had a bath but didn't have a shower and which saw me, every morning, bent over the tub washing my hair with a plastic cup – and the other room, which was everything else. Kitchen at one end, sofa bed at the other and very little space in between. But we weren't paying for it, it was close to the Tube and we were seldom home long enough to mind the lack of space.

'No clothes?' I lifted the box as I passed. 'I like it when I get clothes.'

'Make-up's good too.' Pamela was filling the kettle. 'Did you get some coffee in?'

'No. We don't drink coffee.'

'For guests?'

I pushed her out of the way with the box. 'Here, open this. And guests can drink tea like normal people.' I put two tea bags in the pot.

Pamela crouched down to rip off the tape and lifted my phone to snap the open box.

'Fancy,' I said.

'Yeah, this is good stuff. A new brand from Cornwall, I think. Their Instagram is sick, like, so sick. Look them up before you post.'

I filled the pot and sat down beside her on the floor, cross-legged, and picked out a sparkly blue eye pencil. 'Ooh, colourful.'

'All inspired by the sea, I believe.'

'You have it.' I dropped the pencil back in the box. 'I'll never use it.'

'Well, I will.' She was already picking the pieces out and depositing them in her massive red satchel.

'I know nothing about make-up,' I said, pouring the tea.

'I'd noticed. You need to learn. And start by not saying you know nothing. You know tons. We've been hanging out for months. I have imbued my knowledge into you.' She fake-vomited on me as she reached for her cup.

'At Uni, my pal would do my make-up before a night out. You'd have liked her.'

'Who was your pal?' Pamela asked, leaning back against the sofa bed.

'Mhairi.'

'Was, or is?'

'Was, I guess.' I blew on my tea. 'We had a falling out. I haven't spoken to her for months.'

'That's a shame. Fixable?'

I shook my head. 'Doubt it. It was all about the band. Ricky...' I paused, remembering the way things had gone up north. I took a deep breath. 'Betrayal,' I said, over-dramatically.

Pamela regarded me for a long moment, then shrugged. 'Well, it's kind of good you not knowing about make-up. You're learning as you go. You're learning with your followers. It's authentic.'

'Hmm,' I said, sipping my tea.

'In an inauthentic world, you might be the last bastion.'

I screwed up my face and crossed my eyes at her, and we both laughed.

'There's another box out in the landing,' Pamela said. 'Books or something. Didn't look interesting.'

'Ooh,' I gasped, scrambling to my feet.

I carried the box in and laid it on the sofa bed. We were running out of space fast. There were boxes piled high in every corner and piles of clothes in between.

'Expecting something?' Pamela asked as I tore it open and started lifting out books.

'Is this poetry?' She took a book from me and leafed through it.

'Research,' I told her. 'Thought I'd write some poems.'

'You write poems?'

I wobbled my head. 'I wrote some for my Masters. I quite liked it.'

'You've got a Masters?'

'I do.'

'You're full of surprises today.'

I wriggled a folder out from under the sofa bed and extracted my certificate. 'Ta dah.'

'Wow. Distinction, no less,' she said, scanning the parchment. 'Wait. This was this year. When was your graduation?'

'While Vermillion was onstage at the festival in Arras,' I said with a shrug.

'You didn't go?'

'Nah. Didn't have time.'

Pamela handed it back. 'This is what I was talking about. You should post about this.' She splayed her hands out in the air. 'Jo-D. MA in Creative Writing.'

'It's hardly on-brand, is it?' I slid the folder back under the sofa bed.

'Hmm, maybe not,' Pamela said, taking her own phone out of her bag. 'Never saw the point of university.'

'Did you not go to Uni?'

She shook her head, scrolling through some messages. 'Straight to work. Learned on the job. What I know can't be taught – like, can *not* be taught.' She looked up at me. 'Have you seen the time?'

I grabbed my phone. 'Shit.'

'I need to go too,' she said, draining her cup and reaching up to the counter to drop it in the sink. 'Work beckons.'

'No,' I wailed. 'Don't go. Help me.'

'I have helped you.' She chuckled, fastening her bag.

'No, help me get ready. Tell me what to wear. Look at my hair.' I lifted an Ikea sack full of clothes and emptied it on the floor in front of her. 'And you can share my Uber.'

She was shaking her head, but started rifling through the clothes, so I knew I had her.

'This is no way to store your outfits.'

I stripped off my leggings and t-shirt and reached into the bathroom for some deodorant.

'What is it tonight?' she asked.

'Lava party.'

Pamela lifted a black, strapless bodycon dress from the pile and threw it to me. 'This. Have you shaved your pits?'

'Yes.' I stepped into the dress and pulled it up over my bare chest.

'You can't wear knickers with that,' Pamela said, standing up. 'Where are the Kirkwoods?'

'The what?'

'The gold shoes with the strap.'

'I can't walk in them.' I stepped out of my pants and pulled the dress back down. It reached just past my knees.

'Yes you can,' Pamela said. 'And you're lucky to have them. There's a waiting list, as of last week.' She opened the closet in the narrow hall. 'But wear your Uggs until you get there.'

She found the shoe box and extracted the sky-high gold heels, slipping them into their white cotton shoe bag and pulling the string. 'No jewellery. No make-up. Your hair is fine as it is.'

I picked up my hairbrush.

'No,' she said. 'Leave it messy. The shoes are all you need. Make it look like you haven't tried.'

'I haven't.'

'You call an Uber. I'll pack your bag.' And she sprayed me with perfume before I had time to close my mouth.

CHAPTER 24

The Uber dropped me in the narrow alley and I was buzzed into an anonymous brick building after looking up at the discreet video camera. I'd been here before; I knew how to do this. They buzzed me through the next door after I climbed the stairs. I walked down a neon lit corridor following the music and opened the door of Vermillion's temporary recording studio. I was in an anteroom with a massive L-shaped grey sofa and all the recording equipment. The actual studio was beyond this, seen through a glass window the size of the wall.

The boys were just finishing the last chorus of 'My Conscience'. The sound engineers, or whoever they were, were busy at their buttons and knobs. So I perched on the edge of the sofa and put down my clutch and shoe bag. This back area of the room was dark, but the recording desks were lit with spotlights and the studio beyond was daylight bright. The air stank of musty men, although a fan blew cold air from the ceiling. I slid along the sofa, away from the chill as the song ended. Matteo stepped towards Lee to give him a high five, but Ricky was shaking his bowed head.

'Can you play it from the second chorus?' His voice boomed into the anteroom.

'Jeez, Ricky.' Matteo's voice was quieter, being nowhere near his mic. 'It was good. It was perfect.'

'No,' Ricky shook his head. 'Listen.'

The just-recorded song started up again, and the boys stared off into space, listening. It sounded fine to me, but what did I know? Ricky held up his hand before the end, and the music stopped. There followed a heated discussion about third verse transition to chorus and I pulled out my phone to check Instagram until Zhou got up from behind his drums and left the room.

'Where the fuck are you going?' Lee shouted.

'Toilet,' Zhou replied, nodding at me as he passed.

I smiled back and was still smiling as Ricky spotted me through the glass, shielding his eyes from the lights.

'Five minutes, then we do it again,' he said, coming out to see me.

I didn't stand up, but instead spread my arms out along the sofa and crossed my legs in what I hoped was a seductive manner. Ricky grinned as he approached, then dropped one knee onto the sofa beside me and leaned in for a kiss. I wrapped my arms round his neck and there we stayed for at least five seconds until we heard Lee say, 'I'm going for a smoke.'

Ricky pulled away and sat on his folded leg beside me. 'Five minutes, tops.'

'Fuck off,' Lee replied as the door swung shut.

'Why do you smell of perfume?' I asked.

'What?' Ricky pulled his t-shirt up to smell it.

'You smell all girly. Who's been here?'

Ricky took a long, extravagant inhale. 'I smell as masculine and fabulous as ever. No one's been here.' He threw an arm around the room. 'Men have been here.'

Had I imagined it? The smell? Obviously, I had. 'Never mind. How's it going? Nearly done? Damien will be here in a minute.'

Ricky frowned.

'Interview? Lava party?'

'Oh, for fuck's sake.' Ricky dropped his head to his hands, his mop of black hair flopping forward to cover his face.

'What?' Matteo said, coming towards us with his guitar still slung over his back. 'Looking swell tonight, Jo-D.'

'Ricky forgot it's the Lava party,' I replied. 'And thank you for noticing, you charming man.'

Ricky looked up from his hands. 'You're wearing Ugg boots.'

'And a bitchin' dress.' Matteo took my hand, kissed it, then bounced down on the sofa beside me. His guitar clattered against my hipbone.

I raised my eyes at Ricky.

'Yes,' he said. 'You look lovely. You are lovely.' He sounded far from sincere. 'Did *you* remember?' he asked Matteo.

Matteo had pulled a rag out of his pocket and was diligently wiping along each guitar string. 'I never forget a party,' he said through the guitar pick held in his teeth.

'You've gone over the wrist,' I said suddenly, noticing Matteo's newest tattoo creeping an inch onto the back of his hand.

'Well spotted.'

'I thought you had to stop at the wrist. Are they still called sleeves if you go past the wrist?' I asked.

'We'll just have to be late,' Ricky interrupted. 'We need another take.'

One of the sound guys – the producer was the only one I knew, and he wasn't there – turned on his swivel chair. 'No can do. We're out of here. Party.'

'Oh, for fuck's sake,' Ricky moaned as Zhou came back in.

'We're finished?' Zhou asked. 'I'm going home to shower, so I'll see you all there?'

We waved him off.

'What is the point?' Ricky groaned. 'No one gives a shit.'

'Tomorrow's another day.' I stroked the back of his neck.

'It's coming together, Ricky,' Matteo said. 'It always seems like it's not, but it will. It's going to be a great album.'

'The greatest,' I said soothingly.

'But what's the point?' Ricky said. 'Maybe it'll be good, but who listens to albums nowadays anyway? There're no hits. We need a hit.'

'Well, 'Give In' is a hit. Or it will be a hit,' I said.

Ricky raised his eyebrows at me, and even Matteo grimaced. They were right; it wasn't that good. Catchy but forgettable. And mildly annoying after a while.

'A hit pays for years,' Lee said in his loud East End accent. I hadn't seen him return. He was leaning against the wall by the door, arms crossed. 'A bullseye a radio play adds up.' His dyed white-blond hair was florescent in the glow of the neon lights from the corridor. And with his black-clad skinny frame, he looked like a magic wand.

'How much is a bullseye?' Ricky asked.

'Fifty pounds,' I replied, not because I knew London slang, but because I knew what a radio play paid.

'If it's money you want,' Matteo said, taking the pick out of his mouth, 'you need to get the hit in a film.'

'How do you do that?' Ricky asked, looking up.

Matteo shrugged. 'Connections.'

'If it's about the money,' I butted in, 'look no further than product endorsement. There're thousands in it. Hundreds of thousands if you've got a big enough following.'

'Is that right?' Matteo asked.

'Ignore her,' Ricky said. 'She's been on at me for weeks about this. Just because she gets sent free make-up that she never bloody uses anyway.'

My phone buzzed with a message. 'Damien's downstairs.'

'I want to talk to you about this later,' Matteo said, rising from his seat with a wave of BO. With his Instagram following, he'd be mad not to monetise. He propped his guitar on a stand inside the studio. 'We'll see you there.'

Lee held the door open for him.

'Shower, then food,' Matteo said as he passed him.

'Nah, man. I'm marvin, chippy on the way,' Lee replied as the door closed behind him.

I stood up and straightened my skirt. 'Let's just keep building your profile and then find a product or area that you're comfortable with.'

'It's not about the bloody money. Jeez.'

I put my tongue in my cheek and looked at him.

'It's the songs, Jo. It's the music. I haven't written a song since we got here. I can't write here.' He waved his arm round the room, but I knew he meant London.

'It'll come,' I said, glancing at the sound engineers behind me. I didn't want them to know Ricky had writer's block. I reached down and tugged at his arm, but it was as limp as an empty jacket. 'Sunday morning's free,' I whispered. 'We'll get up early. Head somewhere green. Be inspired.'

He rolled his eyes and slouched back on the sofa, pulling his t-shirt sleeve up to scratch at his shoulder. Only a rippling vein broke the taut skin on his bicep. My phone pinged in my bag. It would be Damien waiting. I leaned down, moving Ricky's limp hand round to my bum. 'I'm completely naked under this dress,' I whispered.

He was up like a shot.

CHAPTER 25

Outside, the black SUV's door was open, and I clambered into the back seat beside Ricky, pulling the door shut quickly as the car moved off. I slid back onto the cream leather. Damien was on his phone in the front seat.

'Evening, Ali,' I said.

'Jo-D,' the driver mumbled, nodding his head slowly.

Ricky was staring at the back of Damien's head and bouncing his knee fast, his head bobbing along to every other bounce. I wasn't sure if he was going over a song in his head or just waiting for Damien's attention. I took his hand and held it on the empty seat between us as we turned out of the alley onto a busy road.

It was autumn, my favourite time of year, but the only way you'd know it was autumn in the centre of London was by the changing displays in the shop windows. I watched the stores slip by and allowed myself to miss Scotland for a moment.

Ricky let go of my hand as Damien finished his call. 'I want to get a song on a movie soundtrack. How do we do that?'

184

Damien swivelled in his seat to peer at Ricky over his shoulder, then looked at Ali.

'A movie soundtrack,' he snorted.

'What's wrong with that?' Ricky punched the back of Damien's seat.

'You want to be Chris Martin now, do you?'

'No. But I want to be famous.'

'Or Elton John.' Damien hooted. 'All he does now are Disney movies. Write me a Disney theme song and we'll see.'

'Fuck you.'

Damien took his glasses out of the inside pocket of his banana yellow tweed jacket and perched them on his nose. 'Let's just get today done first, eh?' He swiped up on his phone. 'Right, joint interview for CelebToday. Photos done last week. Approved?'

He looked at me over his specs.

'Approved yesterday,' I replied.

'So, stick to the script. Loving London… can't believe how lucky we are… roller coaster… living the dream… happy, happy. Ricky, I'm talking to you.'

'I hear you,' he said, still huffily looking out the window.

'No stories from the festivals. No drunken tales. And no mention of Reading – either of you.'

I pursed my lips.

'I've given her fifteen minutes, so make it thirty and make it look like you're doing her a favour.'

I nodded.

Damien slapped Ricky on the leg. 'Got it?'

'Yeah, yeah,' Ricky grumbled.

We knew how to do this. Stick to the script because

god forbid anyone should get the real us. No one needs to know the real us. I looked at Ricky tapping a tune out on his knee, at Damien in his silly clothes flicking through his phone, at the plush interior of the car shielding us from the world. Maybe this was the real us. Maybe this was the truth now. I wasn't sure I knew anymore.

'Where's it at?' Ricky asked.

'Sandersons,' I replied. 'And then we're close to Soho for the party.'

'Jo,' Damien continued, 'I'm sending some sample merch over tomorrow for you to look at. Get Ricky to approve it ASAP.'

'Christmas sales merch.' I took out my phone to make a note. 'Yip.'

Damien slid his specs onto the top of his head. 'And then you need to start thinking about the album launch in April.'

'Yeah.' Ricky was suddenly engaged again. 'I've been thinking about that.'

'We want a big party, obviously,' Damien continued. 'Media. Bloggers – Jo, a list? Celebs. VIP invites only. Maybe a competition for tickets? On Instagram? Jo?'

'That would work for Matteo's.'

'And I'm thinking live stream on YouTube –'

'And I'm thinking...' Ricky splayed his hands out like a banner. 'Old school rock and roll theme.'

'Are you?' Damien asked sarcastically. 'You're a fountain of ideas today. Let's hear it.'

'Ok.' Ricky glanced at me, grinning. 'I'm thinking eighties west coast America. I'm thinking skinny bleached jeans and back-combed hair. I'm thinking bandannas.'

'Spandex. Hairspray,' Damien continued for him. 'Yeah, I remember. I was fucking there.'

'No,' Ricky said. 'Not spandex. Ok, more sixties. A bit of eyeliner. Black turtlenecks. A battered electric and an old Vox ac-30. You know? Just the music; just the rock and roll.'

'So we've gone from Whitesnake to the Rolling Stones,' Damien said.

'Three chords and the truth.' Ricky laughed.

'And a left turn straight to Nashville.' Damien laughed along, shaking his head. 'Well, you keep working on that theme, my man. Winning at life!'

'Two minutes,' Ali warned us.

I reached down to get my heels out of the shoe bag.

'Ali's going to drop me off, then come back round for you two,' Damien said. 'We good?'

'Yip,' Ricky said, rubbing his hands.

I finished buckling the skinny gold straps around my ankles. The heels were so high I had to sit sideways. I found the mints in my bag and popped one in Ricky's mouth and one in mine, then ran my fingers through my hair, shaking it up a bit.

'Looking fine, Miss Jo-D,' Ricky said, smiling at me.

I leaned in to give him a quick kiss. 'I'll never walk in these shoes,' I said. 'I'll need your arm.'

'You got it.' Then to the car he said, 'Jo's going commando tonight.'

I couldn't believe it. 'Ricky! What the fuck?'

'Don't say that in the interview,' Damien ordered as the car pulled up in front of the hotel.

In the front seat, Ali didn't even flinch.

CHAPTER 26

Four hours later, Ricky and I arrived at the Lava party. We were crazy late, probably the last to arrive. Anonymous dance music drummed a steady, loud beat, but the too bright lighting confirmed this wasn't a dancing sort of party.

'I hope it's catered,' Ricky said, pulling me through the crowd by my hand.

'Oh god, yes.' I was busy smiling and nodding at faces I recognised. There'd be time to network later. Right now, I had to put something in my belly.

'Look.' Ricky tugged me forward. 'It is. Quick!'

We arrived at the centre of the room where a long, white-clothed table lay piled with food platters, overseen by a massive centrepiece of pink orchids.

'What is it tonight?' I asked, scanning the table and hoicking my dress up over my chest a bit.

'Asian. Oh, my god. Look at those prawns.' Ricky popped one into his mouth and rolled his eyes.

'Tiny spare ribs in chef's hats!'

We stood facing the table, cramming small morsels of

food into our mouths. After a while, I spotted the plates, pink with gold trim, and handed one to Ricky. We stacked them with food and turned round to rest against the buffet and scan the room.

It was packed. Small groups stood about chatting and people drifted between them. There were plenty of young trendies and quite a few middle-aged men still in their business suits.

'Have you noticed we're the only ones eating?'

Ricky nodded as he bit into a spring roll. 'We're always the only ones eating,' he mumbled. 'We're the poor people from Scotland.'

I was holding a spicy prawn, but I put it back down on the plate and put the plate on the table behind me. 'Maybe we shouldn't eat at these things. Maybe it's not the done thing.'

'What? Be more like them?' Ricky pointed at the room with another spring roll. 'Try and fit in?'

'Yes. Maybe.'

'You want us to deny who we are?' He looked at me in mock outrage.

I laughed. 'Yes! Exactly. We need to be more like them. Or, rather, we need to actively be the opposite of who we are.'

'But I'm Ricky Steele,' Ricky stated proudly, nodding.

At which point we spotted Damien marching towards us through the crowd.

'You're very late,' he began. 'But not offensively late. But you've got a room to work and not long to do it.' He took the plate off Ricky and dropped it on the table behind us. 'There are photographers here, for crying out loud. What we don't need is a photo of you dripping chilli sauce down your chin. What we do need is a photo of you talking to Sam Devine and anyone else that passes for a celeb.' He turned round to scan the room. 'Him.' He pointed at the back of a very tall man with a massive afro. 'Who's that? I recognise him.'

'Big Brother star?' I ventured.

'And those two. Who are they?'

This time he was pointing at two glittery blonds in complimentary skintight jumpsuits.

'Also from Big Brother.'

'Good,' Damien said. 'Talk to them. Not you.' He pointed at me. 'Just you, Ricky. Photo with Ricky Steele playing the field, as it were.'

I raised my eyebrows unnoticed.

'I don't know them,' Ricky said.

Damien ignored him. 'But both of you talking to the other guy. But just Ricky talking to Sam Devine. And long enough to get a photo. And don't mention the Asia tour.'

'The Asia tour?' I asked.

Damien pulled a face. 'Ah, yes. There may be an Asia tour. Maybe not. Maybe late next year. The stats are looking good. But maybe not. Just ideas.'

'An Asia tour.' A massive smile was creeping over Ricky's face. 'Like Japan? And China?'

Damien took hold of Ricky's arm. 'Do not mention the Asia tour.'

'I want an Asia tour,' Ricky said, making me laugh. He wanted everything.

'And you might get it if you don't mention it.' Damien let go of Ricky's arm and started heading away. He turned on his heel to face us. 'Go, go, go.' He clapped his hands at us before he melted into the crowd.

We looked at each other.

'An Asia tour,' Ricky said.

'Maybe not.' I widened my eyes.

'Maybe.'

'But first, work,' I said. 'You start with the girls, then I'll come rescue you to do the bloke together and then you can see Sam as that's easiest as you know him.'

'Do we know their names?' Ricky asked.

'Nope.'

'There's Zhou over there by the window. I'll maybe just talk to him first. I need to talk to him anyway. He knows that third verse isn't right.'

'No, you can't.' I pushed him off toward the first target. 'Wish me luck.'

'Luck.'

But he didn't need it for as soon as it was obvious where he was heading, the matching girls opened their arms to receive him, fussing and pawing over him like he was their favourite pet. I had five minutes to fill before I interrupted. I was considering a trip to the ladies when Zhou arrived at my side.

'Hey,' he said, glancing at the buffet.

'You eating?'

He shook his head. 'Not that.'

'It's good.'

'No, it's not. It's not good. This is made up. Pretend.'

'Ah,' I smiled. 'Not authentic enough for you?'

He looked at me, aghast. 'I have offended you.'

'I don't care. I didn't make it.'

191

He nodded, relieved. 'I miss good food. I've looked and looked, but…'

'There's no place like home.'

'Yes. You look very nice, Jo.'

'Why, thank you kind sir,' I said, bowing.

We stood together in silence, scanning the room. Ricky was still being patted by the blonds and his shoulders were looking tight.

'Go join Ricky,' I said to Zhou, pointing. 'He looks like he needs help.'

Zhou headed towards them and I set off to the loo, stopping to greet and hug some Lava people and Vermillion's record producer on the way. It should be a good night, all in all. There should be some press from this, and image, as I had come to realise, was everything. And the paps and the junk press that I worked for were in full control of it. They were gods – one false move and they could stamp us out.

By the time I got back to Ricky, he was looking like a deer in the headlights.

I linked his arm and led him away.

'They are bonkers,' he muttered.

I sauntered us up to the next target, who, again, had seen Ricky approach.

'My main man,' he hollered, thrusting his hand at Ricky and hauling him into a manly back slap.

The photographer was on us and Ricky was all smiles and compliments to this unknown, hardly famous person who was, in fact, no different from us. Just trying to make it. Trying to climb the celebrity ladder. Trying to get some press, one picture at a time. I linked arms with the stranger and we all posed for the snap. But once it was taken, I took Ricky's hand to lead him away.

'It was so nice to meet you at last,' I said, pecking the bloke on the cheek. 'Please excuse us.'

'That was rude,' Ricky said.

'It's getting late. We need to get Sam Devine before he leaves.'

'I hate this fake photo stuff,' Ricky whispered. 'These bloody paps! They make their living off us. They're like leeches.'

'No,' I said back. 'It's the other way round. We need them. Especially now. We need to grow our profile, Ricky. This could all disappear.'

I spotted Sam, Lava's CEO, who was worryingly close to the door, and hauled Ricky off in that direction. Ricky had barely said hello to him when a tall, middle-aged woman appeared beside us.

'Sam, darling,' she began in a posh drawl. 'It's been an age.' She kissed him on each cheek, her sharp grey bob barely moving.

Sam turned to give her his full attention. 'Olivia, what are you doing here?'

'You invited me, darling.'

'I always invite you. You never come.'

'Well, here I am.' She flung an arm onto one hipbone, her loose navy suit swishing in a dance. 'Now, introduce me.'

Sam turned back to Ricky.

'No, not him. Her.' The woman pointed at me with her chin, her eyes boring into me through her dark red glasses, which matched her dark red lipstick perfectly.

Sam didn't miss a beat. 'Olivia French, Jo Duncan.'

She looked me slowly up and down, then tilted her head slightly to one side. 'Jo or Joanne?' she demanded.

'Jo's fine.'

Sam took Ricky by the shoulder and led him away. What was happening?

'How do you know Sam?' I ventured.

'Oh, we go way back. In the eighties we were the bright young things.'

Should I know her? I certainly hadn't seen her before, but the name rang a bell.

'Do you know who I am?'

'I'm sorry, no.'

'I'm a literary agent. I run a literary agency.'

Of course! I'd read about her. She was a notoriously ruthless agent, one of the best. And elusive – no writer could get to her and, yet, here she was.

'I've read your Masters portfolio.'

'What? Sorry?' I blinked a few times, trying to catch up. 'How?'

'They send me the best every year.' Her hand was still on her hip as she studied me. 'I've read your column.'

'Thank you,' I replied, graciously, trying to hide my astonishment.

'I did not say I liked it.'

I swallowed.

'I think the column is the least you're capable of. If you ever rise to something better, call me.' And with that, she handed me a business card and walked out the door.

Well. That was weird. But kind of cool. I tucked the card into my clutch. Suddenly, my feet were killing me.

The gold Kirkwoods were sky-high and the balls of my feet were throbbing. I needed to sit. Across the room, on a raised platform, was the only seating area in the cleared party room. Someone had arranged a couple of plush chairs and a velvet bench around a very low glass table. And in the middle of the bench, I could see Lee's white hair glowing like a beacon. Excellent. I'd sit beside him for a minute and have a think about what just happened.

I propelled myself forward just as a waitress, carrying a shoulder-high tray of Champagne glasses, came into view out the corner of my eye. I was heading directly into her path, so I stopped – or tried to stop, because my forward foot kept going forward at the same time as the heel of the other shoe slid sideways. I reached out for support, but there was only air and I was going down. The waitress saw me, reached an arm forward to grab me, but only managed to unbalance her tray and the Champagne flutes toppled like dominoes. My bum banged to the floor, sending my forward leg up high in the air as the Champagne glasses rained down on me. And, right on cue, a flashbulb went off.

CHAPTER 27

And, of course, the photo was everywhere. For weeks. But I rode it out, laughing along with everyone, ignoring the comments on Instagram. It even spawned a 'hilarious' meme for a while. But it all died down. And by the new year it was long forgotten – by the media, if not by me.

It was a stormy January day, and the wind was whipping against our apartment window. But that was all I could tell about the weather as there was no sky to see, just some daylight and the grey building opposite. I had to rely on weather forecasts when deciding what to wear.

I was lying on my stomach, hanging off the side of the sofa bed so I could type without disturbing Ricky, who was snoring lightly behind me with his hand on my bum. I'd woken up with the complete draft of next Sunday's column pasted like a word document in my head. I couldn't risk losing it. Ricky was finally sleeping after days of insomnia and I was trying not to wake him. He'd spent the previous nights pacing round the table and generally fidgeting, unable to rest. It was the album. It was always about the album just now. With only two months to go until release, he was wound up like a spring.

Ricky's hand moved across my backside, then gave a light squeeze. I wriggled in response. The mattress shifted as he rolled towards me, his other hand sliding up my waist.

'Morning,' he mumbled.

I hit print before rolling back up onto the bed to join him. His eyes were still closed, and I gently stroked a finger along one eyebrow. Across the room, the printer clicked and burred into action and Ricky's eyes sprang open.

'What is that?'

'My new printer. I got a printer.'

'Why?'

'To print stuff.'

'What stuff?'

'Stuff. I can't think on the computer. Or I can't edit. I need it on paper.'

He closed his eyes again. 'But why so loud?'

'Oh, I'm sorry.' I shifted a leg over him and pulled myself up. 'Is the noisy printer hurting your precious ears? How can I possibly make it up to you? Please tell me.' I kissed him lightly on the side of his temple, then his forehead, breathing in his scent.

'I am incredibly offended.' His voice assured me he was anything but.

'Oh, please let me try.' I kissed his other temple, then gently brushed my lips over his.

In an instant, he grabbed the back of my neck, smacking his lips tight to mine and flipped me over. I curled my legs round his back and kissed him deeply, pulling him to me.

He pulled back and grinned down at me, all dark lashes and bed hair.

'Please,' I said in a silly, sexy voice. 'Please let me try.'

He cupped my breast hard, and I was arching up to him when the buzzer rang out. We both jumped this time.

'Who's that?' Ricky looked completely put out.

'What time is it?'

'I don't know.' He let go of my hands and climbed off to pick his phone up from the floor. 'Ten past eleven.'

'Pamela,' I said as he padded over to the intercom. 'You've got that photo shoot at twelve.' He hit the buzzer without checking who it was. 'The photo shoot you've already done,' I continued. 'The photo shoot that there was nothing wrong with the first time.'

'Everything was wrong with it,' Ricky said, pulling on a pair of boxers. 'They put lipstick on me, for god's sake.'

I chuckled as I sat up and reached for a t-shirt. 'But the photos looked fine.'

'Fine is no good,' he said, filling a glass of water at the sink. 'It has to be perfect.'

I climbed off the bed and walked to the door to unlock it before stepping into the bathroom for a pee. 'Well, it'll be perfect this time. You'll have Pamela.'

'I should've had Pamela the first time. She's the only one I trust.'

'You need to get ready.' There was a knock on the door. 'Open,' I shouted and in came Pamela.

'It is very cold out there. Like, *so* cold.' She glanced at me through the bathroom door. 'And good morning to you.'

'Sorry.'

She kept going into the flat, unwinding a lengthy electric blue scarf with one hand, the other holding a cardboard coffee tray. 'I brought coffee.'

'No tea?' Ricky asked.

'Ricky!' I shouted as I washed my hands.

'Sorry. Thank you, Pamela.'

'You're welcome.' She sat down beside Ricky on the unmade bed. 'And it looks like you need a high-octane caffeine injection more than a polite cup of tea.'

'He's not sleeping,' I said, climbing onto my side of the bed and crossing my legs before taking my coffee.

'I've never had a polite cup of tea in my life,' Ricky said, accepting his paper cup. 'I drink my tea in mugs, like the rock god I am.'

Pamela pulled a face. 'Well, let's try and make you look like one today, shall we?'

'Ricky, you need to get in the bath.' I poked him in the back.

'No, wait,' Pamela said, taking out her phone. 'You're in the pages again.'

I leaned towards her. 'Oh, let's see. I haven't checked today.'

'It's from the White Tooth night, I think,' Pamela said, scrolling through her phone. 'You look so hot, Jo. Like, so hot.' She handed the phone to Ricky.

He pinched the screen bigger. 'My hair's ok.'

'Vain,' I said, taking the phone and scrolling on. I'd managed to appear relaxed and nonchalant in the photos by turning sideways and shifting one leg forward like Pamela had taught me. 'Yeah, they're ok, aren't they?'

'Who am I with in that one?' Ricky asked.

'I have no idea,' I said.

'Let me look.' Pamela took the phone back. 'Oh, that's that guy that didn't win The Voice. The really annoying one?'

Ricky gave me a look before standing up.

'What?' I said, defensively.

He shook his head and drained the cup.

'I can't know who *everyone* is.'

'Well, just keep me away from people you don't know,' he replied grumpily, walking into the bathroom and sliding the door shut behind him.

'What was that about?' Pamela asked when the water started to run.

I sighed. 'He thinks we should be more selective about who we mix with. Or who we're 'seen with'.' I did air quotes.

'Press is press.' She was still flicking through her phone. 'And I saved the best for last.'

I took a sip of my coffee as she held up her phone, which was open on Instagram.

'Look who tagged you.'

I grabbed the phone off her. 'No way.'

'Yes way.'

'That was at New Year! I told you I'd been introduced to her.'

'It's the shoes. I knew they would work.'

'Eh, *I* knew they would work.'

I was looking at a photo of me and A-list model and elusive socialite, Kiera Dupont, Champagne in hand, chatting away. And I was wearing a tight silver playsuit and my old gutties I'd brought from Glasgow. After the

Lava party fall back in October, I'd refused point-blank to wear high heels ever again. Pamela had tried me in flat boots, pointy pumps, sequined flip flops, you name it. And by New Year I was so sick of shoes I went out in my battered black and white Converse. It was the comfiest night I'd had in months.

'She barely said two words to me, but it looks like we're best buds.'

'Word is, she's on the cover of Vogue again next month. And look how many followers she has.'

'Two point nine million!' I shook my head in awe.

'And you were tagged, let me see, eleven hours ago. Let's have a look at your account, shall we?'

I hadn't even thought of that! I rolled over the bed to grab my phone, swiping it open as I sat back up.

'No way!' I laughed, astounded.

'Yes way. You've just added ten thousand followers. It'll keep rising, for sure. I think you've found your signature look.'

'My what?'

'And I've been thinking how to move forward with this.' She thrust her phone at me. 'These are Jimmy Choo high-tops. Crocodile effect. And these...' She flicked forward a page. 'These are Zanotti. Pink suede. Look at the studs. Very rock and roll. Like, so rock. You could wear them to the album launch.'

'I'll wear my gutties,' I said, draining my coffee. Ugh. 'They're all I need.'

'You can't just keep wearing the same shoes.'

'Why not?'

'Because you just can't! You can't ever wear the same

thing more than once. Twice at the very most. Twice shows you care about the planet. But *never* more than twice.'

'That's stupid,' I said. 'I'm sticking with my gutties. They're comfy.'

Pamela looked at me with a tight face, obviously thinking.

'What?'

'What other shoes do you have, like from before?'

'Before what?'

'Before London. What did you bring with you?'

'My gutties.'

'Seriously? You brought one pair of shoes?'

'I pretty much only had one pair of shoes.' I laughed, a little embarrassed, and pointed at the now famous photo. 'I like that look.'

Pamela put on her thinking face. 'So, you like glitzy tiny dresses with battered plimsolls.'

'Yeah. Why not?'

'Posh with cheap,' she mused. 'Fancy with battered. How about vintage trainers? Or we could get some other plimsolls and mess them up ourselves. Make them look old.'

'Or you can find me something floor length and I can just wear my gutties?' I laughed and Pamela shook her head.

The water turned off in the bathroom, and Pamela got up.

'I'll wait downstairs,' she said, winding her scarf back round her neck.

'We still on for tonight?'

'You bet.' She picked up her oversized leather tote. 'I am desperately in need of a night out. Like, so desperate.'

'Great. And, hey, don't mention the photo to Ricky.' She gave me a puzzled look. 'It's just.' I lowered my voice. 'You know, me and Kiera Dupont, and him and that bloke that didn't win The Voice.'

This time, she raised her eyebrows. 'So what?'

'Please, Pamela.'

She turned to head out the door before Ricky emerged. 'Whatever.'

CHAPTER 28

It was just after nine as I hurried up the stairs at Russell Square and out into the windy night. It was not raining, thank god, as I'd opted for the hoodless denim bomber jacket over a red jumpsuit and, of course, my gutties. I knew I looked good, but the gutties were the only things that felt like me in the entire outfit. Nothing much felt like me nowadays. Everything felt borrowed from some imaginary, near perfect life.

I checked the map on my phone and turned right. I was so looking forward to a few drinks with Pamela, after spending the day staring at my computer screen. A good blether. Hopefully, a seat. She'd assured me I'd get both.

A couple of chilly minutes later, I pulled open the heavy oak door and stepped into the lovely warm fug of an English pub. Pamela waved at me from the bar and I climbed onto the stool beside her.

'This is nice,' I said, looking around. A lot of wood, ambient lighting, not too busy, and a jazz band playing unobtrusively in the far corner.

'Isn't it?' she replied. 'I got you a vodka Red Bull.'

'Perfect,' I picked it up. 'Cheers.'

We clinked glasses.

'So, photo shoot went fine?' I asked her.

'Yip.'

'Well, thanks for helping.'

'Don't thank me. I'll get paid.'

'You know what I mean.'

'I should be thanking you,' she said. 'Guess who reached out?'

'Who?'

'Kiera Dupont's manager. Wants to talk ideas.'

'No way! To be her stylist?'

Pamela shrugged. 'Maybe? Who knows?'

'Because of that photo? OMG,' I laughed. 'Cheers to that.'

We clinked glasses again.

'You'll get too big for me,' I said in mock horror. 'You'll abandon me.'

'Never. And maybe you'll get too big for me. Anyway, nothing's fixed. It might come to nothing.'

'But still. Amazing.'

'Enough of that.' Pamela was all at once serious. 'What was that about this morning?'

'What?'

She made air quotes. 'Don't tell Ricky about the photo?'

'Oh, that.' I wriggled out of my jacket. 'Just, you know, he's having a tough time just now. The album… Well, he's not sleeping.' I sipped my drink. 'And he's not writing either.'

'They're not your problems.'

'No, I know that. But they kind of are. He thinks we should be aiming for a higher…' I looked up to the ceiling for the word. 'Social scene. And he gets annoyed when we don't meet that.'

'Well, I still think that's Ricky's problem, not yours. You're doing everything for him, like, *everything*. Stop trying to appease him all the time.'

'I don't. Well, I do, but it's more complicated than that. It's my job. And it's how we are.' I shrugged, not enjoying this chat one bit.

Pamela gave me a long look. 'Every relationship is different,' she said. 'Until it's the same.'

I bristled slightly. 'What about you?' I asked, trying to change the subject. 'No men on the scene?'

'Several men on the scene,' she replied, sipping her drink.

'Several? Wow. Good for you.'

'Hook-ups. When I need them.' She regarded me steadily. 'A relationship is something I neither need nor want,' she said. 'I have enough plans of my own. Like, so many plans.'

'Don't you get lonely?'

'No. I'm rarely alone. And lonely has nothing to do with being in a relationship or not.' She turned to look out across the room. 'Some of the loneliest people I know are part of a couple.' Suddenly, she spun in her seat to face the bar. 'Heads-up. Two o'clock,' she stage-whispered.

I didn't need to look. I knew what she meant. I shuffled in close beside her.

'Coming straight this way,' she murmured.

I'd been spotted. People – fans I suppose – had been approaching me when I was out and about for a while now. More so Ricky, which was understandable. But me too. I hadn't got used to it yet. I braced myself.

'Jo?' asked a male voice.

I turned with a fixed smile, which instantly broke into a genuine smile as I jumped down off the bar stool. 'Dinger? No way! What are you doing here?'

He gave me a tight hug. 'You've stumbled into my local.'

'Your local? You're in London now?'

'I'm on placement at Arup, yeah.' He let go of me and stepped back. 'How are you, Jo? It's good to see you.'

'Oh, I'm fine.' I took hold of his arm. 'Pamela, this is my old friend, Dinger. Sorry, Donald. Donald Bell.'

Dinger's face instantly blossomed pink.

Pamela held out her hand. 'Nice to meet you, Dinger or Donald.'

'Donald's fine,' he said as they shook hands.

'What news from home?' I asked.

He stuck his hands in his coat pockets. 'Same old, same old. Just how you left us.'

He was very well-dressed, I noticed, in a dark wool coat and polished brogues. He looked older, more grown up.

'And Ricky?' he asked, after a pause.

I smiled. 'He's fine. You should call him. He'd love to hear from you.'

Dinger's face tightened. 'Oh, I don't think so.'

There was an awkward silence. Everything that had happened came back to me on a wave. Everything I'd left behind.

'Well.' Dinger bobbed his head towards the back of the room. 'I'd better go join my mates. Great to see you, Jo.'

'And you,' I said. 'Oh, wait. Give me your number.'

'You've got it. It hasn't changed.'

'I don't have that phone now, though,' I said, struggling to get my phone out of my jacket pocket.

We exchanged numbers, and he left us with a nod to Pamela who was leaning an elbow on the bar watching me.

'That wasn't awkward at all,' she said.

I sighed heavily and sat back up on the stool.

'And are all the men you know like that?'

'What?'

'Handsome.'

'What? Dinger?' I snorted a scoff.

'So? Who is he?'

I gave her a sad look. 'He was the drummer up in Glasgow.'

'Ah,' she said. 'More betrayal.'

I nodded. 'I didn't treat him very well. Any of them.'

'Want to talk about it?'

'Not really.' I looked to the end of the room where Dinger was sitting with his back to me while his mates took inconspicuous glances our way. 'Can we go somewhere else?'

'Sure.'

Outside, I fastened my jacket and followed Pamela down the pavement.

'You ok?' she asked, after a few steps.

'No.'

She stopped and turned to face me.

'I don't know what I'm doing here,' I said.

'We're on the way to get hammered.'

'I don't mean tonight.' I flung an arm out, flapping my hand. 'London. Everything. I don't belong here.'

'Who does, darling? Who does?' Pamela leaned against the building wall and regarded me.

'It's so… false. All of it. All the Instagram and the column and the events with people I don't know. You can't *know* these people. They're all so fucking false. There's no integrity. Honesty.'

'It's just a game, Jo,' Pamela said calmly. 'Try to think of it as a game.'

I was fighting back tears. 'It doesn't seem like a game. I'm sure as hell not having much fun.'

'Thank you.'

'You're fun,' I said, quickly. 'This is fun.'

She chuckled.

'I was having fun. I'm sorry. I'm ruining our night out.'

'Look, you just can't take it that seriously. You've got to stop seeing it as work. It's just a game. A game of who you know, who you need to know, how to get to know them and how to get what you need from them.'

'Yeah, I've heard that. Except it's called contacts, networking, schmoozing and planning. Planning, planning, planning. NO FUN!'

'Oh, my sweet bundle of joy.'

'I know.' I ran a hand through my hair. 'I hear myself. I do. But then the press. Oh my god. They just make it all up. Or they take something true and just twist it. And then it gets picked up and repeated and fed with other rumours and it becomes a fact. It becomes the truth. And the real truth? Well!' I was raising my voice. 'What does *that* even matter? Who even cares. It's all just fiction. It's all just a story.'

'Is this about Reading again?' Pamela said in her slow, calm voice.

'No! It's about everything.' I was breathing heavily. I turned my face up and roared at the patch of sky between the buildings. Roared from the bottom of my lungs until the roaring became laughing and I bent over with my hands on my knees.

'Are you done?' Pamela was still leaning on the wall.

I looked up and nodded through my hysteria.

'Jolly good.' She took my arm and tugged me along. 'That was an excellent description of the entertainment industry. Really nailed it.'

'Don't take the mickey.'

'No, seriously,' she continued. 'You should be a writer.'

'I am a writer,' I shouted.

She stopped again, still holding my arm. 'Well, there you go. *There's* the truth. Right there.'

I felt jolted, surprised. 'Huh! I'm a writer.'

'And again?' she said.

'I'm a writer. Huh!'

We walked on.

'The point, I believe, is what do *you* want to do?' she said. 'You. Not Ricky. You. Now, forgive me as I know it annoys you, but it does seem like all that…' She nodded her head back towards the bar '… has everything to do with Ricky and not much to do with you.'

'But I've told you, that's how it is. That's how we are. He needs me.'

'If you spent a little less time running around after Ricky and a little more time on *your* dreams, how bad would that be?'

I didn't feel annoyed. I felt like the inside of my body, my deep core, was listening. 'Like how?' I asked.

'Like, just for a minute, picture all this without Ricky. You're in London, you're fine, money isn't a problem. What are you doing?'

I thought for a moment. 'I'm not writing for that bloody rag, that's for sure,' I said.

'Good, go on.'

'I'm not writing blogs either,' I continued. 'But I am writing.'

'What are you writing?'

'I'm writing a book,' I said. 'I'm writing a novel. I'm sitting in a cafe after a morning of research in the British Library and my words are flowing out of me and the waiter brings me a huge pot of tea and I'm meeting my friends later and–'

'And life is good.' She turned into a doorway and pushed open a plain metal door.

The pulse of music swept over us, and I had to raise my voice.

'Where are we?'

'We need to dance,' she shouted, tugging me into the dark club. 'This is where I come to dance. You'll like it.'

And I did.

CHAPTER 29

'*How we communicate and share information and ideas is changing. But this is nothing new. Down through the ages, storytelling has changed from dance to spoken word, from cave drawings to graphic novels, from meticulously handwritten religious texts to one hundred and forty character tweets*', I typed.

I was working on a freelance article, which I'd have to publish under a pseudonym, for the much-hyped alternative news website, Really True. The words were pouring out onto the page. And it wasn't hard to lose myself in the writing and thinking being surrounded, as I was, by the deep calm silence of the British Library. Since that transformative night with Pamela two months previously, I'd been coming here to work. I might not be writing a novel yet, but here I was, in the seat of learning, surrounded by other scholars reading or writing or typing. I felt at home. I felt good. I felt like me at last.

The light from my phone caught my eye, and I glanced at the screen beside me. A Google alert. I picked it up through force of habit and scrolled through to the link. A blog piece about Vermillion by a well-known music journo. Press pieces like this were coming thick and fast. It was only a couple of weeks until the album launch and Lava Records were whipping up a storm of hype. Vermillion was everywhere. Ricky was everywhere. I scanned through the text, then stopped and restarted, reading properly.

'Shit,' I said out loud.

The room seemed to tut in unison and I glanced about with an apologetic smile, then looked back to study the words. This was not good:

'Ricky Steele, the lead singer of Vermillion, is becoming a bit of a celeb popstar with a developing habit of turning up to the opening of an envelope. Basking in the glory of their popular, but unremarkable, first single, his opinion of himself has become somewhat inflated.'

I sat back to consider. This was Ricky's worst nightmare. This is what he'd been fearing. I felt the tingle of guilt. Hadn't he told me over and over that he was hanging out with the wrong people, being photographed with the wrong people? I should've been more attentive to that, should've put a stop to the silly fake celebrity events, should've talked to Lava, to Damien. I should've put my foot down. Well, I couldn't help this article, but I could put my foot down now.

I closed my laptop, gathered my papers and set off down the aisle of desks, pulling up Damien's number as I walked. I pushed through the heavy door into the corridor as Damien answered on the first ring.

'Are you with him?'

'No,' I replied. 'He's at rehearsals. I'm heading to King's Cross now.'

'Take an Uber.'

'No. The Tube will be quicker.'

'Has he seen it?'

'I don't know.' I opened my locker with one hand to get out my bag and denim jacket, which I crammed into my bag on top of my laptop and notes. 'I can't see how.'

'Look, tell him this isn't about him. This is about Lava.'

'Oh, I know that,' I said, raising my voice as I exited the building. 'It's about Lava sending him to all those stupid, insipid parties and having him standing around being papped with all sorts of nobodies. And it's your fault, Damien. All publicity's good publicity, is it?'

'Calm down. Calm down,' he said, managing not to say 'dear'.

I walked a bit faster.

'Listen. That journalist has a beef with Lava. Long story. Failure to deliver exclusive. Doesn't matter. But this looks like revenge. It's come out of nowhere. Total left field. Everything's good.'

'Everything is far from good, Damien.'

'Well, it's manageable,' he countered. 'A couple of positive pieces to smooth it out. I'll call in some favours. It'll all go away.'

I slowed down a bit and took a deep breath. 'So can *you* explain that to Ricky?'

'No can do. I'm on the bloody train back from Manchester.'

I already knew that. 'This'll throw him completely,' I said, still annoyed, although I accepted this particular incident wasn't Damien's fault.

'Well, do the best you can.'

I cut him off without replying.

*

Half an hour later, I arrived at the studio south of the river. I'd only been here once before by car and I tucked away my mobile, which I'd needed for a street map. The entire way here, I'd rehearsed how I was going to tell Ricky – if he hadn't seen the article already. Either way, it was going to be a case of damage control. I took a deep breath as I entered the building.

The studio was actually a big bank of studios in a converted warehouse and I signed in at reception and was directed to Studio Four. Through the foyer, out the double doors to a paved courtyard and up a metal fire escape. I could hear Vermillion playing as I approached, but once inside there was no Ricky, just the three boys rehearsing 'Touch and Go', with Matteo singing. Matteo saw me first and the others ground to a halt.

'He's in the break room,' Matteo said.

'Which is?'

He pointed down with his guitar pick. 'Courtyard.'

They were playing again before the door closed behind me.

Back down the stairs, I followed the doors around the courtyard until I found the one with 'Chill' painted on the black gloss. I pushed it open.

It was a big room, dark with lit-up vending machines, a foosball table, pool table, seating area and a small kitchen under strip lighting, right next to a big dining table where the only humans in the room sat.

In the brief moment before my brain could pick out Ricky, I had an overwhelming sense of déjà vu. There

215

were two blokes I didn't recognise both looking at me. The other had his head down close to the table with one hand held to his nose. His head moved forward along the line and then whipped up. Ricky sniffed and wiped and finally noticed me. I was gone before he could react.

A hundred yards down the street, I heard him calling. I quickened my pace to a road junction and had to pause while a stream of vans and cars passed.

'Jo!'

I glanced back, and he was running towards me. I leapt out onto the road. Horns blared and tyres screeched, but I made it across and kept going. I didn't run. Maybe I wanted him to catch me. I just needed a few more seconds to think. But I couldn't think. I was too angry to think.

I stopped and turned just as he reached me.

'Really?' I said.

'Jo.' He hunched over, hands on knees to catch his breath. 'It was nothing.'

'Really.' I crossed my arms.

He stood back up, holding his side with one hand. 'It's no big deal.'

I snorted. 'That's what you said the last time.'

'What last time?'

'Malcky? Back home?'

Ricky shook his head. 'Fuck's sake, Jo. Malcky? We're back to Malcky again?'

'And how long's it been going on this time?' I shouted.

'Nothing's going on,' he said, reaching for my shoulder.

I jerked away. 'And what else have you been keeping from me? What else has slipped your mind?'

'Nothing else. There's nothing,' Ricky said, holding his

hands out, palms up. 'I don't know those guys. They were just there when I went to get a drink.'

'And what?' I thundered. 'You were just being friendly?'

Ricky took a deep breath. His eyes darkened. I was pushing it. 'I don't know what you want me to say.' He shrugged.

We stood in silence for a long moment.

'We've worked so hard for this,' I said at last. 'We have literally not stopped since we got here. And we're close. So close. And you're just going to throw it all away.'

'It's all just work and worry for you, isn't it,' he scoffed. 'I'm not throwing anything away. You just don't get it.'

'Oh, enlighten me, please,' I said sarcastically.

'You've never got it. Every day of my life I've woken up wanting this, waiting for this.' He lifted his arms to indicate… I don't know what. London? The world? 'And now it's here,' he continued. 'I'm living it.'

'Yeah, you're living it alright.'

'Not the coke. I'm not talking about coke. I'm talking about all of it. The places, the people, the music, the work, even the celebrity. All of it. And every day I wake up excited, wondering what's going to happen next. And you, you wake up with your head full of appointments and deadlines and…' I could see him trying to think what else I did. Unbelievable! He didn't have a clue what I did for him. 'Shit,' he said, at last.

'See,' I uncrossed my arms to point at him. 'That's your problem right there. What's going to happen next. Your life isn't a story, Ricky. Nothing happens next unless you plan for it to happen next. This is real. This is how it works.'

'No, you're wrong,' he said, spitting his words out at

me. 'My life is a story. My life will be a fucking great story. I'm writing history here. My life will be a legend and I want it up there with the best of them. With Cobain and fucking Hendrix.'

'What? Dead before you're thirty? Well, keep going and you might get there.' I turned on my heels and set off in the direction, I hoped, of the Tube. 'And by the way,' I said, turning to walk backwards away from him. 'The next instalment of your amazing story hit the Internet an hour ago. You might want to check your phone.'

CHAPTER 30

The roller coaster, I was coming to understand, continues on. Two weeks later the album was released, the launch party happened, and we were all gathered at Lava Records offices for what was being billed as a celebratory breakfast but was actually a strategy meeting for ways to market our way out of the disappointingly lukewarm album reviews.

I walked round the boardroom table to the breakfast buffet where Ricky was considering a Danish. He was wearing his old Pearl Jam t-shirt. It was threadbare, the stitching coming away at the back of one armpit, his lean biceps sliding out of the sleeve.

'You want a tea?' I asked, picking up a cup. 'I think they put it on just for us.'

'No,' he replied, putting down the pastry and walking off.

I watched him take a seat next to Zhou and then I caught Damien's eye. He had obviously observed that small scene. He kept a neutral expression as he regarded me and I looked away first. I put my cup down and headed out into the corridor to call Pamela.

'What news?' she asked.

'Nothing yet.'

'You ok?'

'No.'

'Still not speaking?'

'No.' I couldn't cry. Not here. 'I don't know what to do, Pamela. I've tried everything. It wasn't even that bad a fight. But with the album reviews...'

'He's being such a dick,' she said. 'What's his problem?'

'He thinks it's all my fault.'

'And, as we've been over, it has nothing to do with you. He needs to grow a pair and stop blaming everyone for everything.'

'It's so hard,' I said quietly as someone walked past. 'It's just this silent treatment all the time. I don't know how to reach him.'

'Stop trying,' she said. 'I've said it before. He's acting like a child. Just ignore him.'

A tear rolled down to the corner of my mouth as I turned to face the wall. 'I just love him. I hate it like this.'

I could hear Pamela taking a deep breath. 'You've got to distance yourself a bit, Jo. Stop loving him so much for a while.'

'I can't just stop.'

'What other choice do you have?'

'To keep loving him. To love him more.'

'Well, that's working real well.'

I closed my eyes and leaned my forehead against the wall, and there was the memory of our first kiss in The Shrine. His soft lips, me on my tiptoes, his hand on my lower back, pressing me to him.

'Look,' Pamela said in my ear. 'I've got to go prep for this Kiera thing.'

'Oh, god. I'm sorry. I forgot.'

'It's fine.'

'Tons of luck, Pamela. You'll nail it, no bother. You're the best stylist ever,' I said. 'I'm sorry I've been such a pain. My head's in my arse.'

'You're head's in your heart, that's all. And Ricky's head's in his dick. Chin up, eh?'

'Let me know how it goes,' I said, and followed Sam Devine as he marched past me into the boardroom.

'Right,' Sam began. 'Everyone know everyone?'

A few heads nodded round the table as I took the only empty seat across from Ricky.

'Jan, you start us off,' he continued. 'Where are we at?'

Jan, the deputy head of PR, cleared her throat. 'Downloads sitting one five fifty.'

'Which is strong,' Damien said.

Sam screwed up his face. 'With room for growth.'

Ricky fidgeted on the seat opposite. I could tell he was grinding his teeth.

'Early days.' Damien sounded lighthearted. 'Early days.'

Sam sat back in his seat. 'Let's not play this game, Damien. For the sake of a few fragile egos? The reviews were shit.'

'Well–'

'They were shit. And unless this starts to turn around,' Sam twirled his index finger in the air above his head, 'there's going to be one serious dent in our balance sheet. Jan, what have you got?'

Jan cleared her throat again. 'We're thinking multiple approach. We're thinking temporary price drop.'

'No,' Sam said.

'No,' Jan repeated. 'Good. We're thinking brand partnerships. Sportswear. Energy drinks. There's word Boost-Quake are looking.'

Ricky tilted his head back and let out an audible sigh.

'Ricky?' Sam said. 'Something to say?'

'No,' Damien intervened. 'He's fine.'

Ricky scoffed. I bit my lip. I could tell he was about to explode. He'd basically looked like that for days.

'Look into that, Jan,' Sam continued. 'What else? Emphasis on driving downloads.'

'Social media,' Jan said.

'That seems to be the problem rather than the solution just now, does it not?' Sam replied.

'Well, yes.' Jan cleared her throat one more time.

'Drink some water, Jan. For god's sake,' Sam said.

Jan took a sip from the glass in front of her and glanced at me down the table.

'Sorry,' she said. 'So, we're thinking Instagram. Matteo's audience is strong and Jo-D's numbers have skyrocketed, what with hashtag-flats.' She did some air quotes as an afterthought. 'So, we're thinking, harness their audience.'

Harness their audience? I glanced at Matteo, who was frowning but nodding.

'Go on,' Sam said.

'Candid shots. Impromptu clips of jams – of practice sessions. A last-minute heads-up for a secret gig.'

'Ok, move forward with that.' Sam nodded.

'We'd need access to their accounts.' Jan glanced at me again.

'Fine,' Damien agreed.

'Eh?' I said. 'I don't think so.'

'Jo-D?' Sam said.

'I'm not just handing over my account.'

'Jo-D's account,' Damien put in.

I glared at him. 'Which is me.'

'Not really,' Jan said, squeezing her face up.

I pointed at Matteo. 'Matteo's is his.'

'I don't mind,' he said quickly.

Ricky was watching me with hooded eyes. My rising outrage subsided into the pit of my stomach.

'Bit more of a team spirit needed here, Jo-D,' Sam drawled.

'I think she's concerned about the intellectual property angle,' Damien said.

Was I? Or was I just pissed that something I'd worked my butt off on was being taken away.

'Talk to legal,' Sam said. 'But let's get this moving.' He clapped his hands three times. 'Jan?'

Jan had her hand raised like a schoolgirl. 'So, we're thinking, Jo-D's column in The Sunday Chronicle.'

'What about it?' I asked, bristling again.

She glanced at me and just as quickly glanced away. Was she frightened of me or just frightened generally?

'Turn it into a book.'

'What?' I said.

Sam nodded. 'Rights?'

'Retained,' Jan said.

'What?' I asked again, as Ricky scoffed loudly across the table.

'A rock 'n' roll fairy tale,' Jan said. 'Basically Ricky's biography.'

I snorted. 'I'm not writing Ricky's biography.'

Sam looked at me from the top of the table. 'That's basically what your column is.'

I opened my mouth to reply and then closed it. Was it? Was it basically Ricky's biography?

I looked at Ricky, who was still glaring at me. I'd thought the column was about me. Well, me and Ricky. I thought it was about us. But suddenly, it was blatantly obvious the column was about Ricky. It had always been about Ricky. 'No,' I said.

'We can still publish,' Jan said.

'We need her name,' Sam said. 'Damien.'

'On it,' Damien said.

'Right.' Sam looked at Jan. 'Done?'

'Done,' she replied.

'Speak to Boost-Quake. I want a secret gig by Friday. Call that editor at JP's.' Sam twirled his finger in the air again.

'Sasha?' Jan said.

'Yes, her. Get the columns to her.'

And with that, he marched back out the door, followed by Jan and her minions.

'Well, that was a shit show,' Lee said.

Ricky scraped his chair back and stormed out of the room. I sighed wearily.

'Is he always like this?' Lee asked.

I shrugged.

'The Jools thing, I think,' Zhou said.

'Yeah,' Matteo continued. 'Final straw.'

'What?' I asked. Vermillion was booked to play The Jools Holland Show at the start of May. It was a huge deal. 'What's happened?'

Matteo pulled his finger across his neck. 'We got cancelled.'

'No.'

'Indeed, yes,' Damien said, standing up. 'And we're all disappointed but, Jo, you need to sort him out.'

'How am I meant to sort him out? He won't talk to me.' Everyone apart from Damien looked down at their feet. I swallowed a lump of shame.

'And sort the two of you out while you're at it,' Damien said. 'Whatever's going on, make it go away. This…' He paused, searching for the right word. 'This atmosphere between you has been noticed.'

CHAPTER 31

Ricky was long gone by the time I left the Lava building. He wasn't at home either. I felt a wave of relief to find the flat empty. No more atmosphere to deal with for a while, at least. I made a cup of tea while the bath filled and tried not to think about the meeting. Everything seemed out of my hands, out of my control. And it was all because of this stupid argument between me and Ricky.

I settled the mug on the edge of the bath and climbed into the steaming water. God, it felt so good, like a kindness, a hug. Pamela popped into my head and I remembered her advice. Maybe I would just ignore Ricky. Maybe I should try it, at least. And today would be a good opportunity, as I had no idea where he was. Probably off on a bender, drowning his sorrows in drink. He was never one to deal with bad news well; hated things not going his way. Yes, I would ignore him. I would not think of him.

And the next day found me in bed nursing a glass of water after a bit of a bender of my own. I'd met up with Pamela and her mates to celebrate her successful meeting with Kiera's team and I'd managed to not think of Ricky at all.

I picked up my phone and turned it on, having turned it off yesterday afternoon to at least feel I still had some control. It had been strangely satisfying, but nearly twenty-four hours seemed like enough. I put it down and sipped some more water until it stopped pinging notifications. Then I took a deep breath and picked it back up. I couldn't bear to look at Instagram, so I checked my e-mails first. Three from Jan at Lava and one from the Sunday Chronicle, amongst others. With my thumping headache, I couldn't deal with any of them, so I closed the app. I took another breath and opened Messages, but a quick scan showed nothing from Ricky. I would not call him. I would not. But where was he?

Damien had sent a text telling me to check my e-mail. Pamela had sent a text with the change of venue last night – that would have saved some time had I seen it. But the most recent one that caught my eye was from 'Pap-Dan', who I'd heard nothing from since Italy. I clicked it open.

– *thought you should see. already sold* – it read, followed by a sorry emoji and an attached file. I clicked 'open' and stopped breathing as one by one the jpegs revealed themselves.

Ricky and a blonde woman talking, laughing. Somewhere outside in the dark. I pinched the photo bigger. An alley. Ricky was still wearing his Pearl Jam t-shirt from yesterday. I flicked on through the photos with a sense of dread rising from my belly. Ricky and the blonde – one of those Big Brother girls from the Lava party – hugging. Ricky and the blonde kissing. Ricky holding the blonde up against a wall, her legs wrapped round his waist. I scrolled on. I didn't want to, but I couldn't stop. I didn't believe them, but I couldn't not. I scrolled back to the text – *thought you should see. already sold.*

I put the phone down on the sheets. I stood up and stumbled to the bathroom and vomited last night's booze into the toilet, resting my head against the cool tiles in between heaves. I felt utterly alone, completely empty. Lost.

I got up to wash my face and rinse my mouth out, and caught sight of myself in the mirror. My expertly dyed red hair was piled up in a scrappy bun on top of my head and last night's make-up was smeared under my already-hollow eyes. I looked gaunt, drained, my pale mouth a thin line. I had to call Damien and let him know. Let him get a head start on the clean-up. But I didn't want to. I pushed myself back out of the bathroom and picked up my phone. It was still open on the photos. Sort it out, Damien had said. I couldn't sort this out.

I walked to the window and peered down at the street: cars and buses and people marching along. I couldn't sort this out. This, this *betrayal*. The word came to me from deep within. Betrayal. A massive and, likely to be, very public betrayal. I said the word out loud, causing the glass to steam up. And suddenly I was angry. Like a force it rose up, filling the back of my throat and I ran to the bathroom to vomit again, still clutching my phone.

When I was finally empty, I sat down on the floor and saved the file, then clicked print. I brushed my teeth and cleaned my face properly, then took my washbag out from under the sink and packed it. I opened the cupboard in the tiny hall and pulled out my suitcase, chucking in tops and bottoms, dresses, shoes. I kicked it through to the main room and emptied my underwear drawer into it, followed by my books and notes. I picked up the printed photos, found the tape in a kitchen drawer and started sticking them onto the walls of our flat any old way. If I worked fast, I didn't need to focus on them, and my rage was keeping me working fast. Once they were up, I chucked my laptop, phone and charger into my black tote, pulled on the promotional baseball cap some company had sent me, and left, double-locking the door on my way out. I sent an Uber request on the way down the stairs: Euston Station. I was going home. I'd had enough.

Only once I was safely in the car did I realise there was no home to go to. I couldn't go back to Barinner, to the island. I'd never give my sister the satisfaction of seeing me fail so spectacularly. And Glasgow wasn't my home anymore. All ties had been cut, so to speak.

But maybe not all. I flicked through my phone and there was Dinger's number. He answered on the second ring.

'Jo,' he said. 'How are you?'

'Can I stay with you?'

'What's happened?'

'I just need to hide.'

'Where are you?'

'In a taxi. I was going to Euston, but—'

'I'll find you in Russell Square. Give me half an hour.'

CHAPTER 32

I wheeled my suitcase into Russell Square and picked a bench under a yew tree, away from the cafe. The early afternoon sunshine was warm on my face as I watched the dappled light from a plane tree flit and sway on the path in front of me with an empty mind. I was actively not thinking. It felt like the safest thing I could do right then.

I saw Dinger before he saw me – I still recognised his walk – and raised a hand in greeting. He was in work clothes, shirt and tie, with a satchel slung over one shoulder. He took a seat beside me without speaking, and we sat on in silence.

'Euston Station is right there,' I said after a while. 'I could be home in, like, five hours.'

'Yip. I've thought about that a few times,' he replied.

I felt tears well up behind my sunglasses and sniffed them back down, clearing my throat, which was parched.

'What do you need?'

'Tea,' I said. 'A cup of tea.' I looked at him for the first time. 'No one drinks tea here.'

He smiled back at me. 'What is it with the coffee?

'Everywhere it's coffee,' he said. 'Right, come on. Tea it is. I have tea.'

*

His flat was just a five-minute walk from the square and I followed behind him as he pulled my suitcase along the busy lunchtime streets. Inside his block, an elevator took us to the second floor, and he held the door of his flat open for me. His flat was huge compared to ours. I passed the bedroom and bathroom and on into a massive open-plan living area with floor-to-ceiling windows and a narrow balcony.

'Wow.'

'Isn't it.' He stood my case by the wall and walked to the kitchen area. 'Company flat, though. Came with the placement.'

I wandered over to the window. 'That's almost a view,' I said, gazing out over a wide road junction to a row of shops diagonally opposite. 'It's so quiet.'

'I think the windows are soundproofed,' he said, filling the kettle.

'Soundproofed windows. Huh.'

'It's simple enough. Thicken the glass and leave a wider gap. I keep meaning to measure them to see.'

'Ever the engineer,' I said, taking a seat at the breakfast bar and shaking my hair out from under the cap.

Dinger blushed and tried to hide it in the mug cupboard. With his jacket off, I could see how broad his back had become. He'd been working out, for sure. I decided not to mention it.

'Thanks for this, Dinger.'

He glanced at me over his shoulder and smiled.

'I really appreciate it,' I said. 'Are you meant to be at work?'

'Yeah, but it's fine.' He poured the boiled water into the mugs. 'I said I wasn't feeling well, so I'm all yours for the rest of the day.' He picked up the mugs and walked round to the lounge area. 'Unless you want me out the way.'

'No,' I replied. 'No. I'm glad you're here.'

He blushed again. 'Come and sit. It's comfier.'

I kicked off my gutties before joining him on the plush cream sofa that perched on a deep cream rug.

'This place is amazing.'

'I know,' he replied, rolling his shirtsleeves up. 'So, what brings you to my humble abode?'

I took a sip of tea and looked away from his buff forearms to the massive blank screen of the TV.

'You don't need to tell me,' he said.

'No, I do,' I replied. 'Or I want to.'

'I see they're getting some poor reviews.'

'For the album? Yeah, they've not been great. Have you heard it?'

He gave a half nod.

'It's not that bad.'

'No.'

'It just seems to have turned out a bit pop-y.'

'So, let me guess, Ricky's mad?'

'Yeah,' I said. 'He's mad at the reviews and mad at me.'

'Why?'

'There's other stuff going on. There's just so much stuff going on. All the time.' I felt the tears well up and put my mug down on the coffee table.

Dinger fetched a box of tissues and then rested his hand on the middle of my back while I blew my nose.

'Sorry,' I said.

'Jo, why are you here? What's happened?'

I sighed and pulled my phone out of my bag, ignoring the notifications and opening the text from Dan. I handed it to Dinger.

He scrolled through for a moment and then stood up, dropping the phone onto the table with a clatter.

'Fucking arsehole,' he said, walking to the window.

It seemed to help to hear him say that.

'He is such a dick.' He turned back to me.

I shrugged.

'So, what? These go in the paper tomorrow?'

'Or a website,' I said. 'I don't know. Anyway, that's why I'm here.' I tried to chuckle in a lighthearted way and failed.

Dinger growled and stomped across the room to slam his fists down on the breakfast bar.

That seemed to help me too. I felt a bit lighter.

'And how long has this been going on?' he asked through clenched teeth.

'I think it's new,' I said. 'I think he was just on a bender last night. They got dropped from the Jools Holland Show. It was, like, the last straw, or whatever.'

'Don't make excuses for him,' Dinger practically yelled, startling me. 'Sorry,' he said in a lower tone. 'But he's such a fucking idiot.'

He walked back over and sat beside me. On the table, my phone continued to buzz notifications and missed calls.

'Talk to me,' he said. 'Tell me everything that's been going on.'

So I did. I told him everything – from last summer to yesterday, from the festivals to the studio, from Italy to the apartment. I told him how hard it all seemed, how little fun it was turning out to be. I told him how tired I was. In other words, I had a right good moan. And it was good. It felt really good. 'I don't know why I'm telling you all this.' I laughed after what seemed like ages.

We were on our third cup of tea and the late afternoon sun was slanting through the balcony balustrade.

He rested a hand lightly on my knee and smiled. 'Because I'm your friend, that's why. You're safe here.'

He didn't blush this time, I noticed.

'I feel safe here.'

And I did. I did feel safe. And stronger than before. I drained my cup of tea and laid it on the table, picking up my phone. 'I should deal with some of this.'

'You don't have to,' Dinger said.

My phone was buzzing with an incoming call. I glanced at the screen. 'It's Ricky. I should probably…'

'Take it in the bedroom if you like.'

I slid it to answer and stood up to walk through the room. I could hear Ricky's voice calling my name, but I waited until I'd closed the bedroom door to lift the phone to my ear.

'Jo, are you there? Jo?'

'What do you want?'

'Where are you? I've been calling for hours.'

'What do you want?'

He paused, then: 'To say I'm sorry. I'm sorry, Jo.'

'What for?'

'You know what for. I just freaked out. It was a mistake. Jo?'

I sat on in silence.

'Where are you? Come home so we can talk.'

'I don't think there's anything to talk about.'

'Come on, Jo. It was just a mistake. I was drunk. You know what I'm like.' He was aiming for lighthearted, but all I could hear was insincerity. 'We'll get through this.'

'Like we got through it before?'

He paused again. When he next spoke, his voice was cracking, pleading. 'We'll find a way through it,' he said. 'I know I fucked up, but this is us, Jo. I need you, remember? You need me. I'm your man.'

'You're not my man.' I forced back the tears, my rage carrying me through. 'You're less than a man.'

And with that I ended the call, turned off my phone, then sat staring at the blank screen with my blank mind, trying to hold it together.

After a while there was a gentle rap at the door and Dinger came in. I didn't look up. Couldn't.

He sat down on the bed beside me. 'You ok?'

I shook my head, running my tongue over my dry lips. 'I think we're done. I think that's it, over.'

Dinger lifted his arm, and I rested my head on his shoulder gratefully.

'I love him so much,' I whispered. 'But I don't think that's enough anymore.'

He sighed and gently stroked my arm. It felt good, comforting.

'I've completely lost myself,' I continued. 'I was trying so hard to make it work that I've disappeared completely.'

I sat up to blow my nose, and Dinger let go of my shoulder.

'That's not true, Jo.'

'When people talk about making a relationship work,' I was rising to my theme, 'that's what they mean. One and one do not make two. It's not one plus one, it's one times one. Which makes one. Somehow you've got to make two into one – so you lose part of yourself, little bits of yourself. Until, one day, you see the two of you will never fit and you are much less than what you were.'

'It's not like that, Jo. It's not. It's not always like that.'

'And you know this how?' I snapped.

Dinger shrugged. 'Yeah, how would I know?'

'God, I'm sorry. That was shitty. Sorry.'

'But I do know it's not always like that.' His voice was calm and sure. 'Ricky, he's a taker. He will never chip away part of himself to fit you. You know that, right? You've done all the changing, all the reducing.'

A fat tear rolled down my cheek and onto my leg.

Dinger lifted my chin with his hand to look at my face. At the sight of my tears, he pulled me into his arms and I curled my legs up onto his knees and let him rock me. It felt so good – so familiar. I let the tears fall.

'I'm sorry,' I said.

'Don't be sorry,' Dinger whispered. 'Don't ever be sorry.' He squeezed me tighter. 'When was the last time someone took care of you, Jo? When did you ever let someone take care of you?'

Never, I thought. And I lifted my head from his chest, closed my eyes and kissed him. His lips were firm, unyielding. I opened my eyes and looked deep into his –

holding my nerve until his hand came up to the back of my head and he kissed me back, his lips softening. I wrapped my arms around his chest and I felt his other hand slide under my legs. He lifted me up and over so I was lying on the bed with him beside me. He wiped my hair back off my face and looked me right in the eye, searching, asking, wanting.

This was not the time to be analysing anything, so I tried to pull him back down to me, but he held his ground. 'I want this,' I whispered in reply, in confirmation, lifting my face to meet his lips and this time he didn't resist.

That perfect night would become etched in my memory. Moment after moment of tenderness, as Dinger discovered all the places of my body. I opened myself to him, thinking nothing of the world, of my life, my situation. Thinking only of his touch, his lips, of the very moment I was in. And each time he pulled away, I pulled him back towards me. Each time he hesitated, I guided his hand. And each time he lingered on a stretch of skin, I leaned into his touch. For surely this was the solution, this was the cure.

And when I awoke after sleep had finally overcome me, he was lying still beside me, watching me, wide awake, with eyes full of devotion.

'Morning,' he whispered.

I smiled, and he lifted himself onto an elbow, the light from the window behind him dazzling me. I squinted but couldn't see him clearly.

'Tea?' he asked. 'I'm dying for a cup. I didn't want to wake you.'

He swung out of bed before I could reach to stop him

and padded out of the room. He was gone. And just like that, the real world came rushing back in. What had I done? How had I managed to make everything so much worse? How was I going to explain this to Ricky?

I could hear the kettle boiling and to escape my head I got up, pulling a blanket round my naked body and headed to the kitchen.

Dinger was standing behind the island, head bent over his phone. 'Seventeen missed calls. From an unknown number.'

I settled myself on a stool opposite him. 'It'll be one of those insurance scam things.'

'And a text from the same number.' He scrolled with his thumb. Then he stopped and looked up at me.

'What?' I asked.

He held the screen towards me. 'For you, I think.'

THIS IS PAMELA. JO'S FRIEND. CALL ME NOW. NOW!

I took the phone from Dinger, my heart already hitting my stomach.

CHAPTER 33

I stretched my fingers out on the steering wheel and gave them a wiggle before reaching for the remains of the now cold coffee. It was bitter, disgusting, but I needed the caffeine. I blinked hard and squinted at the dark road ahead, shifting my bum on the seat. We were somewhere between Birmingham and Manchester. I'd stop again after Manchester to stretch my legs, get more caffeine.

Beside me, Ricky was still out cold – asleep or unconscious, who knew. He'd come to, briefly, when I started the hire car after the first stop. Raising his head to peer out at the service station parking lot.

'Where are we going?' he'd asked.

'Home.'

He'd stayed staring out at the dusky scene. Thinking? Not thinking? 'Can you even drive?' he'd asked, as I steered out onto the slip road.

'I could drive before I was fifteen,' I'd replied quietly. 'Go to sleep.'

And he had.

I slotted the coffee back into the cup holder. Twenty-two miles to Manchester, the motorway sign said. So, less than five hours to Glasgow. Another three after that. I glanced at the clock. It was just after ten pm.

*

By dawn Ricky was sitting up, awake, his head resting on the window as we headed deeper into the Scottish Highlands.

'I have no idea where the fuck we are,' he mumbled.

'Scotland.'

Ricky shifted in his seat to sit up. 'Well, I gathered that. Anywhere in particular in Scotland?'

'Next stop Mallaig.' I shifted up a gear as the road evened out.

'Mallaig?'

I glanced at him briefly. 'Home. I told you.'

'I thought you meant Glasgow.'

'No, my home. Barinner.'

'The island?'

'Yeah.' I shifted back down a gear into a corner. 'I thought that would be a better idea, considering.'

'Considering my monumental fuck-up?'

We sat on in silence for a moment as the sun glanced at us from behind the hills to the east. It was going to be a fine day.

'We should probably talk about it,' I said, eventually.

'No thanks.'

Ricky picked up my empty coffee cup and gave it a shake.

'We'll get something at the ferry,' I said. 'The cafe will be open.'

He replaced the cup. 'I appreciate this, Jo.'

'I'm not entirely sure what we're doing,' I said. 'I'm not sure how kidnapping you like this is going to help.'

He started bouncing his knee. 'I couldn't have gone to rehab. I don't need bloody rehab.'

I took a deep breath. 'You OD'd, Ricky.'

'Barely.'

'You could have died.' I gripped the wheel. 'You were unconscious at the hospital when I got there. Unconscious.' I glanced at him again. He was chewing his lip. 'Ricky! Heroin? I mean, what the fuck?'

'I was just…' He shook his head.

'What?'

'Trying it.'

'Trying it?' I was losing my temper. 'That old nugget? Try everything once, twice if you like it?'

'Look, Lee said–'

'Lee?' I shouted, turning to face him. 'Lee, who we left in ICU in an induced coma? That Lee?'

'Look out!' Ricky gasped, clutching the dashboard.

I snapped my eyes forward. A massive deer was on the road in front of us. I swerved up onto the verge to miss it. The car bounced and banged back onto the tarmac. My heart was thumping and I let out a slow breath. In the rear-view mirror, the deer trotted across the road and disappeared into the undergrowth.

'I'm tired,' I said with forced calm. 'Sorry.'

'I didn't know about Lee,' Ricky said quietly. 'Do you think he'll be ok?'

'I don't know.' I shrugged. 'Probably.'

We drove on in silence for a while.

'I'm not sure what we're doing either,' he said eventually. 'I just needed away. I just...' He turned his head to look out at the Atlantic coming into view as we reached a summit on the road. 'I just need time to think. I don't know what's happening anymore. The album.' He turned back to look at me. 'Us. Everything's gone wrong. Everything's out of control.'

I glanced at him, and he looked so lost, so bewildered. I moved my hand from the gearstick and he took it, pressing it to his lips with his eyes closed – reading more into the gesture than I'd meant. I pulled away gently, replacing my hand on the steering wheel.

'Mallaig,' I said, as we passed the thirty miles per hour sign.

'Thank fuck. I can't feel my arse. Do your folks know we're coming?'

'Yeah, I called from London.'

The street was quiet as we headed to the ferry terminal, a few cars, a lorry. But I noticed Ricky slouch lower in the seat.

'Here,' I said. 'Grab that bag in the back. There's a baseball hat.'

Ricky found it and tucked his hair up as he put it on.

'Just until we get to the island,' I said. 'No one will bother there.'

'You think?'

'Yeah, for sure,' I replied as we pulled into the terminal car park and found a parking spot at the far end.

'Have you got my phone?' Ricky asked, as I turned off the engine.

'Yes, but it's off and should stay off.'

He looked at me with his eyebrows up. 'Eh, why?'

'They'll trace us. I just thought, you know, until we know what we're doing...'

'A regular Nancy Drew,' Ricky said.

'Well, I don't know. It seemed like a good idea at the time. I got a pay-as-you-go sim.'

'Did you! Well, maybe wise. A couple of days off-grid to get my head straight.' He took a deep breath. 'What else did you think of? We've got the baseball hats. We've got the burner phone.'

I was regretting this race north. His tone was making me cross. 'I've thought of it all,' I said, twisting in the seat to haul the carrier bag forward. 'Anoraks.' I pulled out a grey and khaki green jacket.

Ricky laughed. 'That's the ugliest thing I've ever seen.'

'No one will even notice you in it. And all our stuff's in rucksacks in the boot. We'll look like hikers. Or birdwatchers.'

Ricky snorted out another laugh. 'You rock, Jo-D.'

He raised his hand to give me a high five, but I left him hanging and opened the car door instead.

'Cafe's this way. Bacon butty and a cup of tea.'

*

The cafe by the ferry slip was warm and steamy, the bell above the door jingling as we entered with our hefty rucksacks. I glanced about nervously, but there were only a couple of workmen, heads buried in their morning papers, drinking their mugs of tea.

'Do you hear that?' Ricky whispered.

The tinny radio was playing one of Vermillion's songs.

'No escape,' I whispered back, then turned to the counter to order.

It was funny hearing 'Give In' playing all the way up here in the middle of nowhere. I looked at Ricky and he pretended to hold a microphone, mouthing the words. I shook my head to make him stop.

The song ended, and the DJ began to speak.

'That was Give In by Vermillion. A tribute to a life cut off too soon.'

I locked eyes with Ricky. Time seemed to stop.

'Tragic,' replied his female co-host. 'We're all in shock here at this news.'

'Yeah, we sure are,' the DJ continued. 'And if you're just waking up, the breaking story of the morning is the death of Lee Castles of the band Vermillion, and the disappearance of Ricky Steele, the lead singer.'

'Information's still coming in, but we know Lee was pronounced dead late last night at the Royal London Hospital.'

'And that Ricky was admitted, but has since...'

'Vanished?'

Ricky was shaking his head, eyes wide. I reached out to touch his arm, and it shook, too. His whole body started to shake. I pulled him towards the door.

'Oi!' the lady behind the counter said. 'You haven't paid.'

I pushed Ricky out ahead of me.

'Give me my phone,' he said.

'Ricky, I–'

'Give me my phone!' he shouted.

'Ok, ok.' I shrugged the rucksack off my back and rummaged for his phone, turning it on as I pulled it out.

He grabbed it and began fast pacing the length of the cafe cabin as it restarted. As soon as it was on, he called up a number and held it to his ear. 'Damien,' he said, almost immediately.

I could hear Damien shouting, even though it wasn't on speaker. 'Where the fuck are you?'

'What's happened?' Ricky said, still pacing.

I grabbed hold of him to make him stop.

'Is Lee…? Tell me it's not true.'

'Oh, it's true,' Damien bellowed. 'You've completely fucked up this time. Completely. The press are going nuts!'

'I'll come back.'

'From where? Oh, I don't care where you are! You can't come back from this.'

'I can fix it.'

'You can't fix this, you complete prick. You can't PR your way out of this one. Heroin? It's not the fucking nineties.'

'I should come back.'

'To what, Ricky? You've been fired. The record company have fired you. Drugs are one thing – you can spin that with a trip to rehab. But a drug death is another thing all together. Lee is dead. They have to be seen to take a firm line on this. And you, my dear, stupid, fuck-up of a boy, are going to take the blame.'

Ricky dropped the phone and staggered against the side of the cabin.

I could still hear Damien's voice. 'This is your fault. This is all your fault.'

Ricky sank to his knees, and the weight of his rucksack brought me down, too. He was hyperventilating, his eyes darting left and right.

'Ricky,' I said, holding his face in my hands. 'Ricky.'

He looked at me then, eyes blank, empty.

'It's finished,' he whispered. 'I'm finished.'

CHAPTER 34

'Well?' Aunt Mary asked as I entered the warm, steamy kitchen. 'Is he for getting up today?'

A heavy weight of exhaustion settled on me. 'I don't know. I don't think so.'

'It's over a week,' she pointed out.

'Nine days,' Alison added slowly, accusingly.

I threw my sister a look.

'Well, it is,' she said, slicing a banana into her porridge bowl.

Dad didn't seem to notice, busy as he was, with yesterday's paper spread before him, making notes on the sea tides, slurping his tea. I squeezed past Alison and slipped a couple of slices of yesterday's loaf into the toaster. Beside me, Aunt Mary was kneading today's dough.

'It can't go on like this,' Aunt Mary said, slamming the heel of her hand into the dough, sliding it forward.

'He just needs some time,' I mumbled.

Alison snorted. 'He's had some time. He's had nine days. And I want my bed back. I'm only home for a fortnight.'

'I'm not enjoying sharing your bed either,' I answered sharply.

'Well, why are you?' she replied. 'I thought you two were a couple.'

'We're not. I've told you. We've split up.'

'Well, what's he doing here?' Alison asked slowly, annunciating every word.

I glared at her over my shoulder as she spooned a heap of porridge into her mouth. Dad calmly turned a page of the newspaper, oblivious.

'I don't think it's time he needs.' Aunt Mary turned the dough, slamming it back on the board. 'He needs professional help, not couped up here with his own thoughts.'

'And you pandering to him,' Alison retorted to me.

'I'm not pandering. I'm just making him some toast. He's a guest.'

Alison snorted again. 'A guest says please and thank you. A guest gets out of bed and…'

I crossed my arms and glared at her. 'And what?'

'And has a conversation!'

'Shh,' Aunt Mary said. 'Stop shouting.'

'A drug addict, on the other hand,' Alison continued, 'lies about all day, taking advantage.'

'He's not a drug addict,' I said sharply.

'That's not what the papers say,' Alison said. 'That's not what the whole bloody internet says.'

'Language!' Aunt Mary whispered loudly.

'He's not a drug addict,' I said to Aunt Mary.

She didn't look at me, but set her mouth in a firm line of disagreement as she scattered a pinch of flour over the dough.

'He's not,' I insisted. 'It was just a mistake. Drugs are everywhere down there. You don't understand.'

'Just a mistake and then somebody dies,' Aunt Mary said, stopping to look at me. 'We might live up here in the middle of nowhere, Joanne, but I wasn't born yesterday.'

Behind me, the toast pinged. I pulled it out of the toaster.

'I promise he's not an addict,' I said calmly, spreading butter. 'It's just his mind. He's had a shock. It's like he has to recover mentally.'

'That doesn't make it easier.' Aunt Mary was still watching me. 'That makes it harder. I just think he needs professional help. I really do.'

'No,' I said, reaching to the shelf above me for a plate.

'Look at what happened at the ferry,' she said, pointing a floury finger at me. 'Imagine if Bill hadn't been there with the van? What would you have done?'

I swallowed down the thought of those terrible moments on the pier before Bill arrived. Trying to calm Ricky, trying to get him to stand.

I slid the toast onto a plate. 'Well, Bill *was* there. So it was fine.'

Alison scoffed. 'Far from fine, I'd say.'

'And you can't expect everyone to keep covering for him forever,' Aunt Mary went on. 'It can't go on like this.'

'They'll track him down,' Alison said. 'Caroline said she saw strangers getting off the ferry yesterday.'

'What?' I asked, panicking.

'In townie clothes and wheelie bags.'

'Och, they were the food inspectors for the pub,' Aunt Mary said, turning back to her loaf. 'But still, they'll sniff him out soon enough.'

'I know,' I said, reaching for a mug. 'But he just needs a bit more time. Please be kind. Please.' I turned to face Alison at the table, but she didn't meet my eye. 'He's just grieving. For Lee, but also for everything else. He's lost everything: his friend, his band, his career.'

Alison continued on with her porridge. Aunt Mary was back to kneading the dough.

'Don't you see?' I filled the mug from the teapot on the table. 'He'd made it. All he'd ever wanted, he had. But it's over.'

No one seemed to be listening. No one seemed to care. I picked up Ricky's mug and the plate of toast. I could feel a bubble of tears rising in my throat. It was all so fleeting. Everything he'd had, gone. Everything we had, gone. And I didn't know what to do. I'd thought I could fix him, but he hadn't spoken to me since we got here. Hadn't uttered a word. And I was getting frightened. He'd never been this low before.

Alison clattered her spoon down in her empty bowl and stood up, meeting my eye.

'So,' she said firmly. 'Exactly how long is it going to take?'

The tears spilled out of my tired eyes. 'I don't know.' I sobbed.

Aunt Mary turned, wiping her hands on her apron. 'Och,' she said, sympathetically.

Dad banged his mug onto the table, making us all jump. 'Right. I've had about enough of this. Joanne, put that food down.' He pointed at me and I lowered the plate and mug to the table, startled. I hadn't thought he was listening, had almost forgotten he was there.

He scraped his chair back and marched out of the

room. Alison raised her eyebrows at me and turned to the door. We could hear his boots stomping up the stairs. In the kitchen, you could've heard a pin drop. Upstairs, we heard the bedroom door bang open and Dad's muffled voice through the floorboards.

'Ricky, I am very sorry that your friend died. But that's enough of this now. You're under my roof and I will not tolerate any more self-pity. Your breakfast is on the table. Joanne will find you some suitable clothes. I expect you outside in ten minutes.'

And with that, Dad's boots made the return journey back down the stairs and out the front door. Alison turned to look at me, her mouth hanging open, her eyes wide. Aunt Mary lifted her eyes to the ceiling as we collectively held our breath. The clock ticked loudly on the wall. Three seconds passed. Five. And then a creak, another creak. And then soft footsteps across the ceiling.

'He's up,' Alison said with a chuckle.

'Go, go, go,' Aunt Mary said, giving me a shove. 'There're oil-skins behind the cellar door. He'll need boots and gloves. And get him a pair of your dad's long johns.'

Alison snorted with laughter.

'Oh, you won't know where they are,' Aunt Mary said, pushing past me. 'I'll get the bottoms.'

Ricky appeared at the kitchen door in his boxers and the same old Pearl Jam t-shirt he'd had on nine days ago. His hair was in a greasy pile over one eye, his face dark with stubble. He lifted a hand to scrape his hair back off his face and looked round the room, bewildered.

Aunt Mary patted him on the shoulder as she passed. 'Morning, love. Eat up quick.'

Alison got up, shot me a look and left the room too.

Ricky sat. I slid his toast and tea towards him across the table and cleared Alison's porridge bowl into the sink.

He picked up a piece of toast. 'Where am I going?'

'To the fish farm,' I replied. 'Hurry up.'

CHAPTER 35

Later that afternoon, I settled myself on the lichen-covered rock and pulled my knees up to wait. It was a beautiful day. Pulled cotton wool clouds were skiting across a pastel sky and the light of the sun seemed to come from the choppy waves themselves, all gold and pure dazzling. How many times in my life had I sat on this rock waiting for Dad to come home? And here I was again.

I looked to the headland and didn't have long to wait before Dad's small boat came into view. I sat on until I could pick out the three figures, then made my way down to the jetty. My shoulders were aching from digging manure into the new community polytunnel with Alison. But it was done and ready for planting tomorrow.

'How did it go?' I shouted as Dad threw me the line.

'Ay, not bad,' Dad replied, pulling the boat into the side. 'He's got a pair of sea legs alright.'

Ricky, who was already hefting the crates onto the jetty with Bill, threw a smile at my dad and then glanced at me.

'Not quite the Amalfi Coast,' I said, securing the line to the metal hook.

'No,' Ricky replied.

I jumped down onto the boat and followed Dad into the wheelhouse. 'How was he?' I asked, quietly.

Dad didn't look up from his notepad. 'He's strong,' he said. 'He did a good day's work.'

Ricky appeared at the door, resting one hand on the roof of the wheelhouse. He still had on the oilskin trousers and rubber boots, but had stripped down to his dirty t-shirt. The armpits were damp with sweat and he had fish guts smeared up both arms.

'Bill says he can manage the crates,' he said to Dad. 'Anything else to do?'

'Yes,' Dad said. 'Have a wash.'

Ricky sniffed his armpit and pulled a face.

'I'll walk you up,' I said.

I picked up the Tupperware lunch boxes and leaped back onto the pier behind Ricky.

'Will I see you later, Ricky?' Bill called from the shed.

Ricky raised a hand in reply.

'You meeting Bill?' I asked.

'Aye. He said he'd buy me a pint.'

'That's nice,' I replied. 'I'm working the bar tonight. I can show you where it is.'

Ricky chuckled and pointed at the Tavern Inn all of ten paces from the jetty. 'I think I can find it. Unless there's another one in this busy metropolis.'

'So, today was ok?'

'Aye,' he replied, head down, trudging. 'Why would you be working in the bar?'

'It's Aunt Mary's bar. Everyone's expected to work here.'

Ricky stopped walking. 'And that reminds me. I want to talk to you about Aunt Mary.'

'What about her?'

'I thought she was your mum. Well, I presumed she was, given the lack of evidence to the contrary.'

I started walking again. 'No, she's Aunt Mary.'

'Jo.' He held my arm to stop me. 'Why did you never tell me your mum died? I made a right arse of myself this morning with your dad.'

'Oh, poor you,' I said, shaking him off.

'Seriously. Why would you not mention that? Why did I not know that?'

I started walking again. 'I don't know. It didn't come up.'

'Didn't come up?' Ricky said, keeping up with me. 'No, I don't buy that.'

I sighed, loudly. 'When I got to Glasgow, I didn't want to be that girl whose mum died anymore. I didn't want it to define me forever.'

'It hardly defines you. But it's a huge part of who you are.'

'See,' I said. 'You're redefining me.'

We walked on a bit in silence.

'I just…' Ricky started, 'Well, I feel like I don't know you.'

I stopped walking. 'Of course you know me.'

'But being here.' He turned to look back at the pier, then out over the still sea. 'The way your dad is. This island. You grew up here. It's part of who you are and I never knew it. You didn't show one bit of it, in all these years.'

I shrugged. 'I just wanted this bit done. I'd had enough of it, you know? When I got to Glasgow, I just wanted something different.'

'You were running away.'

'We all run away,' I snapped back at him.

'Hmm,' he said, crossing the tarmac towards the shore.

I followed him down over the line of seaweed.

'It's beautiful here,' he said, bending to grab a fistful of sand, letting it pour through his fingers.

'Well, in this weather it is.'

Out on the water, there were gannets diving. In close, herring gulls bobbed about in ones and twos. I lifted my hand to the glare.

'It's so quiet,' he said.

I listened to the water lapping, a gull calling.

Ricky dunted my arm with his elbow. 'This was the right place. I'm glad you brought me here.'

I gave him a brief smile.

'How did it all go wrong so soon?' Ricky said, swinging his oil-skin jacket over his shoulder and turning back to the road. 'This time last year…'

'This time last year,' I said, joining him on the tarmac. 'You were playing The Dungeon. But a few months before that you were curled up in a ball saying exactly the same as this.'

Ricky looked at me quizzically.

'The Winston's gig? Gary? The amp?'

Ricky let out a laugh. 'Oh, Jesus. Do you remember? The amp blew up! God, that was a bloody night and a half.'

We smiled at each other for a moment, both lost in memories.

'Happy days,' he said sadly.

'They'll be happy again. But now it's shower time. You smell really, really bad.'

CHAPTER 36

'What'll it be, Bill?'

'A pint for me.' Bill leaned an elbow on the bar and looked towards the door. 'Ricky not coming?'

I picked up a glass and tilted it under the beer tap, watching the amber liquid spill into a thin froth, straightening the glass as it rose to the rim. It was nice to be back pouring pints. It was satisfying. Calming. It was enough for now.

'He said he'd come down with Alison,' I replied, not quite stopping myself from glancing at the door.

'So, you guys hanging about a while, then?' Bill asked as I placed his drink on the mat. 'Now that Ricky's up and about?'

'I have no idea.'

Bill took a first sip. 'Aye, early days.'

The door swung open, but it was the boys from the boat yard guffawing loudly at each other. Bill moved off to join them.

'Joanne,' Aunt Mary called from the side of the bar. She was carrying two crates of mixers.

'Let me do that.' I hopped over to take the top one. 'I can do all that.'

'Och, I'm just used to doing it all,' she said as I lifted the second crate from her onto the floor. 'I forget you're here again.'

I began stacking the bottles onto the shelf under the till. 'Well, I am here. Make the most of it.' I looked up at her. 'In fact, why don't you go home? I've got this tonight. I'm back in the swing of it.'

'No, no.' She shook her head, nodding at the door. 'It's filling up, look.'

I bobbed up from the floor to look. No Ricky, just more locals – the young couple that had taken the farm at the north end, and the Andersons from the distillery. The pub was small, with seating for less than a couple of dozen, so it already appeared full. Although I'd seen nights in the past with over fifty people merrily crammed in, steaming the windows with their sweat and laughter.

I served the customers, finished tidying the mixers, and the next time I had a chance to look, Ricky and Alison were arriving at Bill's table. Ricky was shrugging off one of my dad's wax jackets and shaking hands with the boat yard boys as Alison came to the bar.

'What kept you? Is Ricky ok?'

'We were talking about music,' she said with a snooty smile. 'And he's fine.'

We both looked over at the table. He did look fine, leaning forward on his stool, bouncing his knee, chatting away.

'Well, he's not fine,' I said. 'It's his first day up. This is all quite a lot for him.'

'For him or for you?' she asked, still watching the table.

'What do you mean?'

'Never mind. Are we to get drinks?'

'You can have a drink. But Ricky's having Diet Coke.'

'He'll look stupid sitting there with a Diet Coke,' Alison said. 'Let him have a beer.'

'No,' I replied. But I didn't know what to do. And as if by the weight of my stare, Ricky climbed off the stool and came to the bar.

'Alison, I'll get the drinks,' he said. 'I insist after being guided so charmingly to this venue.'

He bowed, and Alison giggled.

'Well, you'll be lucky if you get a drink,' she said. 'Joanne says you're to have Diet Coke.'

'I didn't say that!'

Ricky smiled weakly. 'Joanne's right. Diet Coke it is.' He pulled himself straighter. 'Good idea.'

Alison tutted and stomped off to the table. I placed a can before him and reached for the glass, plopping some ice in.

'Don't call me Joanne,' I said.

'Everyone else is.'

'It sounds wrong when you say it.'

He chuckled. 'I agree.'

'You ok?' I asked.

'Yeah. I won't stay long.' He glanced around the bar. No one was looking. Not obviously, anyway. They'd have got used to the idea of him being here by now, even if they hadn't seen him yet.

'You're safe enough here,' I said. 'They're good people.'

He picked up his drink and walked away as I turned to serve Caroline.

'He's up then,' she said in a loud whisper.

'He is. What can I get you?'

'Two G&T's please, Joanne,' she said, wrinkling her nose at me in a kind of fake smile.

I was watching Ricky in the mirror as I poured the measures, my back to the bar.

'I heard your dad pure dragged him down the stairs this morning,' she said.

'Hardly.'

'What a drama!' she continued. 'Love a bit of drama, I do. Livens the place up a bit, eh?'

I watched her scroll through her phone and noticed I was grinding my teeth. I'd grown up on the island with Caroline. She was only a year younger than me. I'd never really liked her. She wasn't very likable. Although Alison didn't seem to mind her.

I set the glasses on the bar in front of her. 'One person's drama is another's reality,' I said.

She continued scrolling, oblivious. 'I mean, look at this.' She swivelled the phone towards me. 'Still trending on Twitter. Hashtag Find Ricky.'

I didn't look at her phone. 'Anything else?'

She pulled a tenner out of her back pocket and handed it to me, eyes still glued to the screen. I rolled my own eyes and fetched her change.

'And those photos!' She shook her head slowly, pinching the screen to enlarge an image. 'That's not you with Ricky, right?'

I slapped her change down in a puddle of beer. 'No, that's not me.'

She blew out a dramatic breath. 'Brutal,' she said, turning to glance at Ricky, then back at me.

I busied myself rinsing glasses. 'It'll die down.'

'Doubt that! This ain't going away anytime soon. They're not going to stop until he's back out in the open.' She picked up her drinks. 'Oh, they'll find him all right. Mark my words.'

I steadied myself on the sink as my stomach rose and fell. They would find him. It was only a matter of time. What were we going to do?

Jimmy Anderson was on his feet and had launched into 'Wild Mountain Thyme'. Bill stood on his seat to reach down the bodhran from its dusty shelf and joined in the rhythm as Jimmy conducted the whole pub into the chorus, *'And we'll all go thegether, to pull wild mountain thyme...'*

'Here we go,' Aunt Mary said, and she squeezed past me with a tray to collect the empties.

I continued drying and stacking glasses, keeping my eye on Ricky and Alison. Alison was speaking into his ear, leaning towards him. She'd grown up so much since she'd started at the Gaelic College on Skye, where she was studying Traditional Music. I let out an audible sigh as she rested her hand on his knee. That would need to be nipped in the bud. But it seemed Aunt Mary was already on it. She pushed between them to clear the glasses.

As the song ended and everyone was clapping and cheering, the fiddle was passed along from the games' cupboard, hand to hand, and Alison rose to accept it. She flicked her hair off her shoulder and nodded to Bill before settling her chin in place and launching into a reel. I caught Ricky's eye, and he mouthed 'wow' with a look of mild astonishment. I just shrugged my shoulders and smiled. Nothing unusual in this – a typical night in the pub always slipped into a ceilidh. Everyone was expected to take a turn. Caroline was already removing her boots to prepare for her usual Highland Fling, the only thing she could remember from our early years of lessons.

But as Alison closed off the reel, I heard Bill say Ricky's name. And when I looked, Kevin, from the boatyard, was holding out the pub's battered guitar. Ricky firmly shook his head.

'Oh, go on,' Alison said loudly, giving him a nudge.

And from the far end of the pub, Jimmy Anderson began shouting 'Ricky,' rhythmically over and over.

The colour drained from Ricky's face as he tried to smile, still shaking his head.

Within a heartbeat, the whole pub was clapping and chanting his name – not unkindly, just with a sense of expectation. He was a musician, after all.

Ricky looked at me from the midst of the noise with the same look I'd seen at the ferry slip ten days before. He was about to lose it.

Without a thought, I bent down, flipped a plastic crate over and stood on it. I took a deep breath, closed my eyes and, as loud as I could, launched into 'Gradh Geal Mo Chridh', the Gaelic song I remembered best from my youth. My mind emptied of thought as my out-of-use tongue manoeuvred around the now unfamiliar syllables. How long since I'd sung in Gaelic? I raised my arms to the side for balance and to guide me through the rise and fall of the tune, allowing the words themselves to dictate the timing. The ancient song filled up my soul, turning me into a vessel for it to experience this room, this place and time. I wasn't singing the song, the song was singing me. That was how I'd always experienced it, how it had always been. And when my eyes opened after it was done, all eyes were silently on me and more than one set were wet with tears. I lowered my arms to my side as Jimmy Anderson raised his glass and said, 'Welcome home, lass.'

Glasses were raised across the room, and his words were echoed. I blinked as I came back to myself and stepped down from the crate, grateful to hear Caroline call out to Alison to play something she could dance to. Then I looked at Ricky, who was staring at me, completely dumbfounded, and I indicated the door with a nod of my head. 'Go,' I mouthed, and he rose without hesitation and pushed out the door.

I told Aunt Mary I was taking Ricky home, grabbed my hoodie, scooted round a dancing Caroline, snatched my dad's wax jacket from the stool and made it out the door without making any further eye contact.

Ricky was crouching in the shadow of the seawall, and he rose when he saw me.

'You ok?' I asked, handing him the jacket.

He hung it over his arm, not feeling the night chill. 'What was that?'

'What was what?' I was busy pulling up my hood and zip.

'What was *what*! That! That... I don't know what it was. Singing?'

I walked away from him down the road.

He trotted after me. 'Jo, that was unbelievable! How did you? I mean – how?' He began laughing.

'Don't laugh at me.'

'I'm not laughing at you. I'm just… How can you do that? Your voice! For fuck's sake! It was incredible. I've never heard anything like that.'

'We learned Gaelic at school.'

He held my arm to make me stop and jumped round in front of me. 'But your voice, Jo. It was… oh my god. How did I not know you could do that? I literally do not know anything about you.'

I sidestepped round him and walked on.

'Everyone can do it here,' I said as lightly as I could. 'And, by the way,' I changed the subject, 'Alison has a crush on you. You'd better watch out for that.'

He caught up with me and laughed again. 'Alison? She's a nice girl. You've a nice sister.'

'Just don't lead her on. And don't say nice.'

'Have no fear! You're the only Duncan for me.'

And with that, he wrapped his arms round me with such force that I staggered onto the grass verge.

'Stop it,' I said, harshly.

Instead, he swept his arm down and under the back of my legs, hoisting me into the air to tip me upside down like he used to in Glasgow. I struggled angrily against him, with more force than I ever used back in the day. Freeing an elbow, I slammed it backwards into his ribs. He collapsed to the ground, taking me with him. He was still laughing as I scrambled to my feet.

'Seriously though,' he said, not sounding at all serious. 'Thanks for saving my arse tonight. I really didn't want to perform there.'

'For fuck's sake, Ricky,' I shouted down at him as

he reclined on the grass, head rested leisurely on one propped-up hand. 'I'm sick of saving you! All I ever do is save you!'

He dropped his hand and sat up, the smile slipping from his face.

'What are you even doing?' I pointed at him accusingly. 'You don't get to touch me anymore. Have you forgotten how we got here?' I was screaming, my throat already burning. 'Why are we here, Ricky? Eh? Why the fuck are we here?'

He clambered to his feet. 'I forgot,' he said, hanging his head like a puppy, making me even angrier. 'Just for a second there, I forgot.'

'I'm sick of saving you!' I yelled again, right near his face, then stomped off down the tarmac.

CHAPTER 37

By the time I made it down to the kitchen the next morning, Ricky had finished his breakfast and was rinsing out the porridge bowls in the sink. Aunt Mary was humming to herself as she kneaded the dough, and Dad was engrossed in the paper, pencil in hand. I needed to speak to Ricky, but I hesitated at the door. Alison clomped down the stairs and pushed past me.

'Morning,' she said to the room as she popped her bread into the toaster.

Ricky looked over his shoulder, spotted me, and turned back to the dishes.

'Sleep well?' Aunt Mary asked.

'Apart from Joanne kicking me in the kidneys half the night,' she replied, leaning back on the counter.

Dad folded his paper. 'We'll be off in ten minutes, Ricky.'

'Yip,' Ricky replied. 'All set.'

'Joanne,' Aunt Mary said. 'There you are. Can you get the lunches ready, please?'

'Can't Alison do it?'

Alison snorted in derision and rolled her eyes dramatically as Aunt Mary gave me a look.

'Sorry,' I said, moving to the dresser to get the Tupperware. 'Of course I can do it.'

I watched Ricky walk round the other side of the table and out of the room. I hurried to prepare the sandwiches, slicing the cheese thick, as the soup heated, then slopping that into a warmed flask, grabbing two water bottles and rushing out to catch Ricky.

He was just outside, tying the string of his oil-skin trousers, holding the front of his t-shirt under his chin. He didn't look up as I came out. The gravel was sharp under my bare city feet and I stepped off onto the dewy grass.

'I brought your lunch.'

He bent over to pull on the thick knitted socks and didn't reply.

'It's going to be another lovely day,' I said, looking out at the calm sea and the pale blue empty sky. 'Let's hope this weather holds.'

What was I talking about the weather for? Ricky continued to ignore me as he wriggled his feet into the rubber boots. Dad would be out any second.

'I'm sorry,' I said, still clutching the lunches to my chest.

'What for?'

'For what I said last night. It was mean.'

'It was true.'

'Well, I didn't mean to make you feel bad. You don't need reminded of everything every five minutes.'

He straightened up and looked at me with tired, hooded eyes. He was unbelievably handsome, standing there in the morning light with his bare arms and a night's growth on his face. I could hardly bear it. Would I ever be free of him? I thought as a lump rose in the back of my throat.

I swallowed hard and bent to put the lunches in the cool bag. 'Me shouting at you doesn't help.'

'You were entitled to shout. I deserved it. I deserve it all.'

'No,' I said, wanting to go to him, forcing myself to stay still.

'Yes.' He lifted a hand to rub his bed-head hair back off his face. 'I just don't know what to do. I always know what to do, and I just don't know anymore.'

He looked at me. He looked to me to know, to solve it all. And still I tried.

'You start again,' I said. 'You make a plan and start again.'

He shook his head and moved his gaze out to the sea, his shoulders slouching forward. 'I'm finished, Jo. It's over. It's all gone. My career, the record company, Damien, the band.' He breathed in sharply. 'Lee.'

I stepped back onto the gravel to place a hand on his shoulder.

'And you,' he whispered, looking down at me. 'I've lost you too, haven't I?'

'I'm right here.'

He placed a hand on top of mine and looked back out to sea. 'You know what I mean.'

I could hear Dad getting ready behind the door. He'd be out any second. 'Come on,' I said, swinging the cool bag onto my shoulder and heading across the grass to the lane. 'I'll walk you down.'

Ricky picked up his oilskin jacket and followed obediently. I knew what I had to say, what Ricky had to hear. I just didn't know if he was ready yet.

'You know what?' I began as he caught up with me. 'You're just feeling sorry for yourself.'

He raised his eyebrows. 'That's one way of putting it.'

'Do you know that Robert Frost poem, 'Wild Thing'?'

'Oh, Jesus Christ! Do not start quoting poetry at me.' He quickened his pace away.

I hopped after him on my bare tiptoes, trying to avoid the stones and emerging thistles. 'Hold up. I haven't got any shoes on.'

He stopped and turned to wait. 'I mean it. No fucking poems.'

'Ok. But listen.'

He was listening. Waiting. Waiting for me to fix everything.

'I know you're low and that this all seems completely hopeless,' I said. 'But I promise you, you are not finished. You are not finished because Damien says so. Or the record company. Or anyone.'

'Everyone says so,' he mumbled, slinging his arms into his jacket. Behind me, I could hear Dad's footsteps across the gravel.

'Just shut up and listen. You are not finished because you've broken the rules, or lost the game, or been fired, or whatever.' I reached to his chest and grabbed a handful of his t-shirt. 'You're only finished because you quit. And you are not a quitter, Ricky Steele.'

Dad passed us, slipping the cool bag from my shoulder as he went, marching down the lane towards the front street. 'Let's go, son,' he said without breaking his stride.

Ricky half turned.

'No.' I tugged at his shirt. 'Wait. Listen to me.'

He sighed, but turned towards me again.

'You are not a quitter,' I repeated, trying to send my words deep into his head.

'Ok,' he said, coldly. 'I'm not a quitter. I've got to go.'

'Wait. Let me say this.'

He pulled his t-shirt out of my grip and set his mouth in a thin line.

'I'm just saying, you still have a choice in all this and it's the most important choice you ever have to make. You have to choose whether or not to believe in yourself. In your talent. In your skill. In Ricky Steele.'

He snorted and turned his head out to sea. I wasn't sure he wanted to hear any of this, but I had to finish saying it. I grabbed his chin and steered his face back towards me.

'Other people may have made their choice already,' I said with all the power I could muster. 'But you haven't. And that's all that really matters.'

I let him go. And he turned to jog down the lane to catch Dad.

*

'That's the last of the swiss chard,' I said that afternoon, laying the basket down beside the week's veg boxes.

'It's done well this year.' Aunt Mary was scouring clumps of mud off the freshly dug carrots. 'It's been mild. And there's still kale and savoys in.'

'Aye,' I said. 'Two rows still.'

I straightened my back, bending to the side to lean

into the stiffness. It had been a while since I'd done full days of manual labour and my body was protesting. But I wasn't complaining about the solid, dreamless sleep my exhaustion awarded me every night.

'That should do for the rest of the boxes. There's only six still to fill. Alison's already away with the first load,' Aunt Mary counted. 'Help me pack the rest and we'll call it a day.'

I retied my bandana to catch the trickles of sweat escaping from my brow and neck, and bent to evenly distribute the freshly picked vegetables into the empty crates for the islanders.

There wasn't a breath of wind and with each movement I could smell my own BO. I needed a shower. My bare arms were caked with clots of earth, my nails black, and my old teenage pink and floral t-shirt was sticking to my back. I listened to the sounds of the surrounding island – the garden birds calling and chattering their spring song, the gulls further out, crying and yelping, and the engine drone of the afternoon ferry pulling away from the slipway.

'Penny for your thoughts?' Aunt Mary asked.

'I worked so hard to get away from here. And here I am, right back at the start.'

Aunt Mary sat back on her heels. 'Are you ashamed of us, Jo?'

'No. I'm sorry. I didn't mean to say that. You brought us up so well. I'm grateful. I am.'

'I've found life tends to put you where you need to be.' She squeezed my hand and then bent back to the vegetables. 'Ricky seems better.'

'Well, he's up, which is a start.'

'You don't think he's better?'

'I don't know,' I said. 'He's so low. He doesn't know what to do.'

'Aye, some things take a while. And some things don't leave you, however far you run.'

I let her words sit between us as we carried on our work.

'You love him very much, don't you?' she said.

'Yes. But I need to work out how to stop now.'

She nodded. 'He's hurt you.'

My eyes filled with tears, my bottom lip starting to tremble.

'Oh, Joanne.' She crawled on her knees towards me. 'Come here, love.' She took me in her arms and I leaned my head on her chest. 'You've had all this to deal with and not a minute to deal with yourself.'

'I'm so embarrassed.' I sobbed.

'Of what?' she asked, rocking me. 'What've you got to be embarrassed about?'

'Everything!' I wiped my snotty nose on my dirty arm. 'Those photos. Everyone's seen them. And they're all talking about them. About me.'

'No one's talking about you,' she said calmly. 'Or if they are, it's with kindness. And the folks here are glad to see you home. You've got to talk more. Get it all off your chest. You always were one for bottling things up.'

'I don't know what to do. They're going to find us here.'

'Who's going to find you?'

'Everyone,' I sobbed dramatically. 'The press.'

'And Ricky will have to deal with that himself.' She pulled me upright to look at me. 'You've done enough for him,' she said firmly.

'He needs me.'

272

'Yes,' she said. 'He's very needy. I can see that. But I think you've done enough for him now.'

I could hear Alison on the quad bike roaring through the gate and sat up to dry my face before she could see me. Alison smirking was all I needed.

Aunt Mary clambered to her feet, too. 'Oh, who's this now?'

I looked up, shielding my eyes with my hand as the bike careered towards us across the field. Alison was driving far too fast, with Caroline kneeling behind her. The bike skid to a halt and Caroline leapt off, making a beeline for me at a fast trot.

'They've found you!' she began, panting as if she'd run all the way.

'What? Who?'

'There's a pile of them, down on the slip,' she continued, pointing back the way they'd come.

'Three of them,' Alison said, eyes ablaze with delight at the drama of it all.

'Asking for you by name.' This from Caroline.

'Jo Duncan, they said.'

'To Calum.'

'And what did Calum say?' I asked, heart thumping in my chest.

'He said no one here by that name,' Caroline replied. 'And they just sat down there on the slip.'

'They said they'd wait!'

'It's the paparazzi, for sure.'

'They've got tons of equipment.'

'Where's Ricky?' I asked frantically, turning to Aunt Mary.

She looked at her watch. 'They're probably on their way back. It's after four.'

I dropped the onions into the nearest box and took off at a run.

CHAPTER 38

I crossed the field and through the gate, taking a sharp left onto the lane towards our house. The girls were hot on my heels, with Aunt Mary taking up the rear. I widened my stride down the hill and grabbed the gate post to swing me into our garden, bounding through the open door to snatch Dad's binoculars from the hook.

Back outside, the girls were waiting in wild excitement.

'Alison,' I panted. 'Go and warn Ricky.'

'How?'

'Go to the Point. They'll pass in close there. Get them to come in at the old pier.'

Alison turned to run down the lane as Aunt Mary arrived at the gate, red-faced.

'No,' she gasped. 'Go round the back way. You can't let them see you run.'

Alison set off back up the lane and cut off into a field which would lead her through the back of the village houses, past the pub and out to the Point, a stony promontory at the end of the bay.

'What'll I do?' Caroline asked, obviously delighted with the afternoon's turn of events.

I ignored her and started off down the lane with Aunt Mary. At the corner, the whole of the village would come into view, including the pier. It was only about a hundred yards to the sea from there, and I slowed my pace, crouching close to the ground. I climbed the verge at the corner and crawled on my hands and knees to the boulders on the bluff above the Anderson's house. I lay flat on a rock and peered over the top as Aunt Mary and Caroline joined me.

'See?' Caroline said in a pointless whisper. 'Told you.'

Even without the binoculars, I could see the three people on the pier with their piles of equipment. One was sitting on a box and the other two were standing. 'What are they doing?'

'Waiting, by the looks of it,' Aunt Mary replied.

I cast my eyes out to sea, scanning, and was relieved to not see Dad's boat. There was no sign of Alison on the Point either.

'She'll make it.' Aunt Mary read my thoughts. 'She knows those rocks like the back of her hand.'

The village was empty. No one was out, which was unusual for this time of day. But everyone would have heard by now and were no doubt watching and waiting from behind closed doors.

Finally, Alison appeared round the side of the last house, slowing to a walk and making her way out onto the Point. I brought the binoculars to my eyes to follow her progress. When she was nearly at the end, she lifted a hand to her mouth and a moment later we heard a loud whistle echoing across the bay. I lowered the binoculars to look at the people on the pier. They'd heard it, but turned back to their own conversation without seeming concerned.

Alison whistled again, and increased her pace, falling to her knees once as she tried to run and wave at the same time. The newcomers didn't flinch. In the still afternoon air, I could hear an engine drone. My heart pounded against the rock.

'They're not going to turn,' Caroline whispered beside me. 'They don't see her.'

'They'll see her,' Aunt Mary replied calmly. 'She'll do it.'

And suddenly the engine drone died and Alison disappeared down the far side of the Point, out of sight.

I held my breath, eyes darting from the pier to the Point, until I heard the engine spluttering back to life and fading into the distance. Alison reappeared, steadily making her way back to the village and turning left onto the shore road towards the old pier. She'd done it.

I dropped my head to the rock in relief and took a few deep breaths.

'Now what?' Caroline asked.

'I don't know.' I looked at Aunt Mary.

She shrugged. 'Hide until they go away?'

'They'll never go away.' They didn't know the paparazzi like I did. This was just the beginning. Our time here was up.

I lifted the binoculars to take a better look at the pier. They were all chatting, not doing anything, waiting. Did they think Ricky was just going to stroll up to them? The seated one suddenly stood up, brushing dust or dirt off her bum in such a way that I knew she was a woman. She was shorter than the other two as well. She reached into the top of her rucksack and pulled out a bottle of water, passing it round so they all took a sip. Why would they share a water bottle? I focused the binoculars with my index finger. Their 'equipment' was actually three rucksacks and a pile of cardboard boxes. Why would they carry their equipment in cardboard boxes? There was something else behind the boxes that I couldn't see. Something black? A black case? Maybe that was the camera equipment. The tallest man pulled off his black beanie hat to scratch his bald head as the shorter one squatted down on his haunches, handing the water back to the woman. At the back of my mind, something familiar stirred.

The tallest replaced his hat and bent over to busy himself with the black case. Eventually, he pulled out a white guitar and sat down cross-legged with it, right there on the pier, and began to pluck out a tune.

'Why have they got a guitar?' Caroline sounded as surprised as I was.

The woman reached forward to rub the guitarist's neck affectionately and dropped a kiss on the top of his head before turning towards the village, cupping her hands round her mouth and shouting, 'Jo Duncan! Come out, come out, wherever you are!'

I gasped. The entire island seemed to gasp.

I refocused the binoculars on the woman who was spinning slowly on the spot, arms held wide open, face to the sky as the shorter man laughed at her. And suddenly I knew.

'That's not the press.' I laughed, relief bubbling out of me as I scrambled off the boulder and onto my feet.

'Who is it then?' Caroline asked, still lying down.

'They're my pals,' I replied, pointing at the pier. 'I know them. They're my Glasgow pals.'

'Oh, thank god for that,' Aunt Mary said, climbing to her feet.

I set off down the lane, still laughing with relief. 'Caroline,' I shouted over my shoulder. 'Can you go and get Ricky?'

I broke into a run, waving my arms above my head like a lunatic. 'Mhairi!' I yelled.

'Jo!' she shouted back.

I bounded off the road and down the pier and we collided in a hard, tight embrace, my laughter turning to sobs of joy and gratitude.

'Mhairi,' I cried. 'What are you doing here? I can't believe it.'

She laughed and hung on tighter. 'I knew you'd be watching.'

'Oh, everyone'll be watching. We're a suspicious lot!'

I pulled away to take a better look at her. She looked exactly the same, as if I'd just seen her yesterday.

'I'm so glad to see you,' I said, still crying. 'Why are you here? How did you even…?'

She laughed again, sniffing away her own tears. 'You're making me cry. Stop it.'

'What are you doing here?' I asked again, through snot.

'All right, Jo?' Bob said, stepping forward beside Mhairi.

'Bob,' I cried, releasing Mhairi to wrap my arms round his thick waist.

He patted me on the back, laughing. 'Where is he, then?'

I let go of Bob and wiped my eyes on the shoulder of my t-shirt. 'I've sent someone to get him. He's just in from work.'

'What work?' Mhairi asked.

'The fish farm,' I replied, automatically.

'The fish farm?' Bob guffawed. 'What the actual fuck?'

'I know, right?' I laughed again, realising, all at once, the complete absurdity of Ricky Steele, rock god, working on a fish farm. 'But, stop. Stop. Tell me what you're doing here? How did you find us?'

Mhairi and Bob stepped aside, and there was Dinger.

'Hey,' he said.

And it all came back to me. I blushed from my toes to the top of my head. 'Dinger,' I said, smiling at him as best I could. 'How did you know where we were?'

'You told me you were going home.'

'Did I?'

'In the hospital. In London.'

London, I thought, as more memories flooded back. Only a fortnight had passed. It seemed like a lifetime.

'We thought you might need some moral support,' Mhairi said.

'But your work?' I said to Dinger.

He shrugged. 'I was due time off.'

'And we fancied a trip.' Mhairi was smiling.

I could hear a quad bike engine along the bay and turned to look. The village was busy again with people standing and walking about, no doubt having a nosy at the events unfolding on the pier. The bike slowed at the end of the slip, and Ricky climbed off. Alison was driving, but she carried on up the lane to the house, leaving us to our reunion.

As Ricky came closer, clomping down the pier in his boots, the oilskins slapping together with each step, I could see him pick out the individual faces. His own face was blank. He ran a hand through his hair and came to a halt in front of us.

Bob was the first to step forward, hand outstretched. 'All right, Ricky?' he asked.

Ricky took his hand. 'Bob,' he said, quietly. 'I'm sorry as fuck, mate.'

'Aye.' Bob was still holding his hand.

Mhairi gently touched Ricky on his shoulder. 'And that's all that needs said.'

He turned to her with a weak smile and then grabbed Bob in a hard embrace, both of them slapping each other on the back.

Bob pulled away first and stepped aside to give Ricky a view of Dinger. Ricky put his hand out.

'And you, Dinger,' he said. 'I'm sorry. For it all.'

Dinger hesitated, glanced at me, then took Ricky's hand. 'I'd never have made it anyway,' he said with a laugh. 'Those crowds you've been playing to! I'd have shat myself.'

Mhairi flung her arms round Ricky's neck. 'Come here, you A-list celebrity, you superstar, you. Oh my god, you stink of fish!'

And with that, we were all laughing and talking over each other, letting the low spring sun warm us back to friendship.

'What is all this stuff?' I asked at one point, indicating the boxes.

'It's your stuff,' Dinger said. 'From the flat.'

I bent to open a box, which was indeed full of my folders and books that I hadn't packed when I'd fled the flat. The next box was a jumble of clothes and shoes.

'How?' I was incredulous.

Dinger shrugged. 'We convinced the letting agency we were from Lava and they gave us the key.'

'Who's 'we'?' Ricky asked.

'Pamela,' Dinger replied. 'She sends her love. And she said…'

'What?' I asked.

'Oh, I'll tell you later.'

'Is that what I think it is?' Ricky asked, pointing at the guitar Bob had been playing.

Bob picked it up and handed it to Ricky with a grin.

'My Mustang!' He laughed.

'We couldn't bring them all,' Dinger said.

'I bought this from that shop behind St Enoch's.' Ricky stroked the neck, turning it over in his hands. 'I saved up forever for it.'

'You did not,' I said. 'You used your dad's card.'

He shrugged as we all laughed.

'We brought our camping gear,' Mhairi said. 'And our own food.'

'And beer.' Bob nodded at a couple of slabs behind the boxes.

'There's a pub.' Ricky pointed down the street. 'Wait 'til you see it. You'll love it. Can we go to the pub, Jo?'

'Later.' I smiled. 'Let's get all this up to the house. There's room in the garden for tents. It's a bit cramped in the house, but you can eat with us. And use the bathroom.'

'Great.' Mhairi hefted her rucksack onto her shoulders. 'I'm dying for a piss.'

'Your folks won't mind?' Dinger asked.

Ricky snorted and I threw him a look.

'No,' I said. 'They'll be cool.'

CHAPTER 39

As expected, Dad did not mind. And no one batted an eyelid when I introduced Aunt Mary. Nor did they ask where my mum was. We got the tents up at the side of the house in no time, and Mhairi followed me into the kitchen while the boys settled down on the grass with the beer.

'I've brought tons of pasta,' Mhairi said.

Aunt Mary smiled at her from the chopping board. 'Och, there's plenty of food. I've put lamb in the oven and I'm going to do a winter ratatouille. You girls start the potatoes.'

It didn't take us long to get everything on the hob. Alison came down from her shower and I called Ricky in through the open window to take his. Alison, I noticed as she started laying the table, had blow-dried her hair and was in full make-up. I suppressed all the comments I could think of.

By the time I'd finished showering, everyone had gathered round the kitchen table, chattering and laughing. It was a lovely sight. My family and friends all together. Why had I never invited them here before? Why had I never imagined this scene?

Aunt Mary plonked the lamb in front of Dad, who'd

been sharpening the carving knife all this time. I took the free seat between Mhairi and Dinger, who passed me the steaming vegetables.

'Thanks so much for this, Mary,' Mhairi said.

'It's just nice to have a bit of life around the place,' she replied, dolloping mashed potato onto her plate.

Across the table from me, Alison poured water into Ricky's glass, unnecessarily resting a hand on his shoulder as she did so. He didn't seem to notice.

'So, what news from Glasgow?' I asked.

'Same old, same old.' Bob passed his plate down for some meat.

'Work, rain, repeat.' Mhairi nodded. 'You guys'll have much more interesting tales to tell.'

'Oh, I don't know,' I said. 'It rains in London, too.'

'Not as much,' Ricky added, laughing.

'Come on,' Mhairi persisted. 'Tell us a story. You must have loads. Something with a celebrity.'

'Well,' Ricky said, swallowing a mouthful of vegetable stew, eyes sparkling with beer. 'There's Reading.'

'Yes!' Alison said.

'No!' I replied.

'Yes,' Mhairi said. 'We read about that in the papers. What actually happened?'

Ricky was looking right at me, still laughing.

I glared at him. 'Don't you dare. What happens in Reading stays in Reading. You promised.'

'I did promise.' Ricky carried on giggling. 'Ok. Well, this one time in Bilbao…'

And so the meal passed in a blur of chatter and laughter. Aunt Mary and Alison left after dinner to open the pub and Dad disappeared out to his shed. The boys cleared the table and washed up, while Mhairi and I sat and reminisced, the bottle of wine in front of us.

'I'm sorry we fell out,' I said at one point, smiling sadly.

'You didn't have a choice.' She sipped from her glass, not looking at me. 'What's done is done.'

'I did have a choice.'

She turned to face me. The boys were oblivious, being noisy at the sink, making more of a mess than they were trying to clear.

'I did have a choice,' I repeated quietly. 'And I'm only now realising I chose wrong.'

I looked at Ricky's back, the shoulder blades cutting through his shirt, his dark hair catching the overhead light. I was more than a little drunk. 'I made the wrong choice,' I clarified.

'Stop it.' Mhairi placed her hand on top of mine. 'You didn't have a choice. You were in love. That leaves you with no choice.'

My eyes filled with tears. Why was I so emotional today? The boys had finished the dishes as best they could. I wiped my eyes and told them to take the beer through to the sitting room and let us clear up the rest.

Once we had the room to ourselves, I put my head in my hands.

Mhairi rubbed my back gently, tutting once. 'So, what? You don't love him anymore?'

I shrugged, sniffing. 'He's not perfect. I know that. I know you don't get all the boxes ticked. You don't get perfection – that's just fairytale stuff. And if you hold out for perfection, you can end up with nothing.'

'Is that what you think?'

'Yes. He's not perfect, but he's so many other things. I guess I just choose to focus on all the other things. What's wrong with that?'

'Well, I don't have perfection either,' Mhairi said as she got up from the table and started putting empties in the recycling bin. 'I have Bob. He's grumpy – a lot. I'd prefer a more pleasant disposition. He's bald at twenty five. I'd prefer a bit more hair. But he only sleeps with me. I'm sorry Jo, but there are non-negotiables. The main ones being non-violence and fidelity. You know this.'

I sat where I was. She was right, of course. She reached across me for an empty can. Through the room I could hear a guitar. 'Is that Ricky playing?'

Mhairi listened. 'Well, it's not Bob.'

'That's the first time he's touched a guitar in a fortnight,' I said. 'Thank god you guys came.'

Mhairi sat down on my dad's seat at the top of the table. 'Was it awful?'

I nodded and rolled my eyes. 'He stayed in his bed for nine days.' I pointed to the ceiling. 'Dad got him up in the end. Just marched up there and took him out on the boat.'

Mhairi snorted. 'Wish I'd seen that!'

I laughed despite my mood. 'It was a sight, I tell you. But we haven't really talked. Not about Lee. Not about us. Not about what we're going to do.' I scratched at some dried gravy on the table. 'What are we going to do?'

Mhairi got back up from her seat and pointed a finger at me. 'What are *you* going to do? If you guys are done, then he's got to work it out himself.'

'But I'm in it too. I'm Jo-D.'

Mhairi picked up a dishcloth and rolled her eyes.

'I know!' I said, defensively. 'But I'm part of the story. They'll want the two of us.'

Ricky poked his head in the door. 'Can we get that guitar from the pub?'

'Now?' I asked.

He grinned.

'Sure. Why not head down there? We can all go.' I popped the cork back in the bottle of wine and stood up. 'We need to apologise for the fuss you guys made earlier with your dramatic arrival.'

'Really?' Mhairi asked.

'Well, it would be polite to show face at least,' I said, turning to Ricky. 'You guys go ahead. We'll follow you down.'

Mhairi and I knuckled down to finish up in the kitchen, wiping the table and worktops for the next day, as the boys clattered out the house, their voices receding down the lane. Once we were done, we quickly followed.

The evening air was still and chilly. It was almost dark. We could pick some lights out on the mainland already. The beam from a lighthouse pulsed. The boats clinked and sang as they jostled gently in the harbour.

'It's beautiful here,' Mhairi said, breathing in the cool air. 'It's nice to be out the city.'

'Yeah,' I agreed as we padded down the lane to the front.

'So.'

'So what?'

'So, do you still love him or not?'

'I don't know,' I said. 'How *do* you know? I think I can

see him clearer here. Like I couldn't see him in London, or something. It was all just,' I flung my arms up. 'Too busy, too blurry. I don't know.' Mhairi stayed silent beside me as I sorted out my thoughts. 'It's just hard to look at it all. It's so obvious that I don't really want to look.'

'Well,' she said. 'You have to look. And if you want my opinion, he hasn't changed. Nothing's changed. Ricky is still being Ricky, as he always was. *I* can see that.'

We were near the pub by now. The voices and music were getting louder.

She took my arm, stopping me in my tracks. 'I think you know what you have to do. That's what all this crying is about.'

I wiped my eyes, suddenly aware that, once again, tears were rolling down my face. 'That's just the wine.'

'Oh,' she said, raising her eyes to the darkening sky. 'And another thing.'

'What?'

'Dinger?'

'What about Dinger?' I asked, aiming for nonchalance.

'Ha!' She laughed. 'I knew it. I knew it the moment I saw him. As soon as I mentioned your name he went scarlet. And your face blew up like a beetroot when you saw him on the pier.'

I growled and tugged her towards the pub.

She shrieked with laughter. '*Jo and Dinger, up a tree.*'

'Stop it! Honest to god. Stop it.'

She ground her heels in to stop us both. 'And? How was it?'

'No,' I said firmly. 'Absolutely not ever going to talk about it. Ever.'

'Oh, go on. Give me something.'

'Never. And you can't say anything. Ever. Ricky can *not* know this.'

'I know. I know,' she said, following me to the door.

I swung it open and the warm fug of beer and humans wafted out. I stopped and turned back, making Mhairi bump into me. I leaned towards her ear. 'He was surprisingly good,' I said, and swung myself in through the door as a delighted Mhairi guffawed behind me.

CHAPTER 40

We were given time off the following day to spend with our friends. The good weather was still holding, and Alison and I knew just where to head. And a tough fifty-minute hike later, I paused, lifting my shades to let the warm April sun hit my full face. I looked out over the empty, glistening Atlantic.

Bob came to a stop beside me. 'Fuck me. This was worth that walk.'

'Look at the colour of the water,' Mhairi gasped. 'It's, like, turquoise.'

Alison ran between us, slamming her fiddle case into my chest for me to hold. She whooped in delight and bounded down the sand dunes. 'Let's swim!'

Ricky and Dinger arrived, dropping the crate of supplies that it had been their turn to carry.

'I'll swim,' Ricky said, slinging his guitar off his back and sliding down the dunes to the beach. 'I'm sweating buckets.'

'It'll be freezing,' I shouted after him, laughing.

But he was already stripping off his shirt as he ran.

'I'll dip a toe in,' Dinger nodded, setting off after them.

I lifted one side of the crate with Bob on the other and we slid and bumped our way down and out onto the beach. The white sand stretched left and right half a mile in each direction, and out to sea there was nothing but emptiness all the way to America. We had the place to ourselves. It was the island's best-kept secret.

We laid the crate and the fiddle down beside Ricky's guitar and I kicked off my gutties, rolling up the legs of my jeans. Bob and Mhairi set off, hand in hand, to the south and, after a moment's hesitation, I padded down the cool sand to join Dinger, following the line of scattered clothes. He'd rolled the legs of his khaki chinos up and was, indeed, dipping a toe in.

Ricky had thrown himself into the sea and was screaming expletives at the cold. Alison, who was much more used to the water, was throwing strong front-crawl strokes around him, seemingly oblivious to the temperature.

'They're mad.' I laughed.

'Your sister's a nice girl,' Dinger said, stepping back to join me on the beach.

'Hmm.' I watched her tread water as she tried to push Ricky under.

'How are you doing?' he asked.

'Fine,' I replied automatically. 'How are you?'

'Fine.' He paused. 'It's nice to see you.'

The awkwardness settled in between us. Did he want to talk about it now?

'I'm glad you came,' I said, smiling carefully.

'Don't worry, Jo. I get it. I've always got it.'

'Got what?'

'Whatever I am, I'll never be Ricky,' he said, looking out at the splashing, swearing idiot. 'I'll never be him.'

'Jesus, Dinger,' I said, aiming for a light tone. 'Why would you want to be him?'

He looked right at me. 'I just wanted you to know. It meant a lot to me.'

I was blushing and wished the sunglasses were back on my face and not on top of my head.

'I know.' I had to come up with something better than that. 'It was special for me, too.'

He shrugged in defeat, dropping his eyes to the sand.

'It was good,' I said. 'Surprisingly good.' *Surprisingly good?* What was I thinking?

He screwed up his face in a grimace.

'Not that I didn't think it wouldn't be good,' I continued, unable to stop. 'I mean, not that I considered it before. Or not that I didn't consider it before. Or…'

I managed to stop myself. At least he was genuinely laughing now.

'Do you want to give me a score?' he asked. 'Any feedback. Recommendations.'

'No, I do not.' I laughed, slapping his arm. 'Stop it. You're taking the piss.'

Ricky and Alison were scrambling back to shore, and I slipped my shades back down over my eyes.

'I was wondering,' Dinger said, clearing his throat. 'Maybe the next time you're down south we could go for a drink?'

I regarded him for a moment, allowing a memory of that night to return. His lips on every inch of my body.

The weight of him on me. 'Are you asking me on a date, Mr Bell?'

'Maybe,' he replied without blushing, without lowering his gaze.

'I'd like that,' I answered quietly, as Alison and Ricky burst from the water beside us, splashing our legs.

'Get in there,' Ricky hollered, goosebumps covering his body. 'It's marvellous.'

He made a dash for me, but I jumped behind Dinger, who dodged left and right to prevent a dripping Ricky from catching me. Ricky gave up, turned, spotted Alison heading up the beach, her arms wrapped tightly around her shivering body, and made a dash for her instead. He grabbed her round the waist and manhandled her back to the water as she shrieked with delight.

'We should get a fire lit,' I said, walking away from the sea. 'Those two idiots will need a bit of heat. Oh, what were you going to say about Pamela yesterday?'

'She wants you to call her.'

'Is something wrong?'

'Just call her. Sooner rather than later.'

'Ok.' Worry niggled at my stomach. 'I don't have my phone. I haven't turned it on since we got here.'

He pulled his phone out of his hip pocket and unlocked it. 'Use mine. I'll start the fire.'

I found her number and walked towards the dunes as it started ringing.

'Donald,' she answered. 'You've just caught me. I'm walking into a shoot in, like, two minutes.'

I smiled. It was lovely to hear her familiar English twang. 'It's not Donald,' I said.

'Jo-D!' she shrieked. 'How the hell are you? He found you then?'

'Yes. He's here. I'm fine.'

'Oh, my god. I mean, what the fuck? Like, seriously, what the fuck?!'

'It's a bit of a drama.'

'A bit of a drama? I haven't seen drama like this since Cheryl divorced Ashley. I take it Ricky's with you?'

'Yes.' I noted her disapproving tone.

'I saw the photos you stuck up in the flat. Nice move.'

'Tasteful, I thought.'

'Indeed. Now, look, I've only got a minute. Do you have a plan?'

'No,' I said. 'No plan. How long have we got?'

'Who knows? Days? Maybe less.'

'Seriously?'

'You guys missed Lee's funeral.'

'Fuck.' It hadn't crossed my mind. I was a terrible person. 'Fuck. How was it?'

'It was a funeral. How do you think it was? But Ricky was missed. Everyone was watching for Ricky – like, everyone. But that's not your problem. The Chronicle is your problem.'

I ran a hand through my hair. 'Oh, my column.'

'Yeah, so they're running with the fact Jo-D's disappeared, too. I take it you haven't seen any press?'

'Avoiding it.'

'So, you're the story. Our missing columnist. They're building it up daily. Everyone's on it. All the hacks. Word is it's big money. Like, big money.'

'Fuck.'

'Right? So you need a plan. They're coming. Are you guys on or off?'

'Off.'

'And yet there you are together on some idyllic Scottish island.'

'I know,' I said, sitting down on a tuft of marram grass. 'It looks bad.'

'It's not great. But you've still got a card to play, if you're quick.'

'So what do I do?'

'Find a way to make Ricky front and centre. Make it about him, not the two of you. Push him out front. You stay down. The story's so big right now you could have any interviewer you want. Like, anyone. Think quick and let me know if you need help with contacts. I've got to go.'

'Ok.'

'Jo?'

'Yes.'

'Remember, it's a game. It's all a game, and it's your move.'

'Got it.'

'Love ya, babes.'

'Love you too,' I said as she rang off.

I sat for a moment, my brain working overtime. How to make it about Ricky? Below me on the beach, Ricky and Alison had finally made it out of the water. She was steadying herself on Ricky's shoulder as she tried to pull on her jeans. I could hear her giggles rising in the breeze and ground my teeth. Mhairi and Bob were back with armfuls of driftwood, and it looked like Dinger had the fire going. I started back down the dune to join them.

CHAPTER 41

'What were you up to?' Ricky asked, popping his head out through his t-shirt.

I handed Dinger his phone and accepted the beer can in return. 'Talking to Pamela,' I replied. 'In London.'

Ricky sat down abruptly on the sand. 'What news?'

I took a deep breath. 'Time's up. She reckons days, at the most.'

'Shit,' he said.

'Kind of inevitable,' Mhairi said, shaking a rug out onto the sand to sit on. 'It's all anyone's talking about.'

Bob snorted, shaking his head. 'The big disappearance.' He snapped a piece of driftwood over his knee.

'Give me your phone,' Ricky said to Dinger.

'That won't help,' I answered. 'Don't give him your phone.'

'I just want to look,' Ricky said as Dinger handed over his phone.

'He has to know sometime,' Mhairi said, cracking open her own beer.

Ricky was already online, scrolling, his jaw jutting left

and right as he chewed his cheeks, bare toes pulling at the sand.

I snatched the phone off him and gave it back to Dinger.

Ricky looked up at me, wide-eyed. 'What are we going to do?'

'We're going to face it head on,' I said confidently. 'And if we're quick and smart, we can do it on our terms.'

'How?'

'With this amount of attention, anyone will give you an interview. You're huge just now. You can choose.'

He regarded me as my words sunk in. 'Radio 1?' he asked.

'If you want.'

'Jools Holland?'

I screwed up my face. 'You might have to build back up to that one.'

'Brooke Baxter?'

'The great B.B.?' I said. 'She might do it.'

'OMG,' Mhairi laughed. 'I had such a girl crush on her when I was growing up.'

'Never missed her breakfast show for years,' Alison agreed.

'But you can't do a joint interview,' Mhairi continued. 'She'll tear you apart.'

'Yeah,' Alison said, unpacking the bread rolls and sausages, and not looking at me. 'Let Ricky do it. He's the star, after all.'

'No,' Ricky said. 'She'll want Jo too. Or she'll just go on and on about her if she's not there.'

I put my hands on my hips. 'Well, I don't want to talk

about it in public. Isn't it enough that those photos are everywhere?'

'This is your bloody idea.' Ricky raised his voice. '*I* don't want to do an interview.'

'Stop it,' Mhairi said, reaching across to pull me down beside her.

'Well.' Bob poked a log into the fire. 'Whatever you do, you can't stay here. The island will get over-run when the press find you.'

'He's right,' Alison chipped in with surprising insight. 'There's only so much good will for you, Joanne, and you're using it up fast.'

I glared at her across the flickering flames. She had shuffled right up close to Ricky as she held her speared sausage into the red heat.

'We could go to Glasgow,' Ricky said. 'Face it from there?'

'To the flat?' I asked.

'Flat's rented out,' Bob said.

'To my parents, then,' Ricky suggested.

'God no,' I replied. 'They're too old for that. The press'll camp out on their doorstep.'

'London?'

'With what money?' I said hopelessly.

'Right,' Mhairi said, handing me a raw sausage on a wooden skewer. 'That's enough. There's no good solution right now, so can we just eat our picnic, drink some beer and try and have a nice day out, please?'

I speared my sausage and held it into the fire with the others. The six sausages bobbed and turned sadly on their separate spikes as we sat on in silence.

'Oh, for god's sake,' Mhairi said. 'Alison, play us a tune or something.'

Alison didn't need to be asked twice. She handed Ricky her skewer and pulled out her fiddle, flying straight into a jig. Dinger propped his sausage up on a log and lifted two bits of wood to beat a rhythm out on the rock beside him. Ricky bounced up to grab his guitar, leaving me manning three sausages. And, just like that, the afternoon slipped back into merriment. As if music could fix everything.

Could music fix everything? I wondered, balancing the three skewers in one hand, swigging beer with the other. I let the sounds fill my head, the fire fill my gaze and the beer numb my worries. It seemed like it could as Alison and Ricky took turns to play as we ate our food.

At one point, I saw Ricky pull out his old notebook from his back pocket, jotting down a lyric, asking Bob for a chord idea. Was he writing again? The notebook must've been in one of his boxes. I hadn't seen him with it for months.

'Sing us something, Ricky,' Alison said through a mouthful of roll.

Ricky laughed happily. 'Let Jo sing,' he said.

Mhairi snorted some beer. 'Jo can't sing.'

'Want a bet,' Ricky replied. 'She was singing the other night in the pub.'

'No way,' Mhairi said in disbelief.

I shook my head, smiling. 'I'm not singing!'

'You should've heard her,' Ricky continued. 'It was unbelievably good. She's got an unbelievable voice.'

'Well,' Dinger said. 'She did win the Mod in 2006.'

'How did you know that?' I asked, incredulous.

300

He shrugged, grinning sheepishly at me.

'Only the juniors,' Alison retorted grumpily.

'No, Ricky,' I said. 'You sing.'

He was happily plucking strings on his old guitar. 'What'll I sing? Something Scottish. I'm loving all this traditional stuff.'

'Caledonia,' Bob said.

'Oh my god,' I cried. 'No! Anything but that.'

'Why?' Mhairi laughed. 'It's a great song.'

'It's so cheesy,' I moaned.

'I don't know it anyway,' Ricky said.

'You do,' Bob replied, reaching across the fire for the guitar. He started finger-picking the chords of the tune, and Ricky nodded in recognition. 'Pull up the lyrics on your phone,' he said to Alison, who happily obliged, handing the phone to Ricky.

'Slower, Bob.'

Bob instantly slowed his plucking and Ricky sang, slipping intentionally out of his usual American accent into broad Glaswegian.

Mhairi whistled loudly in appreciation and Ricky grinned as he sang, eyes on the phone screen. Alison picked up her violin and drew long notes in accompaniment as Ricky slid into the chorus, not letting up on his Glaswegian.

As he sang, he lifted his eyes to meet mine through the smoke. And I couldn't help myself. I kept my eyes locked with his, my throat constricting, my eyes dampening as he sang the sentimental words.

I wrenched my gaze away and down to the fire, blinking back tears. I hated this song. Why the fuck was I crying?

He sang on through the second verse, and Mhairi took hold of my hand. I looked up at her and she was crying, too. We smiled at each other – happy and sad at the same time.

'I've missed you,' I mouthed.

She nodded in reply.

As the second chorus ended, Ricky held the phone out.

'Jo, sing the last verse,' he said, taking a swig of beer.

I ignored the phone. I knew the lyrics. Instead, I looked at Bob and pointed up with a finger. 'Key change, please.'

'Yes, ma'am,' he replied, keeping time with the simple tune, rising through the octaves.

I began to sing, and beside me, Mhairi gasped and clutched her chest in mock shock.

'I told you.' Ricky laughed from across the fire. 'I fucking told you she could sing.' He pointed his beer bottle at me, his eyes sparkling in the light.

I rose to my feet, higher than the flames of the fire, and slipped into Gaelic, easily and inaccurately translating as I sang the rest of the verse. Only Alison knew the words I was singing, and she didn't care if I got them wrong. Alison was too busy inching closer to Ricky on the sand. I slipped back into English for the final chorus and everyone sang along.

'That was epic.' Mhairi laughed as the song ended.

'We should do that tomorrow night,' Ricky said, excited. 'In the pub.'

'You want to sing in the pub?' I asked, surprised.

'Sure.' He grinned. 'Why not?'

Because you haven't sung for weeks, I thought. Because I worried you would never sing again. 'Well, I'm not singing 'Caledonia' in the fucking pub,' I said instead. 'I'd rather stand on the bar naked.'

'Don't be a snob,' Alison said, resting a hand on Ricky's knee.

Ricky reached for his guitar and launched straight into the chords of 'Times Like These.'

'Oh, I know this one too,' Alison said, lifting her fiddle back to her neck, easily teasing out the melody.

I stood where I was, watching the scene, thinking, thinking, an idea darting about my head like a firefly.

'Did you see the recording of them playing that at Reading?' Dinger asked halfway through the song, kicking another log onto the fire.

Ricky laughed, letting the notes fall away. 'We were there!'

'Fuck off,' Mhairi said.

'Of course you were,' Dinger scoffed.

'Did you meet Dave Grohl?' Mhairi was all high-pitched.

Ricky grinned at me. 'Did we meet Dave Grohl, Jo?'

'Don't you dare,' I said, throwing him a look.

He grinned up at me. 'Ah, Reading,' he said.

'What the fuck happened at Reading?' Mhairi asked.

'You'll never know,' I snapped.

'We'll find out in the end,' Bob said, swigging from his can.

'Play one of your songs, Ricky,' Alison said, setting her violin back down in its case. 'Play 'My Conscience'. I love that one.'

'No,' Ricky replied abruptly.

'Let's have a go at that new one we were talking about,' Bob said, understanding Ricky's tone and kneeling to reach for the guitar again. 'What've we got so far?'

Ricky flicked through his notebook and hummed the start of an unfamiliar tune.

Bob plucked at the strings. 'What key?'

'Just play it in G. Dinger, can you hear anything in this?'

Dinger moved round to Ricky's guitar case, shutting it over and sitting cross-legged behind it. He began beating out an echoey rhythm with his hands in time with Ricky's humming.

'Yes,' Ricky said. '*Fleeing down the electric road, in my dreams at night I'm screaming,*' he sang. '*The verge is high when the wheels explode. It's the ease of down I'm feeling.*'

'Listen,' I said suddenly, interrupting. 'I've got an idea.'

They stopped playing. I hesitated, mind still spinning. 'What?' Ricky asked.

'You play a gig in the pub,' I began. 'And it goes online, right?'

'And the entire world descends on Barinner,' Alison replied, raising a derogatory eyebrow. 'Good plan.'

'No, listen,' I continued. 'You don't disclose the location. And the next day you play another gig, in another pub, in another place and it goes online too. Right?'

Ricky ran a hand through his hair. His knee began to jiggle.

'And the next day, another pub, another location.'

'A mystery tour,' Mhairi said, catching up.

'Yeah,' I said, pointing at her. 'Like a game. They're chasing you, right? So why not run? Let them chase you. All round Scotland.'

'But where are these pubs?' Ricky asked. 'How the fuck do we arrange daily gigs in pubs we don't know?'

'*We* know the pubs.' Alison shifted onto her knees as she got it.

I smiled at her. 'We know *all* the pubs.'

'That's what we used to do all the time,' she continued, excitement in her voice. 'We just drove round Scotland for our holidays, playing and singing in pubs for lodgings. And beer money for Bill and Dad.'

'No interview. No explaining. Just the music, front and centre,' I said, eagerly, convincing myself as I talked. 'Ricky Steele, front and centre.'

Ricky stared at me and through me, thinking. 'What would I play? I can't play Vermillion songs.'

'Covers?' Dinger said.

'We'll write some songs,' Bob said, lifting the guitar. 'We're writing songs.'

'Covers and new songs,' Dinger suggested.

'We haven't got time.' Ricky shook his head.

'Well, write fast,' Mhairi said.

'But what if no one wants to listen?' he argued. 'The album was shite. I'm a joke now.'

'No,' came a chorus of voices. 'Not true.'

'A temporary hiccup,' I said firmly. 'It'll be all forgotten if you make a bigger story.'

'And it's Easter next week,' Alison chipped in. 'Everywhere will be jumping.'

Ricky continued to gaze through me, thinking. I held my breath. 'You'll all have to come too,' he said, turning to Bob and Dinger.

'No can do,' Dinger said. 'I'll lose my placement. I'm pushing it as it is.'

Bob was shaking his head. 'Sorry mate. I need this job. I phoned in sick to be here.'

Ricky turned to me. 'So, that's that,' he said, shrugging. 'I know you can sing, Jo. But I'll need some sort of band.'

'I'm not coming.'

'What? Of course you are.'

'No,' I said. 'This is the end of the line for me. This would be your plan. Not mine.'

He blinked, silenced by this news.

'I'll come,' Alison said.

'Absolutely not,' I replied.

'She *can* play,' Ricky said.

Alison stood to face me across the fire. 'I can play.'

'You've got college.'

'I'll catch up.'

'You're too young for this. You have no idea.'

'I'm nearly twenty. And what about Bill? Bill could come too.'

'Yes!' Ricky said. 'Bill would work. He can play guitar and that drum thing.'

'Bodhran,' Alison answered. 'Bill will come, for sure. If Dad lets him off work. And he's got a van.'

'I could cover work for a few weeks,' I said, thinking if Bill was there, Alison *should* be ok.

'You're going to stay here?' Ricky asked.

'I don't know what I'm going to do. And it doesn't really matter. Just let's think. What else?'

'Well,' Mhairi said, 'it needs to get big straightaway. What do we do? Just film it on the phone and post it?'

'Not on *your* phone,' Bob said. 'You've only got six followers.'

'Followers?' Dinger asked.

'On Instagram.'

'Oh, I don't have that.'

'I have Instagram,' Alison said.

'No,' I said. 'They'll trace it back. We could send the footage to someone?'

'Someone big,' Ricky said.

'Or someone who can make it big.'

'Someone we can trust.'

I screwed up my face. 'Or someone who will want this more than you do?'

'And that we can trust.'

I held my hands together in a prayer pose. 'Or that can make this trend globally immediately.'

Ricky sighed. 'Who? You obviously have someone in mind.'

'You won't like it.'

'Who?'

'But it will work.'

'Who?'

'Dan.'

'Who's Dan?'

'From Italy. The paparazzi guy.'

'Absolutely fucking no way.'

'No, he's alright. He always gives me a heads-up on stories.'

'He took those bloody photos!' Ricky shouted. 'He's the reason we're here.'

'I know,' I said. 'And he sent me those photos before they came out, which was nice.'

'Nice!'

'But he can make this work better than anyone else we know. Keep your friends close, remember?'

'And your enemies closer.' Ricky shook his head slowly.

'It would work, Ricky. You could send him footage every night. He'll definitely do it. There'll be money in it.'

Ricky snorted with derision, but he didn't come back with more complaints. He ran a hand through his hair again, thinking.

'I could wear a kilt,' he said at last. 'Make it all kind of Scottishy.'

'You could,' I replied, not at all sure.

He turned to Alison. 'I want to do 'Caledonia'.'

'We can do that.'

'And that new song, Bob. Do you think it's got something?'

'For sure. Couple of hours. We'll have it.'

'I can write more on the road. But covers. We'll need a few covers. What about 'Creep'?'

'Radiohead?' Alison asked.

'No!' Ricky laughed. 'Stone Temple Pilots. I definitely fucking belong here.'

'Better with 'Plush',' Bob said, strumming a tune. 'You can do it acoustic easy.'

'I don't know them,' Alison said. 'What about 'Even Flow'?'

'You know Pearl Jam?'

'Of course I know Pearl Jam.'

'Ha!' Ricky laughed again, excitement oozing from him. 'My kind of girl.'

Alison beamed with delight. Mhairi caught my eye and raised her eyebrows.

'And 'Green Day'?' Ricky carried on.

Alison nodded.

'What about 'Basket Case'?'

'Better with 'Good Riddance',' she replied.

'Yes!' Ricky said, grabbing the guitar off Bob. 'Let's try it. Can you sing?'

'A bit.' She grinned. 'I can keep a tune.'

As they started jamming, Dinger rapping out the rhythm, Bob picking at Alison's violin, I wondered if this mystery tour would work. If this was the solution, after all. If it did work, it could set Ricky back on track again. And if it didn't? Well, maybe it was indeed time for him to face that alone. Maybe, finally, it was time for me to stop.

Mhairi picked up two cans of beer and joined me. 'They'll be here a while,' she said, smiling. 'Let's stroll.'

CHAPTER 42

We set off down the beach at a leisurely pace.

'I think Alison may be developing a bit of a crush,' Mhairi said when we were out of earshot.

'Yes. I'd noticed. I'll have a word.'

We walked on, our bare feet on the cool sand. Out on the flat horizon of sea and sky, a bank of clouds was gathering.

'Weather's going to break.'

'Well, it was a bit too good to be true.' Mhairi snapped her can open. 'Why is beer so good outside?'

'I know, right?'

We both took a swig.

'Think it'll work?' Mhairi asked.

I shrugged. 'Maybe?'

'And you're staying here?'

'Maybe. For a while. I can work from here. I've been doing some freelance stuff for Really True.'

'Good for you,' she said.

'How's the teaching going?'

'Hate it.' She shook her head. 'But, bills to pay.'

We walked on in silence. The tide was going out. The

lapping waves dragging all the little stones and shells down towards the water, propping them up on top of small sand ridges.

'I'm so glad you came,' I said.

'I'm glad too,' she replied. 'I was so mad at you for so long. And then when Dinger phoned, it turned out I hadn't been mad for ages. I just missed you.'

'Oh my god, I missed you too,' I said, linking her arm. 'So much.'

'It's not going to be easy.'

'What?'

'Letting him go.'

I took a deep breath. 'I know. But he needs to go. I need him far away from me.'

'True that.'

'It's like, when he's close, he takes up my whole view. I can't see past him.' I sighed. 'You know, it's only been a year? We've only been going out a year. It seems like twenty.'

'You loved him longer than that though, didn't you?'

'I tried so hard to make it work.'

'You shouldn't have to try,' Mhairi said, squeezing my arm. 'Maybe that's the trouble.'

I closed my eyes to feel the breeze on my face, breathing in the salty air. 'What's your trick?' I asked.

'My trick?'

'You and Bob. You make it look so easy. What's your trick?'

Mhairi smiled. 'No trick. I don't know. We don't try, I guess. We just are.'

'Oh, very Yoda.'

'No, I mean it.' She laughed. 'We don't try. We just don't want anything else. We're just…' She searched for the word. 'Us. Together. I don't know.'

'It was never like that with Ricky,' I said, my eyes filling up with tears again.

'It was.' Mhairi patted my arm and tutted. 'You guys were good. You get him. You totally get him.'

I stopped walking again. 'But did he ever get me?' I sobbed. 'Who gets me? Who the fuck has ever got me?'

Mhairi pulled me into a hug. 'Maybe Dinger gets you.'

I pulled away, wiping my eyes and sniffing. 'Maybe. God, I am drowning in self-pity just now.'

'Well, you're allowed,' she said. 'For a while, anyway. Then you can snap the fuck out of it.'

I burst out laughing. 'He asked me out earlier.'

'Dinger? Shut up! Did he now?'

'He did.'

'Well, well. I didn't know he had it in him.'

I picked Dinger out in the group. He had his back to us. His shoulders were broader than Ricky's now. 'He's changed,' I said.

'Yeah, hasn't he? He hit the gym when you guys left.'

I cast my eyes between Ricky and Dinger.

'He took it hardest, I think,' Mhairi continued. 'Bob and I had each other, but Dinger… Well, Ricky just never looked back.'

'And they were so close,' I said. 'I wish we could go back in time.'

'No, you don't. It was meant to be. Ricky was never going to settle for small time.' We let that sit between us for a moment. 'So, what did you say?'

'To what?' I asked.

'To Dinger asking you out?'

I shrugged, smiling.

'Ha!' She laughed. 'He'll be beside himself. He's fancied you forever.'

The others were getting to their feet, gathering cans and folding rugs. Ricky waved over at us.

'Better get back,' I said. 'There's a gig to organise.'

*

We packed up, kicking sand over the fire, and set off for home with the crate full of rubbish and rugs. I walked ahead with Dinger, Bob and Mhairi, reminiscing about the Union, laughing at half-forgotten nights out. Once we were past the dunes, I slowed to wait for Ricky and Alison. They were chatting happily. I couldn't hear what about. I needed to sort this.

'I need to talk to you,' I said to Ricky when they were in earshot. 'Alison, can you give us a minute?'

She shrugged and walked on ahead.

'Sounds ominous,' Ricky said. 'Sup?'

'Follow me.' I branched off the path onto a sheep track. 'Shortcut.'

I walked ahead up the track, which wasn't one track but a maze of tracks branching off in every direction. But these hills were etched in my memory from childhood. In the summer, when the bracken was shoulder height, I could still find my way without trouble.

Ricky followed close behind me. At the crest of the first hill, I paused, watching the others walk on along the path. I felt tipsy from the beer, enlivened by the fresh air. Ricky stopped beside me.

'You stink of smoke from the fire,' I said.

'Better than fish.' He grinned drunkenly at me, then laughed. 'Look at you in your baggy jeans and your messy hair. That's the Jo I remember.'

'I feel like myself again,' I replied, pulling out my scrunchy and shaking my hair loose. 'Not that Jo-D creation. So, anyway,' I turned to face him.

'What's up?'

'Alison.'

Ricky smirked. 'What about her?'

'She's head over heels, Ricky.'

'I'd noticed.'

'You've got to promise me not to go there. She's only nineteen.'

'Nearly twenty, as she keeps reminding me.'

'And she's my sister. Ricky, promise you won't touch her.'

'You're the only Duncan sister I want,' he said. 'Why don't you just come with me?'

'Ricky, don't.' I turned away to look at the sea. I could feel his gaze on me.

'You're the only thing that's been right in my whole life,' he said.

'That's not true.'

He reached for my chin, pulling my face back round towards him. 'I love you, Jo.'

'I know you do.'

He leaned in towards me and I pulled back, pushing his hand away. 'But I fucked up,' he said, nodding.

I fixed my eyes on the mole below his left eye. 'It is what it is, Ricky. It's who you are.'

'I can change.'

'No, you can't. Not really. And that's ok.'

'I'm so sorry, Jo.'

'Stop it. I know you are.'

'I'm more sorry about what I did to you than any of it.'

I nodded, still staring at the mole. 'I know you love me,' I said, as steadily as I could. 'But what's more important, what's bigger than that, is your love of music, Ricky. It's your purpose. I am not your purpose.' My eyes felt wet again. I blinked over and over, watching the mole on his cheek, wondering what my purpose was if it wasn't Ricky.

'We had some good times,' Ricky said quietly.

'We did.' My eyes slid up to meet his. They were glistening in the low sun. Was he crying too?

I reached out and held his bare arm to comfort him, meaning it kindly, but the feel of his skin, the clear shape of his muscle flexing under my touch was like a magnetic force. I tightened my grip, sliding my hand up the length of his arm, unable to stop myself, my lips parting for air.

And then his lips were on mine, our tongues meeting, eyes still open, staring at each other. We pulled urgently at each other's jeans and separated briefly to frantically open our own buttons, which would surely be quicker, surely giving less time for thought. And then Ricky was tugging my jeans down, scraping the zip on my thigh, and I tumbled to the ground. His mouth found mine again as I wriggled his jeans over his narrow hips. On one elbow, he tried to get mine past my knees. I arched to help him, but they were twisted, caught in a tangle of fabric. My searching hands found him, and he groaned as I slid my hand firmly down his length.

'Now,' I said, into his open mouth, and he pulled away, deftly flipping me over onto my belly. An arm swept under my waist, hauling me up and back as I grabbed bunches of heather for support. My knees were tethered tight by my jeans, but he was rock hard and as he pushed into me, we both cried out with relief.

I fell forward with the force, Ricky heavy on top of me. I turned my head so his face was next to mine, breathing the same air as he ground into me. His hands found mine. Our fingers interlacing on the heather, squeezing with every thrust.

'Now,' I said again, and we came together in a wave of warmth and release.

We lay still like that, breathing together, chests rising and falling in unison. Not far away I could hear sheep bleating. Further, a gull calling. I squeezed my pelvic floor muscles just to feel him again, and he chuckled against my neck.

'Sleep with me tonight,' he said.

'This doesn't change anything.'

'I know. But if this is my last night, I want you near.'

He let go of one of my hands and found the bottom of my t-shirt, passing under and up. He pushed his hand under my bra to cup my breast, teasing my nipple with his thumb. I squeezed down on him again and felt him stir.

'Do you remember the first time we kissed?' I asked. 'In The Shrine after your Winston's gig?'

'Of course I do,' he said, his breath warm on my cheek. 'That was the hottest thing ever. It was like I'd never seen you before.'

I thought of that night. Of how determined I'd been. It felt like I'd spent the last year in a state of determination. A wave of exhaustion swept through me. 'We need to get back,' I said, wriggling him out of me. 'Everyone will know what we've been up to.'

He pulled himself up onto his knees to button his jeans. 'No, they won't.'

'Mhairi will know,' I said, rolling onto my back to pull mine up. 'She'll take one look at me and know. And you've got work to do if you're going to be ready for tomorrow night.'

'God, yes.' He bounced to his feet and stretched out a hand to haul me up. 'I've got that song to finish. I need to find Bill.'

'So it's on?' I asked, pulling my bra back into place. 'You're going for it?'

Ricky blew out a long lungful of air, his face falling into grim resolve. 'It's on,' he said. 'Let's do it.'

CHAPTER 43

The next night, the pub was packed. Like, totally heaving. There was barely room to move, and I'd resorted to clambering over the bar when the glasses needed collecting rather than push my way through the crowd. It was sweaty hot, the door and windows shut tight against the wind outside. The weather had broken as expected and a storm was pushing in from the west, but inside, with all these bodies, it was boiling. I'd stripped to my old yellow vest top, aware of the strap of my red bra that kept sliding off my shoulder. I jumped down beside Mhairi and slid the full tray along the bar towards her before settling the strap back in position.

'Tighten that for me,' I hollered above the din and she dried her hands, then swiftly slid the catch further up the bra strap. 'Thanks for this, for helping.'

She smiled as she reached for the dirty glasses. 'I always fancied being a barmaid,' she shouted back. 'I used to envy you that.'

I laughed and looked down the room to check on Ricky again. A tiny space had been cleared by the unlit fire. Bill was settling himself into position on a low stool to Ricky's left and Alison was perched to Ricky's right, fiddle on lap, calmly watching Ricky tinker with the tuning of Bill's ancient acoustic guitar. He looked nervous. His knee was battering against the edge of the guitar as it bounced. Alison reached a hand out to steady it.

'Did you talk to Ricky?' Mhairi asked, seeing what I was seeing.

'Yes,' I replied, sighing. 'For what it's worth.'

Aunt Mary handed me two straight vodkas and an encouraging look as she squeezed past us to serve further down.

'But I'm thinking it might be inevitable. I mean, look at them,' I said, as Mhairi dried her hands. 'I'm practically making it happen, sending them off like this.' I handed her her drink. 'Maybe I should go instead.'

'No,' Mhairi cried. 'No. You stay. He goes.'

I blew air into my cheeks.

'You knew it wouldn't be easy. But you've got to let go. Push him away,' she said. 'Now, drink your fucking vodka.'

I downed it in one, resisted the urge to refill it and looked across the room instead to check on Caroline.

I had been unamused when Ricky agreed to let her do the filming on the tour. I didn't think she could be trusted, but she was super keen to be involved. She'd begged to go with them and they did need someone to film. And maybe, just maybe, she'd distract Ricky from Alison.

Caroline was in position behind a tripod, holding the phone steady on top of a low table by the window. Her face was all concentration as she wiped the lens on the front of the phone with the sleeve of her shirt, thriving on being in

319

the centre of the drama for once instead of flitting around the edges. Bob, Dinger and my dad were standing in an arc to prevent the table from being jostled. Their beer needed topping up, I noticed.

Did Ricky have a drink? I turned to look. He did. There was a pint sitting behind him on the mantlepiece. I took a deep breath. They could start anytime, really. There'd be no dramatic entrance. There was no running on stage like he usually did.

As I watched, he looked over at me, the weight of what was happening sitting heavy between us. Moments passed as I held his gaze. Moments that held the memory of last night, the memory of all that we'd been.

'Oh my god!' Mhairi cried from her place beside me. 'You had sex with him again.'

'What? Shush,' I said frantically.

'Are you denying it?'

I pulled my eyes away from Ricky to Mhairi.

'Jo!' She slapped my bare arm. 'Why?'

I shrugged. 'I was horny.'

'Oh, for fuck's sake, I give up,' she said, downing her vodka. 'I hope you used a fucking condom.'

I looked back at Ricky and saw him nod to Bill, who lifted the bodhran onto his knee. Ricky raised his hand into the air and dropped his head. From the front to the back, the room fell silent. A few throats were cleared, a stool scraped the stone floor, a glass clinked. And then he started clicking his fingers: once, twice, three times, four times… and Bill came in with the drum, beating dum-dee, dum-dum, dee-dee in time. Alison lifted the violin and began drawing out the melody to 'Good Riddance'.

A single whoop from one of the boat yard boys as Ricky settled his fingers onto the strings. And then he was playing too, thrumming the chords through four bars. And then he sang. Instantly, the back of my neck prickled and I let out a long, slow breath. Mhairi flung an arm round my shoulder, grinning. It sounded good. It sounded fantastic. This might just work.

Straight through the two verses, letting Alison play the guitar solo on her violin, raising back the energy to the final chorus, then a hard stop, Bill alone on the bodhran as Ricky looked directly at the bar and said, 'I hope you had the time of your life.'

The pub exploded in stamping feet and cheering, but Bill didn't let up, changing the beat to a steady one-two. Alison lay her fiddle down and took the guitar from Ricky, beating the same beat on its body with the palms of her hands.

Ricky stood up, placing one foot on his stool so the kilt swayed about his knees, tapping his heel in time. Without a microphone, his hands were free, and he held them out as he began singing loudly in broad Glaswegian.

'*Hark when the night is falling. Hear, hear the pipes are calling.*'

That would be the money shot. That would be the picture the press pulled from this gig. Ricky knew that, too. Defiant. Still standing. Unbeaten. The crowd erupted in stamping feet.

And on he sang through the first verse and chorus of the familiar Scottish pub song. He smiled as he let the room finish the last lines, settling himself back down with his guitar before playing the first bars of the new song.

Alison and Bill sat quietly watching him as he waited for the room to still.

'This is for Lee,' Ricky said, not lifting his eyes from the guitar. 'I'll miss you, man.'

I allowed myself a glance at Caroline, just to be sure she was paying attention, recording everything. Dinger was watching me and I sent him a grin, blushing. He did not blush, nor look away. He just watched me steadily. Since when did I blush and he didn't? I wondered.

Eyes back to Ricky. He was singing hard, eyes closed, putting his life, his future, into this performance. Surely this would work. As the song finished, the pub cheered and stamped.

Alison picked up her fiddle for 'Even Flow'. But when she started playing, it wasn't 'Even Flow'. They must've changed their minds. I'd been busy all day, flying round the island, rounding up the locals, packing Ricky and Alison's bags.

Alison was pulling long notes with her bow. I listened in to catch the tune. What were they playing? Ricky started strumming the chords, Bill beating gently in time on the bodhran. The crowd noise fell to silence as Ricky started singing the lyrics to 'Wild Horses'. His voice was electrifying. It cut through the air. I held my breath, hands raised involuntarily to cover my mouth. Ricky raised his eyes to meet mine as he sang The Stones' lyrics.

He was singing this song to me. He'd changed to this song on purpose. This wasn't the plan. The plan was Ricky and his music. I was meant to be left out of it. He was going to blow his chances.

I was aware of people turning to me, of phones pointing in my direction. Caroline wasn't the only one filming. I knew Dinger would be looking at me, too. But I daren't look. I dropped my hands instead. Pulling myself straight. Eyes on Ricky's. Unsure what was happening. Why was he doing this? I listened to each word he sang, letting him work slowly through them all as Alison teased out the plaintive melody.

By the third verse, I knew. He thought I was more important – more important than this gig. This was his apology. This was his very public apology. And tears were streaming down my face. I let them fall, blinking to clear my eyes, frozen to the spot. Mhairi slid her hand into mine, but I didn't flinch. I had to hear this out. I had to bear this out to the end.

If there was clapping at the end of the song, I didn't notice. I headed straight out the back of the bar into the passageway to the cellar, followed by Mhairi.

'You ok?'

'What was that?' I wailed. 'Why would he do that?'

Mhairi wrapped her arms round me, holding me firm, shushing me until I calmed down. I could hear Ricky singing 'Caledonia', the planned last song. At least they were back to the plan now.

I pulled away, wiping my eyes with the heel of my hand.

'Go wash your face,' Mhairi said gently. 'It's nearly done. And then I was thinking you should come stay in Glasgow with us for a bit.'

'Thank you,' I sniffed. 'But I've got to cover for Bill. I've promised Dad. And it's Easter. The tourists.'

'Well, as soon as,' she said.

I washed my face. I could hear Alison singing the last

verse in Gaelic. The whole pub was singing along as the guitar faded to a stop.

'It's nearly done,' I said to myself in the foggy mirror.

I came back behind the bar. People were lining up, holding their empties, waiting to get served. Shouts of 'more' were erupting from different corners. Ricky was shaking his head, smiling, shaking Bill's hand, accepting a hug from Alison, shaking Mr Anderson's hand, being clapped on the back by others. Caroline was lifting the phone off the tripod.

'I need to…' I said to Mhairi, who was pouring a pint.

'Go, go,' Aunt Mary shouted from the till. 'We've got this.'

I climbed over the bar and shouldered my way through the bodies. Dinger already had the phone, as planned. He'd downloaded a file sharing app earlier and was busy preparing to send it to Dan.

'Wait,' I bellowed, reaching Dinger at the same time as Ricky.

'Aw, mate,' Bob said, clapping him on the back. 'Awesome.'

'Do you want to see it first?' Dinger asked.

'I'm not doing it again!' Ricky laughed, placing a hand on the small of my back. 'Send it.'

I moved out of his reach. 'No, wait,' I said. 'Cut the Stones first. Cut 'Wild Horses'.'

'What?' Ricky asked. 'No. I want that left in.'

'No,' I said, risking a glance at him. 'It was too…'

'Too what?'

'Private?' Dinger answered for me, still holding the phone in front of him, ready to send.

'Personal,' I said. 'Isn't it enough the whole Island saw it?'

Ricky looked at me, incredulous. 'That was me apologising to you, Jo.'

'I know.' I was embarrassed everyone could hear this.

'I want everyone to see that. I want the whole world to see that. That's how much this means to me.'

'It would be a nightmare to edit,' Bob mumbled.

'Let's get a drink while we have a think,' Caroline said, eyes sparkling with delight.

'Argh!' I groaned in frustration, grabbing Ricky's t-shirt. 'Outside. Now.' I started shoving my way to the door. 'And do not send that,' I shouted back at Dinger.

CHAPTER 44

I had to lean my full weight against the pub door to open it. The wind was blasting in from the southwest as the storm bore down on Barinner. I was hot from the heat of the pub and the wind was strangely warm against my bare skin. Ricky followed me out, and the door slammed shut behind us. I marched across the road to the seawall. Below me, the sea boiled and crashed against the stone.

I turned to face him, the wind whipping my hair in front of my face.

'Did you not like it?' he asked.

'Of course I liked it,' I said, raising my voice above the weather. 'But why would you do that? I know you're sorry. But you're risking everything.'

'Did you listen?' he asked, turning a shoulder against the battering wind. 'Did you hear what I sang?'

'Yes, Ricky. But...'

He took hold of my arms. 'I need you, Jo,' he said, steadying us both as another gust of wind rocked us. 'Come with me. This is us. Together forever. Remember?'

I placed a hand on his chest to stop him from getting any nearer. 'I gave you last night.'

'I want forever.'

I screwed my eyes shut against it all. 'Stop it.'

'I love you,' he said.

'Stop it,' I screamed, unaware that Alison had come outside too.

'What's going on?' she shouted, reaching us. 'Why are you crying, Jo?'

'Just give us a minute, Alison,' Ricky said.

And then Dinger appeared at the door of the pub.

'Will I send it?' he shouted.

'No,' I bellowed back.

'Yes,' Ricky countered. 'Send it now.'

Dinger hesitated, looking at me.

'Dinger,' Ricky screamed. 'I'm not fucking joking. Send it now.'

And Dinger ducked back into the pub.

'Argh!' I cried, pushing Ricky away, anger bubbling up inside me.

'What the hell, Jo?' Alison hollered. 'Do not fuck this up for me.'

I laughed like a maniac. 'This isn't about you, Alison. Go away!'

'It's not about you either,' she shouted back. 'This has nothing to do with you anymore.'

I stepped towards her in a white-hot rage. 'Jesus Christ!'

A wave crashed over the sea wall, spraying us with icy water.

'We should go in,' Ricky said.

'You have no idea what it's like for me,' Alison continued. 'Being stuck up here with nothing when you have everything.'

'What are you talking about?' I yelled.

'You!' She stabbed me in the chest with her finger. 'You with your perfect life and your perfect boyfriend. I'm the talented one. It's my turn!'

I laughed. I laughed from deep in my belly all the way to the top of my head. I howled with laughter. And then she slapped me hard across my cheek, knocking the laughter right out of me.

'I hate you!' she shouted.

'Come on,' Ricky said. 'Let's get inside.'

And without another thought, I raised my hand and slapped her right back, with all the force I had in me. She staggered backwards in her silly platform shoes, holding her cheek, a look of incredulous astonishment on her face. And then she turned and ran.

'Shit,' I said, instantly regretting my action.

I took after her round the back of the pub, calling her name. Out of the wind, I heard Ricky's footfall behind me. I slowed, turning on my heels.

'You go in. Let me handle her.'

'But Jo. Say you'll come with me.'

'Argh!' I cried, quickening my pace away from him, towards Alison.

Once out of the lee of the pub wall, the wind hit me again. I squinted my eyes against the dark and the wind, picking out Alison's white top ahead of me. She was heading out onto the Point. She'd break a bloody ankle on those rocks in those shoes.

'Alison,' I shouted. 'I'm sorry. Hold up.'

I caught her up at last, grabbing for her arm. But she tugged it away and kept stumbling on.

'I'm sorry I hit you,' I yelled.

She spun, her blond hair billowing out towards the sea. 'You've always hated me,' she cried.

'What are you talking about? I don't hate you.'

'You've always hated me.' She sobbed, snot and tears mixing on her face. 'You couldn't wait to get away from me.'

'Why would I hate you?'

'Because I killed Mum,' she screamed.

'What?' Ricky asked, appearing beside us.

'Is that what you think?' I yelled. 'Jesus, Alison. Of course you didn't kill Mum.'

'You've always blamed me.'

'I have not.'

'What?' Ricky asked again.

I sighed, picking a strand of hair out of my mouth. 'Our mum died in childbirth, having her,' I said, pointing at Alison.

Alison wailed and took off again over the scrubby grass and rocks. I leapt after her, finally catching her arm as she neared the narrow end of the Point.

'This is my turn,' she cried. 'Don't take this away from me.'

I spread my legs to steady myself against the rushing wind. I could hardly see her through her hair, which was flailing about any which way.

'I'm not taking anything away from you,' I yelled, clinging onto her arm.

'You're trying to wheedle your way into this tour. I know what you did last night.'

Ricky arrived, squatting low on the rock, using his hands to balance like a proper townie.

'Guys,' he shouted. 'This is not good. Let's go back. You can talk behind the pub.'

'Shut up, Ricky,' we shouted back in unison.

Alison wriggled her arm, but I held her firmly.

'You don't deserve him,' she cried. 'He's everything you're not. He's fun and talented and you're just really, really boring.'

'You know nothing about us,' I yelled back. 'All that stuff you read – all those stupid clippings you've got stuck on your stupid wall – none of it is real, Alison. You don't know him.'

'I know him,' she cried, high-pitched in her anger.

'Oh my god! He is not interested in you,' I yelled at her, at all the girls he'd ever crossed paths with. 'He's with me. You are nothing to him. You are invisible to him.'

'Oh, really?' she cried. 'Let's ask him, shall we? Ricky?'

We both looked down at the crouching lump beside us.

'Can we please just get off this very exposed precipice?' he hollered, trying to stand. 'And Jo, in all honesty, I don't think you're helping the situation.'

The wind cleared the hair off Alison's face for a second so I could see her smirking face.

'Fine.' I let go of her arm. 'You fucking have him.'

I turned away just as a violent gust slammed into us. I staggered two steps towards the water before managing to drop to the rock and hold my place. As soon as it passed, I looked behind me. Alison was flat on her belly, hanging over the edge of the Point with her legs splayed. Ricky was nowhere to be seen.

CHAPTER 45

I crawled towards her on my hands and knees and peered over the edge.

She was holding Ricky's wrist with both hands. 'Oh, thank god.'

I slithered forwards as far as I could get without sliding down to the water myself, and grabbed the same arm Alison was holding.

'I'm sorry, Alison.'

Her face was an inch from mine.

'I'm sorry, too. Let's pull him up.'

'I can do it myself if you'd let me go for a minute,' Ricky shouted.

His feet were in the water, the waves dragging his kilt left and right, and his free hand was raking the rock, looking for purchase.

'Well, get up then,' I shouted over the ledge.

But right at that moment, a wave engulfed us. I had water in my mouth, the roar of the sea in my ears. I blinked my eyes clear. Alison was still lying beside me, forehead pressed onto the rock, arms over the edge.

'Ricky!' I screamed.

He was coughing, spluttering, and when he looked up, I saw he had a gash above his right eyebrow, the blood running with the sea water down his face. He flung his free hand up and grabbed my wrist.

'Pull!' Alison yelled.

We tugged with all our might and barely moved him. I brought a knee round to my side, but my plimsolls couldn't get purchase on the wet stone. Alison was kicking off her shoes to better grip the rock. And then another wave.

'It's too slippy,' I shouted.

We were both drenched. Alison's soaked hair was covering her face. Over the edge, Ricky was still clinging onto me. He was trying to get one foot on a tiny hold at belly height, but it just kept skiting back into the water as the kilt dragged him.

We locked eyes, his expression telling me he'd reached the same conclusion I had. He was stuck.

Alison turned her face to me. 'It's the kilt,' she said. 'It's too heavy, with the water.'

'I know,' I said. 'I think the tide's still coming in. We're going to need a rope.' I saw the sea pull back. 'Brace yourself,' I yelled at them both.

Another wave crashed over us.

'Jesus Christ,' I cried. 'Alison, go get help.'

'You won't be able to hold him.'

'I'll hold him.' But I wasn't at all sure. 'I can hold him.'

'No, you can't,' she said. 'But the wind's from the southwest. The current will take him to Cockle Bay.'

I shook my head frantically. 'Are you insane? He'll drown.'

Cockle Bay was the first stretch of sand after the headland, and it wasn't far. But in the water, that was another story. And in this storm – in April – the sea couldn't have been more than seven degrees.

Alison rubbed her face across the rock to move some of her hair and looked at me. 'I'll take him,' she said. 'I can do it. I'm a strong swimmer.'

'No!' Alarm coursed through me. 'No!'

'It's the only way,' she replied, letting go of Ricky and jumping to her feet. 'You go get Dad.'

Instantly, Ricky's weight started pulling me forward, and my legs scrambled to keep their place.

'No!' I screamed. 'Alison!'

I locked eyes with Ricky as I slid forward. Time seemed to slow as he realised he was dragging me down. He let go of my arm. His other wrist slipped out of my grasp as I saw Alison swan dive into the sea behind him. And then they were gone into the broiling, churning darkness of the storm.

'Dear God,' I whispered as I clambered to my feet. I'd never prayed in my life. 'Please. Please.'

It was dark as I ran. Pitch black. But I kept my eyes on the village lights. The wind was behind me now, shoving me along. I fell twice, but clambered back up both times, oblivious to the pain in my knee. My wet jeans were heavy on my legs and I realised it was raining now, hard. I pushed myself forward, lungs screaming for air as I hit the coast road and ran straight into Dinger.

'Jo,' he said, steadying me. 'You're drenched. What's going on? Where are the other two?'

'In the sea.' I gasped for breath. 'Go and get my dad. Tell him Cockle Bay.'

'In the sea? In this?'

'Cockle Bay! Hurry.'

I wriggled free of him, but he caught my arm.

'Wait.' He was sliding his arms out of his down jacket. 'Put this on.'

I let him get one of my arms into a sleeve before setting off left, away from the village, along the track to the north end. I was running in darkness. But I could see the beach ahead, the white sand glowing in the black. I stumbled over the verge and leapt down onto the sand without a thought to broken ankles.

The wide beach was shallow, and the waves weren't as high here, but still they rolled in. I ran down to the surf, peering at the water. I cast my eyes about, searching for anything that wasn't white waves and black sea.

I scanned and scanned. And then, there they were. I splashed through the waves as the sea lit up with the headlights of dad's quad bike and Mr Anderson's Land Rover. Alison was swimming sideways, holding Ricky by the chin.

'You can stand,' I yelled as I ploughed through the waves, oblivious to the cold.

I was waist deep, legs spread wide against the push of the water as Alison struggled to get her feet down. I made it to them and swung Ricky's free, limp arm round my shoulder. He heaved and coughed. Oh, thank god. The kilt was gone, I noticed. He was naked from the waist down.

We half dragged, half swam, until Dad and Bill arrived to take over, powerfully hauling him ashore. Alison and I stumbled onto the sand.

'Are you ok?' I asked, my hand on her back as she bent to cough and wretch.

'Once I'd got the kilt off, yes.' She pulled herself upright, looked at me, and laughed. 'Fucking hell!'

I drew her into my arms, and we clung tightly to each other. 'I'm so sorry,' I cried. 'I'm so sorry I've not been there for you, Alison. I love you so much.'

She squeezed me tighter. 'I've really missed you.'

'Let's promise to never fight again,' I said.

'We always promise that.' She laughed, pulling away, her teeth chittering. 'But Jo.'

'What?'

'I am going with Ricky. On the tour. And I'll be fine.'

'I know you'll be fine,' I replied. 'But will Ricky?'

Up the beach, Ricky was being manhandled into the back of the Land Rover, smothered in towels and blankets to restore his modesty. Alison set off towards what was quickly becoming quite a crowd, pushing her way through to get to Ricky.

'You are such a townie,' she shouted at him as Aunt Mary wrapped a tartan travel rug around her.

Bill was trying to pour whisky from a flask into Ricky's still spluttering mouth.

'It was slippy,' he wheezed.

Alison batted the flask away. 'Do not pull a stunt like that again. I swear to god, I'm not spending the whole of this tour saving your ass.'

His body was vibrating with violent shivers, his skin tinged blue. 'I'm sorry, Alison,' he mumbled.

Alison let out a derisive snort and climbed onto the waiting quad bike behind Dad, as the Land Rover doors slammed shut on Ricky.

Mhairi was peeling Dinger's saturated jacket off my

back to replace it with her own, and I grinned as I realised they were going to be ok – Alison and Ricky. I could let them go. I could let Ricky go.

EPILOGUE

I tugged up my leather-look leggings to smooth the knees and wriggled my shoulder to rearrange my baggy black mohair jumper as Pamela had instructed. I could feel my hair, which hung in loose manufactured curls, sway against the middle of my back. After a four-hour ordeal in a Mayfair salon, I was sporting massive extensions that blended seamlessly with my freshly dyed, rose-gold hair – the latest colour, according to Pamela. I had never worn my hair this long. I looked like Alison.

'Here.' Olivia French, my agent, thrust a copy of my newly printed hardback book into my hands. 'And hand me your phone. I've marked the page you're reading. Just from the highlighter to the end of that chapter, which should be twelve minutes, tops.'

I looked down at the book, turning it over in my hands. My book. I'd written a book. It was still almost unbelievable.

Olivia patted my arm. 'You'll be fine. You're perfectly capable. We've rehearsed the questions. Relax. Enjoy. You have earned this.'

I gave her a weak smile and she turned on her heels and strode away. My nerves were getting the better of me. From my vantage point in the shadows behind the partition panels at the edge of the makeshift stage, I could see out into the marquee, which was filling up quickly. But there, in the second row, was my gang – my London gang. There was Pamela, head down, busy on her phone. I was amazed she'd found the time for this, as she was a celebrity in her own right now. In the last year, her career as a stylist to the stars had totally taken off. In fact, she was dashing back to London after this to fly out to Milan.

And there was Mhairi beside her, also on her phone, but this time taking selfies, phone in the air to get the crowd in in the background. Yes, she was living in London now, too. I'd wrangled her an internship at Olivia's agency and she'd just been offered a copy editor's job covering maternity leave. The pregnant copy editor was married to a hedge fund manager and had bought a house out in Weybridge. I doubted whether she was coming back anytime soon – I wouldn't – so the job was pretty much Mhairi's.

Bob and Dinger were there too, nattering away like a pair of old fish wives, arms crossed, looking bored but resigned to the ordeal. Bob had a job with some tech start-up. I'd no idea what they did, even though he'd tried to explain it a few times. Computer stuff. And Dinger had been taken on permanently at Arup.

Dinger. I smiled softly as I watched him from the shadows, my shoulders relaxing. He was my rock. My champion. He'd been there for me for every hard-wrought word of this book, for every all-night rewrite. He'd talked me down, or up, from every collapse of confidence I'd had – and there'd been many. But more than that, he'd made me feel loved and safe in his arms. I only had to look at him to feel calm and, I don't know, content, I suppose. Quite the opposite of how I'd ever felt with Ricky, who, right now, was thousands of miles away across the Atlantic on tour with Alison. Which was fine. Which was good. Far away in distance and far away in my mind.

After the storm, from which they both recovered with only cuts and bruises and a good story to tell, they'd set off on their mystery tour as planned. And I had let Ricky go, as planned, cutting all ties as best I could. We exchanged the odd text, but all my information came from Alison, who was having the time of her life. Mhairi had been right, I needed the distance to cure myself of him. I took a deep breath. I was nearly there. Nearly cured. I had to believe that. I focused back on Dinger, sitting patiently in this tent in Wales, his shoulders as wide as Bob's, his city confidence oozing from his bones. I'd made the right choice, I reminded myself.

The marquee was nearly full. People were walking up and down the aisles looking for seats. Mhairi was getting up to let someone pass. But no, she was embracing someone. And now Bob and Dinger were rising, too. Who was it? And then the woman flicked her hair in an instantly familiar way. It was Alison! What was she doing here? I was about to step forward out of the shadows when someone tapped my shoulder. I turned. And there, beside me, filling my view, was Ricky.

My stupid heart thundered in my chest. 'What are you doing here?'

He grinned down at me, smudged black eyeliner not hiding his crazy brilliant eyes. 'I pulled the famous card and they let me backstage,' he said. 'Alison's here too.'

'I didn't mean here. I meant here, in Wales.'

'At the literary event of the year? How could we miss that?'

I was incredulous. 'You're meant to be in Nashville. You're playing Nashville tomorrow.'

'Yeah, we just flew in. Back out tonight. Bonkers really.' He laughed. 'The car's waiting for us.'

'Your hair.' I lifted my hand to touch his shaved scalp.

'*Your* hair,' he replied, taking my hand and making me spin a turn on the spot. 'Jo-D, you are smoking hot.'

'But, Ricky.' I thought I was going to cry. 'Alison never said.'

'Yeah. A surprise. Alison said you'd want us here for support. She's actually very bossy. I'm not sure she likes me.'

I croaked out a laugh. No matter how many times Ricky had thanked her for saving him from the sea, she'd never forgiven him for falling in in the first place.

'Is it ok that I'm here?' he asked.

'Yes. Of course. I'm glad you came.'

'It's weird seeing you.' He still had hold of my hand, one finger moving gently over my wrist. 'I mean, I've thought about you, but seeing you…' He shook his head as if to clear it, not taking his eyes from mine. 'I didn't think I'd feel…'

'Ms Duncan.' A man appeared beside us, sporting a wireless headset and a black clipboard. 'We're ready to go when you are. This is Ms Baxter, who'll be interviewing you.'

I let go of Ricky, my hand burning from where he'd held it, and turned to Brooke Baxter.

'Hi,' was all I could manage.

'Lovely to meet you,' she said, shaking my limp hand. 'And Mr Steele, I see.' She took in Ricky with a raised eyebrow. 'Are you joining us on stage?'

'God no.' He laughed. He grasped Brooke Baxter and kissed her lightly on both cheeks. 'Good to see you again.'

'It's been a while,' she replied. 'The Mercuries, was it?'

He nodded.

'America going well?'

'Yes. Totally. Nashville tomorrow.'

'And yet, here you are in Hay-on-Wye.'

Ricky chuckled and folded his arms, and Brooke Baxter turned to me.

'Right. So, no surprises. You've seen the questions?'

'Yes.'

'Fifteen-minute chat. Ten-minute reading. Ten-minute audience questions.'

'Sounds good,' I replied, smiling weakly.

'And your agent said 'Joanne', not 'Jo'?'

I lifted the book to show my name on the cover. 'We're going with Joanne now.'

'Got it. Let's get going then.' And with that, she marched confidently out onto the stage to loud applause.

It was happening. My book launch was happening. I looked at Ricky.

'Go on, Joanne,' he whispered, pushing me lightly on the small of my back.

And I followed Brooke Baxter onto the stage and sat down on the spare seat beside her.

'What a lovely warm welcome,' she began. 'Good afternoon, everyone. I'm Brooke Baxter and it is my immense pleasure to introduce one of the most exciting new authors to emerge from these shores in a generation – Joanne Duncan.'

More applause. More flashbulbs popping. I blinked, smiled, sat upright, nodded and crossed my ankles as Pamela had shown me. I did not, could not, make eye contact with Dinger even though I could feel his gaze upon me. And by force of will, I did not turn to look back at Ricky either, although I knew his attention was fully on me. Instead, I focused on Brooke Baxter's words. This moment was about me. And as I sat there listening, I chose, finally, emphatically, to focus on myself. I chose me. I chose Joanne.

'Although most of us know her as the social media superstar, Jo-D, regularly rubbing shoulders with celebrities, she has left that life behind to follow what is undoubtedly her true calling, delivering to us her bold, honest, groundbreaking, rock and roll roller coaster of a first novel, 'Going all the Way' – a no-holds-barred story of a young woman's journey from obscurity to glory and back again. Joanne, if I may, how much of this remarkable book is fiction and how much memoir?'

I took a deep breath and began.

ABOUT THE AUTHOR

A nn Lilley is a coffee drinker and a lover of wild places. She has a science degree and a literature degree – one of which pays the bills. She grew up on a Scottish island and now lives near Glasgow with her daughter. Vermillion Days is her first novel. She has no idea what happened in Reading. Do you?

Instagram @annlilleyauthor
Website www.annlilleyauthor.co.uk

 Matador

For exclusive discounts on Matador titles,
sign up to our occasional newsletter at
troubador.co.uk/bookshop